PRAISE FOR *A TOUCH OF GOLD*

"A dazzling retelling full of adventure with a dash of betrayal, *A Touch of Gold* will grab your heart and not let go."

BRENDA DRAKE, *New York Times* bestselling author

"Sullivan spins an engaging tale of insidious curses and abandoned gifts. *A Touch of Gold* is a thoughtful addition to the myth of King Midas, told through his daughter Kora's perspective. I dare say it should have been Kora's story all along."

EMILY R. KING, author of The Hundredth Queen series and The Evermore Chronicles

"Land and sea, riches and curses, despair and love—this book has it all."

New York Times bestselling author WENDY HIGGINS

"Utterly charming! This fresh take on a classic tale will be treasured by fans of myth and romance alike."

SARAH GLENN MARSH, author of the Reign of the Fallen series

"With high-seas adventures and a swoony romance you can't put down, *A Touch of Gold* is an imaginative and heart-pounding retelling of King Midas. Full of pirates, curses, sirens, and thieves, Sullivan captures the thrill of first love—and first betrayal—on the high seas."

ASHLEY POSTON, author of *Heart of Iron*

"A charming tale with a heart of gold."

ELLY BLAKE, *New York Times* bestselling author

A
TOUCH
~ OF ~
GOLD

ANNIE SULLIVAN

BLINK

To my family, with love:
Mom, Dad, Katie, Patrick, Michael S.,
Danny, John, Maggie, and Michael K.

PROLOGUE

Once upon a time, a little girl helplessly watched as liquid gold spun a web across her tiny frame, racing to wrap her up in an icy cocoon. Her mouth hung agape. Her limbs stayed outstretched toward a father she could not reach. Her legs refused to respond, to carry her far away. Only the sound of bones crackling, drying into rigid metal fossils, sliced through the night air.

The gold hummed a haunting lullaby as it pooled in her ears, and specks of gold whirled across her vision. She had time for one last breath, but her throat hardened before the air ever reached her lungs. Finally, a burst of gold clenched her heart and squeezed until blood ran out of it, hardening like candle wax as she succumbed to the golden curse.

She could neither hear nor see the outside world. All she could feel was the constant, icy pressure of the gold on her body. Her limbs tingled, liked they'd fallen asleep, but this tingling never went away. It increased with each passing moment; tiny swords pricking her skin over and over again, leaving behind invisible wounds. If her hands could move, she would've clawed the gold from her skin.

Over and over again in her trapped mind, she replayed the way her father's face had recoiled in horror, how his upper lip receded and his brow crinkled over bulging eyes as he pulled away from her.

What had happened? What had she done to deserve this?

She asked the questions a thousand times as the gold weighed down her body.

All she'd done was run into her father's arms as she had every time he came to look for her in the palace rose garden. But this time had been different from all the rest. She'd frozen at his touch, becoming a statue every bit as lifeless as the stone swans spewing water atop the nearby fountain. And just like those swans, she couldn't fly away from this nightmare.

Because the nightmare had started long before the mysterious stranger had turned up at the castle that morning.

In fact, it began long before the little girl was even born. Her father and his brother, Pheus, had been poor farmers, coming through the mountains to sell cabbages in town. Their donkey had twisted a leg on the rocky mountain passes, and the little girl's father had wanted to turn back. But Pheus convinced him to keep going and was so sure they would make it that he left his brother with the donkey and went on ahead to secure a market stall.

What neither brother knew was that the Great Oracle had arrived in Lagonia's capital that day. She had seen in a vision that the king would die before midnight. He had no heirs, which meant a scramble for power and subsequent bloodshed unless the country could unite behind one leader, one she prophesized would have a prosperous rule. She said that the kingdom of Lagonia would find such a future king in the market that very day. He would be leading a limping donkey.

Thus, when the little girl's father led his lame donkey into town, the people had scattered away in shock before cheering. He was crowned the next day, and for a time, Lagonia prospered.

The king married a beautiful princess from the north and had the little girl.

But despite having come from a simple background, the king quickly developed a taste for the finer things in life. In a matter of years, he'd spent most of the treasury on feasts and expensive adornments for his castle. The treasuries grew depleted. Pirates roamed the seas. And his people were going hungry.

The little girl's father and uncle talked endlessly of how they could resolve the issues, but neither time nor money was on their side. Years passed. War came and went. And Lagonia grew ever weaker, ever poorer.

But everything changed when an old beggar arrived at the castle selling cabbages. The king remembered his own humble beginnings and took pity on the man. He welcomed him in and bought several cabbages, even though he had few coins to spare.

As soon as the money touched the beggar's palm, he revealed himself as Dionysus, the trickiest of the gods, the one known for amusing himself by purposefully leaving chaos in his wake. Dionysus admitted he had disguised himself with the intention of entrapping the little girl's father and punishing him when he did not offer kindness to a god. But since the king had shown him mercy, Dionysus instead would reward the king with anything he wanted.

Without thinking, without remembering how Dionysus was known to twist words, without pondering why no one had outsmarted Dionysus before, the little girl's father asked for the power to turn things to gold.

Dionysus had laughed, granted the wish, and disappeared.

And so, the little girl's father had thrown a feast celebrating The Touch that would save the kingdom, the same feast the little girl had snuck out of to go hide in the rose garden. For she knew her father would come looking for her. He would sit on the fountain ledge with her and hold up the tail ends of his embroidered cloak like a mask as he reenacted in a shaky, mysterious voice the Great Oracle's prophecy that had made him king. Then, the little girl would beg him to continue the story all the way to the part where he met her mother. That was her favorite story.

But the little girl didn't hear that story in the garden that day. In fact, after turning his daughter into a golden statue, the king never told the story again.

The little girl stayed in her icy, metallic prison while her father searched for a way to save her. For days, he prayed for an answer, surviving only on water, as the food he touched turned to gold before it reached his mouth. He searched every book. He consulted every healer he could find. He even sent men to search for the Great Oracle, but none could find the way to her cave. Only Dionysus could undo the curse. And so, night after night, the little girl's father cried out from the towers of the castle for Dionysus to return, to remember the kindness he had shown him.

Finally, Dionysus returned.

The little girl's father was so relieved that he didn't stop to consider *why* Dionysus would return. The trickster god was not known for his mercy or his kindness. Still, the little girl's father listened eagerly as Dionysus told him to wash everything he'd turned to gold in the river that ran into the nearby ocean. He'd said water was too pure to be corrupted by magic, and the river would wash away the gold and his power if he submerged in it before the sun set that very day. With his lips curled in a wicked grin, Dionysus cautioned that if everything did not get washed as he instructed, there would be unhappy consequences.

The king ran to the river as quickly as he could, with four men carrying the statue of his daughter. The moment she was submerged in the water, the little girl sputtered back to life again, her hair once more shades of brown rather than gold. Her father leapt in beside her, and when he emerged, no trace of his power remained. He wrapped the little girl in his arms, and didn't let go for a long, long time.

The king was so happy to be able to hold his daughter once more that he forgot about the other items he had turned to gold—the pheasant he'd tried to eat, the platter it rested on, the knife meant to cut his food, the large table he'd tried to dine at, the two chalices he drank from, the three coins he'd weighed in his palm, a rose he'd plucked to give his daughter, a rolled-up tapestry, and the necklace that had belonged to his wife. By the time he remembered the other objects, the sun had set completely.

When the moon appeared, the table and knife and rose and all the rest gleamed brighter than the stars. Amazed, the king turned toward his daughter, only to see a gold sheen creep back over her skin. He raced to her side, but instead of turning back into a statue, the princess remained a living, breathing girl. A girl whose skin sparkled in the moonlight and whose eyes flashed metallic and hard when her father cried out in shock.

As the days passed and it became clear the little girl's skin would not return to normal, they kept her locked away inside the palace for fear of what others would think of her, of what greedy or superstitious people might do, though the girl was just seven years old. And they counted themselves quite lucky that her skin was the only reminder of the curse others could see. For what they discovered soon after about the little girl was not to be spoken of. This they kept secret.

And since the little girl's father could no longer turn things to gold, everyone believed him when he said the curse was gone. So the kingdom went back to normal, and the little girl and her father, King Midas, lived happily ever after . . . or so everyone thought.

CHAPTER 1

>>>>>>>>◉<<<<<<<<

I've only ever turned one person to gold, and that was an accident. It was before I knew what I could do, before I knew that people were right to fear me.

Although the nobles don't know about my powers, money still changes hands at the tables before me as they bet on how long my newest suitor, Duke Wystlinos, will last. Some brokers even take bets on whether he'll scream when he sees me.

I roll my eyes—not that anyone can see it beneath my thick veil. Only one of my former suitors, Lord Primtim, had screamed. Thankfully, we'd been out in the rose garden, where most people couldn't hear.

The light coming in from the stained glass windows reflects off the sliver of golden skin visible in the gap between my gloves and sleeves. I quickly yank the material down before folding my hands back in my lap like I always do to keep from touching things.

You can never be too careful. Not when it comes to gold. Or to curses.

I pray that a trip out to the garden is all it will take to dissuade Duke Wystlinos. Once he sees my skin, he'll flee like all the rest, and I can retreat to the library to read about the mythical island of Jipper that I'll never get to visit.

I stifle a yawn. I was up too late reading last night, trying to put Duke Wystlinos's visit from my mind.

"Don't let the duke see you yawning like that, Kora," my cousin Hettie says. She towers over me as she leans on the chair beside mine. She inherited the same height as her father and mine, while I share my mother's more petite frame.

Her auburn curls bounce and her curvy lips pout forward as she plops down and pulls a platter of grapes closer. A servant brings her a tray full of cheeses, dark brown barley bread dripping with honey, and several olives that threaten to roll off as the servant's hands become shakier the closer he gets to me.

"Good morning, *Hettiana*," I mutter, putting extra emphasis on her full name. I'm the only one who uses it—and only to annoy her.

She ignores me. "We don't want you scaring Duke Wystlinos away until he's had a chance to see what other maidens the kingdom has to offer." She sighs dramatically. "Then again, I suppose that's what you want, isn't it? Me, an old maid like you." She examines the remaining grapes in the cluster before selecting a particularly plump one.

What I *want* is to put an end to the suitors—Hettie can have whichever one she wants. I'd let Hettie marry Duke Wystlinos in a heartbeat, but with the palace coffers what they are, Uncle Pheus made it quite clear that I'll need to marry into wealth to give my family any hope of holding on to the throne. He'd pushed me to accept an offer from the duke, should one be made, because in addition to deep coffers, Wystlinos will bring stability to the kingdom as it continues its recovery from the Orland Wars.

Hettie knows the state of the kingdom as well as I do, which is why she's hoping some dashing lord will come along and take her far, far away from Lagonia. And I can't blame her. How many times have I dreamt of leaving since my father turned me to gold ten years ago?

I just wish Hettie wouldn't bring up all my suitors so often. But since she's one of the few people in the world who isn't afraid of me, I tolerate her and her single-mindedness.

She squishes her barley bread into the pools of honey that have slid off the top.

I look away. I already ate this morning in my room. It's too hard to eat in front of others when you're wearing a veil, and my stomach is in knots anyway.

"I wouldn't mind being the hostess of all those parties Duke Wystlinos throws," Hettie continues. "I've heard he brings in performers from as far away as Kalakhosia."

I suppress the urge to roll my eyes again. I've received invitations to his parties because I'm the princess, and it'd be a grave insult to be left off the guest list entirely. Though, as a cursed girl with golden skin, it's understood that I'll never attend.

A voice at the back of the main hall cries out, "His Majesty, King Midas," and I wish I'd tried a little harder to avoid this meeting. To avoid exposing myself to one more duke or lord who will spread tales about me and look at me in disgust. Maybe if I asked my father—really asked—he would stop the parade of suitors. That is, if he could stand to be in the same room as me for more than ten seconds.

After my skin reverted to gold, our relationship effectively ended. He couldn't stand the sight of me—still can't—and it broke my heart. The times we talk now are mumbled greetings necessitated by the presence of others in the room. Otherwise, we avoid one another entirely.

It's not like I expected my father to apologize for turning me to gold. It was an accident, one he wishes didn't happen as much as I do. But he didn't even come to comfort me when the nightmares began. He didn't take my hand and tell me that it would be all right, that we'd get through this together. He left me to deal with the curse alone. I've never figured out if it's due to guilt or disgust, and I've never had the courage to ask because I'm not sure I want to know.

All around the hall, benches and chairs scrape across the stone floor as the nobles rise to their feet.

Right in front of the dais where I sit is Archduke Ralton, with his polished bald head on full display. As expected, he's positioned near the king's table. He wants to see me fail, to make sure the monarchy stays weak. I've even heard rumors he's gathering funds to raise an army against my father. Ralton keeps saying we need to focus more on fighting the pirates pillaging our coasts and less on finding me a husband, which my uncle always points out is due mostly to the fact Ralton doesn't want a strong line of succession in place. As both my father and the kingdom grow weaker, it becomes more likely the archduke will make a bid for the throne one day—and we may not be strong enough to stop him.

That's the other reason Duke Wystlinos is here.

He's Archduke Ralton's nephew. They supposedly had a falling out a few years back, but Uncle Pheus seems to think having a blood relation in line for the throne will appease Ralton. Or at least make him think twice about attacking.

I turn my gaze to the figures working their way down the main aisle. I can just make out my father's stooped form clinging to my uncle's arm. Long gone are the days when I could spot him in any crowd due to his stature and merry laugh. People call me a ghost because of the way I cling to the shadows of the palace, but the moniker applies more to my father. His skin is as pale as mine is gold.

While his legs struggle to shuffle forward, my father's eyes dart again and again in the direction of his tower. The same tower where he probably spent most of the morning sitting in a small wooden chair next to the twelve objects he'd turned to gold years ago. Minus me, the unlucky thirteenth object.

From anywhere in the palace, I can sense the items—a side effect of once being among them. But I'm not drawn to them the way my father is. For years, the gold has greedily called to him, begging for his attention every moment of the day, telling him he can never part with it, making him believe he can't live without it. Eventually, the lies the magic whispered came true. He needs the gold. If he goes too long without sitting near it, he grows visibly weaker, as if being near the gold is the only thing keeping him alive. And every day, he must remain longer and longer to gain enough energy to face the day.

This is one of the consequences Dionysus warned my father about, another way for his "gift" to plague my family. I have no doubt the cruel god enjoys the irony—my father asked for power over gold to revive his kingdom, but now the gold holds power over the king.

I don't ever want the gold to have power over me like that. That's why I avoid reaching my mind out to it, afraid I will become dependent as well. Sometimes I wonder if my father could survive without being near it, as he's proven he can survive without me.

Hettie's elbow jabs into my side. "Do you see him yet?"

"No," I reply, exasperated. If she can't see Duke Wystlinos, there's no way I can.

I knot my fingers together to resist the urge to pull my golden braid over my shoulder and twirl the end through my fingers.

A group of women bow, and I glimpse a dark head bent toward my uncle, who whispers something. As Uncle Pheus finishes, Duke Wystlinos throws his head back and laughs. The sound echoes around the room. Duke Wystlinos then confidently strides forward, one arm holding his sword hilt as if that's the most natural position in the world.

He turns to several nobles as he passes, clasping outstretched hands.

He bypasses his uncle without a glance. For his part, Ralton makes a show of turning up his nose and looking away. While I'm glad my family isn't the only one who has drama, I can't help but doubt that putting Duke Wystlinos on the throne will appease the archduke. His nephew appears to be the only person he despises more than my father and uncle. Well, and me.

The duke is tall and can't be more than a few years older than me. Tousled black hair falls around his face. He's muscular without being large, and his square jaw is balanced by a straight nose. His face is all angles, but they come together in a way that makes it hard to look away.

I can see why all the housemaids were in a tizzy when his visit was announced. He's certainly lived up to his reputation.

He's wearing a bright purple jacket laced with intricate designs. Silver thread swirls up and down the sleeves, chest, and back, giving him the appearance of a living tapestry and making him stand out against my uncle's less-adorned black jacket. He reminds me of the daring sea captains I read about who go off in search of lost islands and distant shores.

He spots me. A smile spreads across his lips.

I suck in a breath. I tell myself it has nothing to do with the way that smile makes me want to smile back. The breath is only to steady me for what's to come.

The entire party comes to a stop before me.

My father's graying hair contrasts with Pheus's dark locks, so much so that you'd think they were separated by decades instead of only two years. It's one of many differences between them, and not a day goes by that I'm not thankful for Pheus's presence and concern for me. He's the glue that has been holding the kingdom together as my father grows weaker, the one who runs every council meeting and judges every dispute brought before the crown.

"My daughter." My father stumbles over the words. He seems to collapse inwardly like he always does when he's in the same room with me. I notice his clothes are rumpled, and I can't remember if they're the same ones he wore yesterday.

Thankfully, Uncle Pheus is there to not only support my father, but to finish the introduction. "Princess Kora, may I introduce Duke Aris Wystlinos."

"Princess." The duke bows. He doesn't drop the smile as he addresses me, which either means he's not nervous or he's very good about hiding it. I'm not sure which I prefer.

He flicks dark hair out of his eyes as he straightens. "I am honored to make your acquaintance."

I offer the smallest curtsy in return. I'm not sure if it's low enough or not. Maybe if my tutors had stuck around after I'd been turned to gold, I would've executed it without concern, but these days most of my education comes from books and books alone. After deciding I don't care if the curtsy is proper enough, I raise my head and finally meet Duke Wystlinos's gaze.

"Welcome to the palace, Duke Wystlinos," I intone. "We are most honored by your visit." Everyone in the room knows I'm lying, but we're nobles. We're used to playing this stupid game of saying things we don't mean.

Uncle Pheus smiles in encouragement, and Hettie keeps shifting next to me, as if she thinks by moving enough, the duke will eventually be forced to look at her.

Instead, his eyes stay locked on mine. Or where mine would be if the veil weren't covering my face.

"Princess, if you're finished with your meal, perhaps we could walk together in the rose garden?" The way the duke says it holds such confidence, even though I know he's been instructed by Uncle Pheus to take me to the garden, where I can be embarrassed in peace. Still, he almost manages to make the visit sound intriguing, like something I should want because he wants it.

I'm not drawn in by his easy self-assurance. I've dealt with men like him before, ones who rely on their charm and bravado to advance them politically. But I have my own reasons for wanting to go to the rose garden. Nothing brings out my skin tone more than glints of sunlight, and nothing scares a suitor away faster.

"Of course," I say.

Uncle Pheus nods. As usual, my father refuses to look at me, and I wonder if he feels as ashamed as I do by this charade.

I wait for Duke Wystlinos to make his way around the head table so we can venture outside and get this over with.

He holds his arm out to me. It's an unexpected move, and I freeze.

My breath catches in my throat, and my hands clench together, my heartbeat thudding loudly as I stare at his outstretched arm.

What if he's wearing gold?

Seconds tick by. Too long. I've kept him waiting too long.

Surely Uncle Pheus checked. Because Archduke Ralton would have us removed from the palace in a heartbeat if I turned Duke Wystlinos to gold in front of everyone.

My eyes frantically search for Uncle Pheus, but he's helping my father up onto the dais. I'm out of options. And time.

I pull down my sleeves so they're flush with my gloves—the fabric is already beginning to fray from the repetitive action—and take a calming breath.

I pray Uncle Pheus did check because I have no other choice than to unclamp my hands and loop my arm through the duke's.

CHAPTER 2

There. Nothing happened.

I exhale, and my heartbeat settles. I should've known Uncle Pheus would check. He always does.

Duke Wystlinos and I take stiff steps toward the balcony door. The cool air hits me once we're outside, and I sense him relax. I breathe in and out, happy to not have the tepid indoor air continually circulating under my veil.

Past the long stretch of gardens and the labyrinth of houses beyond the palace wall, tall mountains loom in the distance, the same mountains where the Great Oracle is rumored to live. I've always hated those mountains, always felt like she must be up there watching us, wondering why we haven't lived up to her prophecy—of making Lagonia prosper.

An early spring snow still rests on the highest peaks, but down here, temperate air drifts in from the sea on the other side of the palace. I look away from the mountains and breathe in the salty scent to calm my mind.

We walk down the steps toward the maze of hedges. Morning light casts shadows on the pathways, which lead to several small courtyards containing fountains and benches. In between these courtyards are corridors lined with newly blooming roses that lazily bob their heads as morning dew drips off them.

My father's prized birds chirp in cages hidden throughout the garden. For a few moments, that's the only sound, as Duke Wystlinos is yet to speak.

I prefer the silence. When my first suitor arrived, I'd foolishly harbored hope that I'd finally have someone to talk to. But, like the others after him, all he'd wanted to discuss was my father's gold. So rather than hope for the best, I mull over any number of topics I could bring up to scare Wystlinos away. My father's curse. My curse. The gold. The empty treasury. But I don't—not yet. He'll inevitably ask about each subject on his own sooner or later, and that way, when Uncle Pheus asks, I can pretend I tried to give this suitor a chance.

"Your uncle told me you like to read books on sailing," Duke Wystlinos ventures.

This is a new tactic. "Yes."

I answered. That counts as trying, right?

"I've sailed extensively," he replies. "Is there any place that particularly interests you?"

"Jipper," I blurt out before I can stop myself. But it doesn't matter. In fact, mentioning a fantasy island that no one has ever set eyes on and is rumored to move around the sea might even help.

When I'd asked my second suitor, the merchant's son, about Jipper, he rushed off to respond to the imagined call of his father. Apparently, mentioning an island most of the world doesn't believe exists has that effect, so I steel myself for the duke's response.

He doesn't laugh or run away. He just looks at me, smiling slightly. "To my knowledge, no man has ever set foot on Jipper."

I almost sigh. A typical diplomatic answer. Neither an

agreement nor a disagreement that might upset the other party, just a simple restating of a fact. He must've studied under my tutors after they abandoned me.

It's probably better for everyone if I end this now. I reach for the edge of my veil.

"But I wouldn't mind being the first," Duke Wystlinos continues.

My hand stops. "Really?" I pull back on his arm and study his face, waiting for a mocking tone that simply isn't there.

His gray eyes are intense and focused. "Just because something's rumored to be enchanted doesn't mean we should dismiss it. In fact, I think that makes it worth pursuing all the more." He squints and stares at the sun as if he's trying to remember something. "I think the closest I've ever been to where Jipper's rumored to have been sighted is Halpen."

"Halpen," I groan with envy. What I wouldn't give to see that coast. Its white cliffs are said to reflect the colors of the sunset and look prettier than any tapestry ever crafted.

Duke Wystlinos becomes more animated as he talks. "My crew and I once fought pirates off the coast of Halpen Cove." He grabs a stick from the hedge and begins jabbing it into the foliage. "The cutthroats thought they could get the best of me, but I set them straight." He gives the bush one final thrashing before ramming his makeshift sword into it as a deathblow.

I stare at him for a moment before bursting out in laughter. Any servants who may have seen him fighting a bush will likely think him as crazy as they do me. In some small way, that's comforting. In fact, this could be the first time since being turned to gold that I feel like someone might understand me.

The duke looks a little embarrassed, but he's grinning. He

drops the stick back into the hedge and tugs down the sides of his coat.

"How noble of you," I say. "Vanquishing pirates is no small feat."

We would know. We'd been trying to get rid of the ones that took up residence during the Orfland Wars, not to mention the ones that started the war itself. Orfland ships, under the guise of seeking to destroy pirates that had targeted their choppy coastline, were allowed to sail through our territory, but they used their access to attack the Tiberian Isles—the islands that served as the resupplying port for almost everyone who crossed the Seraph Sea—claiming them as their own. From there, they used the isles as a base to start attacking other nearby locations, cutting off our merchant supply and trade routes with many of our allies. We'd known it wouldn't be long before they came for us. They'd always wanted a closer port to the rich Seraph Sea. It had taken all our resources to drive Orfland's ships back to their own territory and force them to accept the terms of our treaty.

But defeating Orfland didn't mean we'd beaten the pirates, who flourished while the Royal Armada was away and we struggled—still struggle—to rebuild it. Uncle Pheus recently traveled to several of our port cities to investigate the rumored return of one particularly cruel pirate, Captain Skulls. We'd thought he'd died during the war, but no one was sure. And Captain Skulls's obsession with collecting the skulls of his victims—the one that had earned him his name—made finding witnesses quite impossible. Thus, no one Uncle Pheus talked to could confirm if the pirate was alive or if the one we'd learned of was a copycat. We prayed it was a copycat because no one wanted to believe the alternative.

I swallow down the thought and turn my attention back to Duke Wystlinos.

He smiles at me as we pass under a canopy of hanging flowers. Long vines nod and sway amongst climbing roses above our heads.

"Well, when you're as familiar with the sea as I am, it's easy to take care of pirates, and I have the fastest ship on this side of the ocean." A faraway look overtakes his face.

He doesn't say it to impress me. His tone is the same one I used in the past whenever I told my father about all the books I was reading, which was years ago now.

"I've fought pirates several times," Duke Wystlinos continues, "most recently during the Orland Wars, when they took an important document from me. I hunted them down to get it back." He plucks a rose from one of the nearby trellises and hands it to me. "Have you spent any time at sea?"

I twirl the rose between my gloved fingers. Its sweet perfume lingers in the air. As a child, I used to wear a rose in my hair every day, in memory of my mother. But after being transformed, I didn't want any reminders of the garden, of what had happened there.

"No, but I would love to," I say.

"We'll have to make that happen, in that case," he says, then pauses. He slides the rose from my fingertips.

As he leans forward, I'm lost in his gray eyes for a moment. There are hints of dark blue streaking through them.

His face stops mere inches from mine. His breath pulses through my veil.

"May I?" He touches the edge of the material and waits for my permission to lift it.

For some reason, my heart sinks. I've been enjoying our conversation. Now I wish it'd go on a little longer. It's nice to have someone besides Hettie to talk to, especially someone who believes in Jipper.

We haven't even talked about my father's treasure yet. Every suitor brings up the gold before asking to see my face.

Some flaws can be overlooked if there's enough money to be had.

I exhale. It's better to get this over with now than to fool myself into thinking he'll last the day, so I nod, signaling he has permission to remove my veil.

He gingerly lifts it over my head.

I turn away. I have no desire to see his face, the way his lips will recede into a mask that mirrors my father's face the day he turned me to gold. The thought of it stings, recalling wounds that haven't fully healed, ones that reopen each time someone new arrives at the palace.

But it's not a look of disgust that sends my heartbeat spinning; it's his touch. He pulls my cheek back toward him and slides the rose behind my ear.

My hand goes to the spot where he'd made contact. "You're not afraid?" My mind is reeling. Everyone is afraid. I can't even remember the last time another person touched me without my gloves or veil getting in the way.

His eyebrows pull together. "You're not the first person I've met who's had to suffer because of someone else's curse."

"What do you mean?" I don't know anyone else—besides my father—who's been cursed. Of course, there are speculations that over the years Dionysus and his love of chaos have cursed many people by trapping them with twisted words and intricate facades. But I've only ever heard the rumors people tell about me. Like that I turn back into a statue at night. Or that if you look into my eyes, you'll turn to gold. Or that I leave golden footprints where I walk. My third suitor actually insisted on walking behind me to see if that one was true.

Duke Wystlinos looks away. All hints of his earlier laughter have disappeared from his face. He bows his head, watching his feet. Thick locks of hair fall forward and eclipse his eyes.

"Just as your father reportedly asked Dionysus for the ability to turn things to gold, and Dionysus twisted his words so *everything* he touched turned to gold, my father had his own wish granted by the god," he says slowly, carefully. "He wished for a pile of money so large he'd never see the top of it. And what'd he receive? He was buried by riches. I wasn't fast enough to dig him out because, for every coin I removed, another one slid down from the top of that unending pile. My father got exactly what he wished for. He never saw the top of that pile. Only the bottom." His voice cracks, but he hides his emotion well.

"I'm not scared of your skin," he continues, "because you're still the same person. What your father did to you doesn't change who you are. You aren't your father's mistakes. You aren't your father's curse. Your legacy rests with you." He resumes his place at my side and continues walking. "At least, that's what I tell myself."

I wish I had words to comfort him, but it's been so long since anyone used any on me that I have none ready to supply.

The duke walks onward in silence, and as he does, his shoulders slowly straighten. He's picking himself back up, putting the wall that's been supporting him for so long back into place. I've done it a thousand times myself.

"I had no idea," I reply, moving to walk beside him once more. I'd heard his father died after falling from a horse he was trying to break. But I understand better than anyone why you'd want to cover it up.

"That's why I had to come here," he says, meeting my gaze once more. "I had to find someone else who'd understand. I had to find you." He looks younger somehow, his eyes more desperate.

I don't even know what to say. He came looking for me?

"I'm sure your other suitors brought you lavish presents equal to your station and beauty, but I prefer simpler, more meaningful gifts." He hesitates. "I was thinking perhaps I could take you on a tour of my ship." His dazzling smile is back.

The entire garden could have turned to gold around me, and I probably wouldn't have noticed because I'm so focused on his eyes, the way one eyebrow rests slightly higher than the other as his face tightens with expectation. Hope brews behind his eyes, making them glint in the morning light.

No one's ever smiled at me like that.

"Thank you." For the first time, I don't retreat into myself. I don't fear that if he looks into my eyes, he'll see the part of me that I've always held back. Because he'd only be seeing the reflection of his own pain, a pain he understands.

I make a mental reminder to thank Uncle Pheus. I didn't give him enough credit. Maybe he'd known that Duke Wystlinos wasn't just a man the kingdom needs, but a man *I* need.

And since Uncle Pheus already seems to like him, maybe he would let us go sailing someday. We could even find Jipper. I imagine standing at the bow of a ship and feeling the sea breeze rush over my unveiled face. When my reverie breaks, I realize where we are in the garden.

My stomach drops, and my hand clenches around the duke's arm as I suck in a breath.

We're about to turn the corner into the courtyard with the swan fountain.

Even now, the swans loom large in my mind. Three swans with their wings spread wide and thrown back form the top of the fountain. Water shoots out of their open beaks.

I used to love swans.

I pull back, my feet faltering.

Duke Wystlinos stops immediately. "What's wrong?"

"That part of the garden isn't very pretty," I stammer, trying not to sound as breathless as I feel. Bile creeps up my throat. If I think about it too hard, I swear I can detect a metallic taste. I swallow it back down and take a deep breath. "Let's go this way." I tug him back down the opposite path.

"Of course," he says with an easy grin. He loops his arm back through mine, eyeing the visible wing of one of the statues. "Don't like swans?"

I shake my head, but the tension doesn't release. I can't concentrate as Duke Wystlinos recounts the time he got chased by a one-legged swan as a child.

We emerge from behind a tall hedge. Before us, stairs lead up to the terrace. The palace windows gleam in the sunlight, and the building's tall towers cast long shadows across the thick stones that cover each wall.

As we near the end of the garden, the duke pauses and takes my hands in his. "Is it too much to ask to extend our walk a little longer?" he says.

I squint. His smile is soft and welcoming, and I want to say yes. But a headache has been spreading since we almost entered the courtyard with the swan fountain, and all I want to do is lie down and close my eyes.

"Perhaps tomorrow," I say. "I'm afraid I have a bit of a headache at the moment." I press my hand against my temple as a burst of pain radiates outward. It pulses behind my eyes. I try to focus my thoughts, but they only slip farther away.

Duke Wystlinos grasps my elbow. "Are you all right?"

"I think I've just been in the sun too long." I take a few blurry steps toward a fountain topped with mermaids perched upon shells. Each one has an arm raised in one of the cardinal directions. Below them, fish jut out of the fountain's base and spit out steady streams of water. A wide stone ledge encircles the fountain, and I press forward toward the ledge. If I can simply rest a moment, I'm sure I'll be fine.

But before I reach the ledge, screams erupt from the palace. I try to locate the exact direction of the sound, but my heartbeat pounds too loudly. The metallic taste returns to my mouth. At my side, the duke jumps, his attention seemingly torn between helping me and seeking the source of those screams.

The hedges loom large overhead and begin to sway as my vision narrows, dark edges creeping in until all I can see is what is directly before me. I reach the cool stone of the ledge and put a hand down to steady myself. Then two ledges appear before me as everything blurs.

A moment later, the pain in my head sears into my vision with a bright gold flash. My knees give out, and distantly, I hear my head striking the stone as I fall.

CHAPTER 3

The sun is still overhead when I open my eyes. Not that it means anything. When I was turned to gold, I spent three days trapped as a statue without realizing the duration. Any amount of time could've passed now, and the thought makes my stomach spin.

A blurry figure silhouetted by the sun moves into my line of sight. Slowly, the top of the mermaid fountain comes into focus, and I move a hand to shield my eyes from the sun, grateful I can move at all. Bit by bit, the pain in my head recedes slightly, and I make out the duke hovering above me. He has one hand holding up my head.

"Are you all right?" he asks.

I groan and sit up. Am I all right? I inspect my body. It's no golder than usual. I touch my hand to my head, where my headache seems to be throbbing with extra force. My gloves slide across something slick.

Blood. It stains two fingers of my glove as I wipe it away.

Duke Wystlinos leans in close. "Let me see." His fingers gently prod around my forehead. "It's a small scrape. It'll only bleed for a little bit." He tears a small scrap from the sleeve of his shirt. "Press this against it."

I take the silken fabric and press it against my head. "Thank you, Duke Wystlinos."

"You can call me Aris, if you like, Princess."

It's a daring move. And yet, I do feel like I've known him much longer than I have. So to repay the kindness he's offered me, I reply, "Thank you, Aris."

He relaxes on his haunches. "Do you think you can stand? Should I send for a chair to be brought out?" Wrinkles crease his forehead.

"No, I'll be fine." I balance between his arm and the fountain to gain my footing. My vision blurs once more before settling. I check the scrap of cloth, and the bleeding has slowed considerably.

"I thought I heard someone screaming in the palace," I add. Maybe they were my own screams. Everything after leaving the part of the garden with the swan fountain is hazy in my mind. I press my hands against my temples to massage away the last of the pain.

"I heard it too," he says quickly. "But I didn't want to leave you."

"We should go see." I lead him up the steps toward the palace, and as we near the top, Uncle Pheus's voice booms and rattles the glass windows. His words are unintelligible, but he sounds furious.

I drop Aris's arm and rush into the main hall. The head table has been thrown aside. Grapes roll across the floor. Puddles of honey ooze beneath overturned platters. Servants and nobles mingle together around the largest table, poking and prodding one another to get a better view.

"Where is the healer?" Uncle Pheus bellows.

I'm forced to push through the crowd because no one's noticed that it's me. Otherwise, they'd be coiling away from my touch.

Aris appears at my side. "Make way for the princess," he shouts.

Immediately, people slink away from me. A hush falls over the crowd.

People whisper about my exposed skin, but I barely hear them because, at the center of the circle, my father lies on the ground. His arms are sprawled out to either side, and his crown has rolled several feet away. His eyes are closed, almost as if he's sleeping. The chair he'd been sitting in is overturned behind him, as if someone flung it out of the way.

"The healer. Someone find the healer." Uncle Pheus's face is red from shouting.

"What happened?" I rush forward and fall to my knees by my father's side. I reach out to touch his chest, but then pull back. I hold my breath until I see his chest rise and fall. My father has often looked like he's been sleeping through council meetings only to bolt upright mumbling about the gold.

This is different.

"He began grasping his head and then collapsed," Uncle Pheus says. He puts a reassuring hand on my shoulder.

Servants appear carrying a couch between them. They lift my father onto it.

I pick up the fallen silver crown and ignore my own distorted reflection before placing it back on my father's head.

"Please wake up," I whisper.

My father doesn't stir.

A small man pushes through the crowd and straightens his

cap, re-concealing his balding head. He bows. "I'm the healer," the man says. He's breathing hard, likely from running all the way here.

I remember the man. He's the one who'd been called in to try to turn my skin back to normal.

He'd had me sit in a windowless room in the heart of the palace for a week, claiming seven days without sun would bleach my skin clear. When that cure didn't work, he'd covered me in every concoction imaginable. All he'd succeeded in doing was leaving me smelling like sap and rum for days, a result that doesn't inspire much hope in me now.

The healer lifts my father's eyelids, listens to his breathing, and checks for a pulse. He takes a tiny vial of yellow liquid from his bag and unscrews the lid. He waves the vial under my father's nose. My father doesn't react.

"I'll need to do a more thorough examination," the healer says, clearing his throat.

"Of course," my uncle replies. He motions for everyone to leave the room.

As everyone slowly disperses, I spot Archduke Ralton at the edge of the crowd with a smug look on his face, but he's quickly lost in the shuffle of people, each dragging their feet hoping to catch one last glimpse of the king or a snippet of dialogue that's being reserved for behind closed doors.

I take a deep breath when the doors to the hall shut.

Aris remains behind, and I'm actually thankful he hasn't left. His presence adds strength I didn't know I was missing.

"He doesn't appear to be in any immediate danger," the healer says, "but he won't come to his senses. What happened before he entered this state?"

"He was eating, as we all were," Uncle Pheus says. "I believe he was having head pains."

My stomach tightens and threatens to expel my breakfast. I'd thought the headache had been from being too near where my curse had started. How had my father felt it too?

"And he started muttering about the gold," Hettie says.

My heart clenches and stops for a moment. I twist my hands together.

I can't keep my eyes from closing, my mind from opening, from seeking the aura that marks the locations of each enchanted gold piece. For me, sensing the gold is like seeing a candle far in the distance on a dark night. Faint but noticeable, and brighter the closer I get.

Normally when I sense the gold, I shove it away. I don't ever want to think about gold, to let it in, to let it overtake me.

But today, I have to.

The auras are harder to locate today, but eventually, I find one. The golden table. It's right where it's always been in the tower. But when I keep searching, I realize I can't sense the pheasant or the goblets or any of the other golden objects.

My mouth goes dry. My eyes snap open.

"No," I whisper.

I grab the hem of my dress and dash toward the door. Someone shouts my name, but I don't stop. I rush down the corridor and up a flight of stairs. My braid thumps against my back in time with my heart.

I skid to a stop at the bottom of the second staircase. Blood drips down the stairs, and I leap away from the puddle seeping into the carpet. Each drop that rolls off the steps seems to confirm my fear.

I stare at the ceiling as I gingerly step around what becomes a stream, keeping one hand against the wall as I inch forward.

A guard's headless body limply hangs over the top step. I clutch my stomach and look away before I vomit, fighting to breathe as the metallic tang of blood creeps in around me. I struggle forward as much to get away from the sight as from the smell.

Ahead, the woven tapestry of several dancing ladies lays crumbled on the floor, exposing the pieces of the door and staircase it concealed. My feet slide into the grooves in the stone steps worn away by my father's continual trek up to the gold. As I climb, I suddenly wish I had a weapon.

At the top, the other door has been kicked in. No lamps are lit in the room—there don't need to be, at least not for me. An ever-pulsing glow ebbs and flows from inside, inviting me in as it did ten years ago.

My breathing quickens. I shouldn't be this close to the gold, to the room where I nearly killed a man last time I was in it. No, where I *did* kill a man.

But my father can barely survive without sitting next to the gold. Every day his eerie connection to it saps more of his strength, consumes more of his mind, makes him need its presence in order to keep going. What would happen to him if the gold really isn't in the tower?

Before I let my fears overtake me, I shove off the wall and into the round, windowless room.

The golden table rears up in front of me, and the glow overwhelms me, like I've stepped into the sunlight of the garden. I freeze. My breath catches in my throat. It's been years since I've seen real, solid gold. Not since the incident.

I swallow down the bile crawling up my throat. I force myself to inhale. No matter how much the room smells like metal, you can't inhale gold. I hope.

Still, my fingers itch inside my gloves. I clench them into fists and take one step farther into the room. Closer to the golden table. Its hulking legs look like columns of twisted gold, and its top could easily fit Hettie and me lying side by side.

It's the only object too big to steal. The other eleven objects are gone. Round and square outlines of dust are all that remain of the three coins, two chalices, rose, platter, pheasant, knife, tapestry, and necklace that my father had turned to gold.

My father's gold has been stolen.

CHAPTER 4

〉〉〉〉〉〉〉〉◉〈〈〈〈〈〈〈〈

T he wooden chair my father uses to sit near the gold lays in
pieces on the floor. I pick up what used to be the seat of
the chair and hold it like a shield across my chest.

Footsteps pound up the staircase toward the tower room.

Maybe it's the ghost of the man I killed. Still lurking here,
waiting for me to come back after all this time. Or maybe whoever decapitated that guard is still nearby. I shouldn't have run
off on my own. I shouldn't have come here at all.

My eyes widen when a figure does appear. I stumble backward until I collide with the wall. I clutch the broken chair
fragment closer to my chest.

It's not a thief or the man I killed come back to haunt me.
It's Aris.

"You shouldn't be here," I say. "It's not safe." *I'm not safe* is
what I meant, but I can't tell him that. I tighten my hold on the
chair fragment, willing myself to look at him and not at the table.
Oddly, that seems to help. My rising panic subsides the longer I
look in his eyes.

Still, the ever-pulsing glow doesn't let me forget that it's
there. Just one touch away.

"What's wrong? What's happened?" he asks breathlessly. His
eyes are wide as he takes in the room.

"It's gone," I say, my voice strangely hoarse, as though being this close to the gold has strained that too.

"What's gone?" The words echo hollowly around the room. He takes a hesitant step forward. He must've taken the same staircase I did. Bloody footprints trail behind him.

"My father's gold."

"We'll alert the palace guard. The thieves can't have gotten far. Come on." He reaches out to me.

"No." I answer as much to his statement as to his waiting hand. I'm afraid to step closer to him. Not with the table so close.

"Why not?"

I take a steadying breath. We'd never told anyone outside the family about my . . . ability. My curse. Most people have realized something was off about me, something more than just my gold skin. But we never confirmed it. Uncle Pheus always said it was better to let them wonder, to dream up their own ideas, than for us to confirm any weakness.

And yet, I feel that if anyone is going to understand my family's curse, it will be Aris. There is nothing else to lose anyway.

"The gold my father . . . created was stored in this room." The dingy space looks even dimmer with just one large gold table in the middle. Spider webs cling to the corners of the rafters. Oddly, none lace their way around the table legs, as if even the spiders are afraid to touch the gold.

"All of it?"

I nod. The whole reason my father had wanted The Touch in the first place was because the treasury was nearly empty, and he knew war was on the horizon. But he hadn't turned many things to gold before turning me to gold, after which he'd refused to touch anything.

"Surely your father can survive without a few gold pieces." Aris runs his fingers across the top of the table, leaving trails in the dust.

I shiver.

"That's just it," I force out, dragging my gaze away from the gold. "He can't. Dionysus was very specific after my father begged to be released from the curse. The god told him to take everything that had been touched down to the spot where the river met the ocean to be washed before the sun set on that very day."

I'd so often heard my father and uncle repeating the words Dionysus had said to them: "Make sure everything gets washed as I instructed, or there could be unhappy consequences. For my gifts take on a will of their own sometimes, and if it's not fully cleansed, especially from humans, well, sometimes they find their own ways of surviving."

"My father bathed in the water," I recount to Aris, "and had me carted down as well. My skin turned back to normal, and after that, he forgot about the other objects." I ignore the memory trying to surface of suddenly finding myself underwater and a halo of white light shining through the deep blue water as I sputtered back to life.

"My skin was gold again at sunset." I shudder, remembering how I thought I was turning back into a statue. My skin never hardened—it just took on its awful hue. "And the next day, my father started showing his first signs of weakness," I continue. "He'd lost the ability to turn things to gold, but everything he'd already turned was still enchanted, still contained a piece of him."

At first, I didn't understand the turmoil the gold was causing in my father's life. I didn't understand magic has a way of seeping into the soul like a poison bent only on making its victim do as it says. And the longer my father left the objects in their golden state, the more the magic pulled at him, convincing him that he needed the gold.

I toss the chair fragment back into the pile at my feet.

"Then we have to get it back," Aris says. "For your father."

Pheus appears in the doorway. "You shouldn't be up here." He's talking to me, but his gaze switches to Aris. He starts to gesture for the duke to leave, but he must've overheard part of our discussion and decided it was too late for that.

"I'm all right," I say, pulling Pheus's gaze back to me. It's not exactly the truth. I'd rather be anywhere else in the palace right now. Even the swan fountain.

He displays no emotion. "So, it's gone. I expected as much."

"Who could have taken it?" I ask. "No one else knew it was here." Pheus had carried the table up with the help of several servants who'd been paid off. But the servants had never known about the other objects.

"I don't know," Pheus replies. "I've alerted a few of my most trusted guards to discreetly search the city and check what ships were in port this morning."

"Why can't we just tell the people it was stolen?" Aris asks. "It would make it almost impossible for the thieves to sell it that way."

"If we did that, we'd have to tell them why the gold is so important in the first place," I say. Everyone knows all the palace gold was exchanged for silver ten years ago, when my father and Uncle Pheus learned that keeping gold around me was danger-ous. We'd dealt in silver ever since. Announcing the gold had been stolen would eventually lead someone to question why that particular gold had been kept, why we needed it back now.

"Whoever has that gold," Pheus adds, "holds the fate of the kingdom in their hands. We don't want to start an uprising, and we can't have the monarchy appearing weak." He clasps his hands. "I doubt they'd ransom it, and even if they did . . ." He trails off before admitting we couldn't afford it.

The kingdom has barely survived on the meager tithes people can manage after the Orland Wars ravaged so much.

"What else can we do?" I say. Now that I know the gold is gone, I want to leave the room and its memories behind. But if I don't get answers now, I'm afraid my uncle will shut me out of the discussion about what should be done for my father.

"I fear there's not much else we can do," Pheus says. "Your father is being moved to his bedchamber as we speak. I imagine he'll continue to weaken as the gold moves farther away. Unless my guards find the gold before the thieves smuggle it away, I'm afraid the healer might be our only hope."

My uncle sighs. "I'm sorry, Kora." He turns to leave, no doubt to take up vigil next to my father's bed as he's been doing for years.

The glow coming from the table seems to increase along with my heart rate. I try to catch Aris's eye, but he seems fixated on the table.

His tale about his own father echoes through my mind, how he'd tried to dig his father out but had been too late. I can't let that happen to my father.

"Wait," I call, stalling Pheus, and praying I don't regret my words. "I might be able to find it."

"What?" Pheus's eyebrows shoot up. "How?"

Aris's eyes jump to mine.

"I can . . . I can sense the gold," I say quickly. I wring my hands. If nothing else, it prevents me from reaching out to the table.

This isn't exactly how I hoped Aris would find out about one of my side effects. Actually, I had hoped he'd never find out. Especially when it came to the other one.

I'd never told Pheus about my ability to sense the gold for the same reason I never told anyone else. I didn't need everyone watching my eyes, seeing if I was looking toward the tower, waiting for the day the gold would take over my thoughts. Things were bad enough after I killed that man, and though I was young, I'd learned to keep my mouth shut, even around my family.

"What do you mean?" Pheus asks cautiously.

"Ever since . . . it happened, I've been able to sense the other objects my father turned to gold. That's how I knew to come here . . ." I trail off, staring at the floor.

"Why have you never mentioned this before?" Pheus looks around the room to make sure it is secure for such a conversation.

I'm afraid to look at either of them. "I . . . I don't know." I can't admit I don't want them to think I'll lose my mind to the gold like my father has.

"How could you keep this from me, Kora?" Pheus demands.

"I'm sorry."

Uncle Pheus looks like he's about to snap at me, but instead he takes a deep breath. "No, this is good news. I just wish you'd told me sooner. By now, the thieves may have already departed on an outgoing ship or have a lead on us over land. Can you sense the gold now?"

"I can't pinpoint its exact location," I say. "It's more like I know when I'm getting closer." I close my eyes and try to steady my breathing. I've never looked outside the palace. But I can do this. I have to.

I reach out with my mind. I don't know how long it takes—it feels like I stand there forever, eyes closed and fists clenched. But eventually, I sense a familiar aura, and I follow the light. After the table, the tapestry is easiest to find because of its size. I locate it with the other objects. They keep sliding up and down. I've never concentrated on the objects for so long. I wonder if they're bouncing up and down because I can't control my connection with them.

I shake my head to break the connection. I then stretch out my hand in the direction they're traveling and open my eyes. "There." I point to the far wall. Toward the ocean. "Somehow, they're moving. They must be on a ship."

"This certainly changes things," Pheus says, rubbing his chin.

"I could take one of my father's ships and go after it," I say. My heart, already beating quickly from having to track the gold, skips several beats at the thought of sailing out of Lagonia's harbor and straight for the gold.

"You're much too valuable here," Pheus replies. "If something were to happen to your father—"

"I'm the only one who can find the gold. How long do you think my father will survive without it?"

Pheus frowns, troubled by my question. "You haven't been out of the palace since you were a child. You're not ready to face the world outside. It wouldn't be safe."

"If you'd allow me, I could go with her," Aris says.

I shoot him a look of surprise. I can't believe everything he's learned about me, about what's going on, hasn't scared him away.

His generosity, his loyalty to the crown, makes my chest swell. I haven't encountered kindness like this in years.

"Thank you, Duke Wystlinos," Pheus says. "But I'm not sure I'm comfortable sending my niece away with a man I don't know."

His words threaten to send a blush creeping across my cheeks. Despite his gruff demeanor, Pheus has always looked out for me, more than my father has in the past ten years. And despite his desire to keep me safe, I know Pheus can't come. Someone has to look after my father and the kingdom, to make sure Archduke Ralton doesn't try anything. Pheus is the only person I trust.

"I have to be the one to go," I add, pleading. "No one else can track it."

"It could take two weeks or more to outfit the Royal Armada for such a journey." Pheus's eyes jump around as he makes calculations. He lowers his gaze, his shoulders deflating like my father's always do. "Even if I let you go, you might not make it in time."

My eyes land on Aris. Maybe we don't need an entire armada.

"What about Ar . . . Duke Wystlinos's ship?" I blurt out.

Aris's face brightens as he steps forward. "My ship is much faster than anything in the Royal Armada, and I could have it ready to sail with tomorrow morning's tide."

"Yes," I practically shout. "And his crew has experience dealing with thieves and pirates."

"Indeed," Aris replies. I can already see the adventurer in him rising to the surface. It's like seeing one of the heroes from my books come to life. "With your ability to locate the gold and my crew, we'll have no trouble getting the cursed items back."

Pheus paces the length of the room several times. I watch

him, saying nothing. It's always better to let him think than to force him into a quick decision, and this decision could mean my father's life or death.

I rub my fingers together to keep them from shaking.

"We could pass it off as a suitor taking the princess out sailing for a few days," Uncle Pheus says slowly, "since that's something she's always wanted to do."

If I wasn't so nervous about what happened the last time I touched a person in this room, I would hug him. "Thank you, Uncle Pheus. I promise, I won't let you—or Father—down."

"Then it's settled," Aris says with a nod. "We leave in the morning." He gives me a reassuring smile, which I return, even though the reality of what I'm about to do starts to sink in.

The three of us depart from the tower, and the golden table sends its flashing shadows chasing down the winding steps after me. It's only when we reach the hallway below that I feel I take my first real breath since stepping into the room.

The guard's body is gone by the time we reach the stairs, but I can't help but overhear one of the other guards say that they haven't been able to find the head.

My stomach clenches.

Maybe the rumors about Captain Skulls are true. Or maybe it is a copycat. I pray it's only a coincidence. But it doesn't matter. I'm still going to have to face whatever twisted soul is capable of doing that.

CHAPTER 5

>>>>>>>>◉<<<<<<<<

'm frozen. My father's shapeless, faceless form comes at me in the night. His arms snake out toward me and coil around my body. He grasps me so tight I can't breathe. My lungs burn. Tears escape down my cheeks. When he releases me and recedes back into the darkness, I watch helplessly as liquid gold slithers up my body. My flesh crusts over with a thick golden coating.

I claw at the gold before it can reach my arms. My fingernails screech against the metal glaze, but it's no use. The gold continues on unhindered. It constricts across my throat, crushing it so I can hardly breathe. Gold pools in my mouth, further choking me as it slides down my throat. It heads straight into my lungs and weaves its way toward my heart. It always ends at my heart. One beat. Two beats. There are no words to describe the agony of feeling your own heart stop.

I bolt awake. Beads of sweat dot my brow. Morning dawns through the window, but I don't feel rested at all, having dreamt of gold and thieves and headless corpses all night long.

My skin glows ever so softly in the darkness, and I hold up an arm to inspect it. Where freckles should dot my skin, a metallic sheen shimmers. It looks like someone has taken golden flour and doused me in it. I drop my arm back down and get out of bed.

I dress myself in a simple green dress—no maid wants to

touch a cursed girl, so I've never had the luxury of wearing complicated outfits. That's also why the dress hangs limply on my slim form, since no tailors will get close enough to measure me. They just guess and send over their best estimates. Unfortunately, their estimates aren't very good.

I look around my room, wondering what else I should bring on my trip. Haphazardly, I toss a few more dresses into a trunk, followed by shoes and cloaks in case we run into bad weather. I linger over my bookshelves, running my fingers over the spines of the thick leather books I've taken from the palace library. The ones like *Captain Corelli's Account of the Sea*. After I'd forgotten what the real sea smelled like up close, the ocean smelled like the ink and mustiness of its pages.

A few seashells sit in front of the books.

My mother had come from Sunisa, a country known for their seafarers. Before she died, she would take me to the shore to collect seashells, and after she was gone, I imagined every shell that tumbled out of the surf at my feet was sent by her. I'd look at my reflection in their glossy surfaces and for one second pretend that it was her looking back at me.

My trips to the seaside stopped after I turned to gold, but that was all about to change today.

I go back to my preparations, tying my waist-length golden hair into a thick braid. I've always wondered if I shaved it all off, would it grow back its original color—a deep brown like my mother's?

Once I'm fully dressed and packed, I pull on my gloves, but my hand lingers on my veil. For once, I want to feel the breeze wash across my face. I want to see the streets of Lagonia. But that means leaving so much of my skin exposed. It's not just the ridicule I fear, but the knowledge that if someone touched my skin, they could be hurt. Killed. Turned to solid gold.

I must be feeling brave or crazy because I leave the veil where it sits. Praying I don't regret the decision, I pull out a cloak and tie it around my neck, yanking the hood low over my face.

My stomach is in knots while I direct a servant to take my trunk outside, to where I hope Aris is waiting. The servant tries his best not to look at my face as I speak, but he chances a few furtive glances. When he finally sets about his task, I linger in the hallway outside my room, debating whether I should go to my father's room to say good-bye. My stomach twists even more, and I decide against it. He can't bear to look at me on a good day. I don't want to make him worse. He'll need all the strength he has left to survive until I can bring back the gold.

The palace is quiet as I make my way through the halls, and once I'm outdoors, I find a small wooden cart waiting. Not exactly a transport fit for a princess, and I smile slightly, knowing Hettie would throw a fit if she were asked to ride in it.

My heart pinches slightly when I see Aris hasn't come to escort me himself; instead, Uncle Pheus waits next to the cart, looking as nervous as I feel. To my surprise, he pulls me into a hug.

"Be safe," he says. "My brother's life is in your hands."

His words pierce my heart, and I nod numbly as he pulls away.

"You can do this," he adds, patting my shoulder, reminding me of all the times he's been there to protect me, to guide me when my own father couldn't. It's the reassurance I need to climb into the cart.

I stay far out of sight from the horse. Animals haven't always reacted well upon seeing my skin.

The driver puts up a good show of not trying to scoot farther away from me. But he does.

Uncle Pheus waves good-bye, and I turn for one final look at the palace. I spot Archduke Ralton standing on one of the balconies overlooking the courtyard. No doubt he's wondering where I'm off to. Hopefully Uncle Pheus's excuse about Aris taking me sailing works because I'm unnerved by Archduke Ralton's watchful gaze.

As soon as a few last-minute supplies are loaded into the cart, the driver snaps the reins and the horse trots forward. Its hooves clop against the cobblestones in the almost-deserted courtyard.

The last time I rode down the streets was ten years ago during the Rose Festival, an annual tradition in Lagonia. My father and I, and my mother before we lost her, would toss rose petals from the carriage windows. They were supposed to bring good luck if they landed on you. After the carriage had passed by, the people lining the streets would rush in and grab handfuls of the petals and toss them at one another.

That all stopped after The Touch. Though the festival continued, we didn't go out into the streets and toss rose petals. We didn't celebrate. We didn't have any good luck.

I can't imagine how the streets have changed in the past years.

We arrive at the palace gates, and they open, the metal screeching on its hinges. As we leave the royal grounds behind, city air rushes over me, clinging like oil to my skin.

On the wealthier houses close to the palace, old columns race upward to support tiled roofs. Those buildings give way to the small shops tucked away behind intricately carved archways that line the avenue. Narrow, twisted alleyways that lead into the less savory parts of the city flank the shops. Inside the shops, darkness presses against the closed shutters.

It's too early for most people to be out and about in town, and I feel strangely disappointed that I don't get the chance to see more of my kingdom's people, no matter how much I worry about their reactions. I see a few merchants carting their wares to the main avenue and setting up under the arches. Around them, men haul olives, others roast almonds in a giant pan over an open flame, and others lay out woven rugs and tapestries for sale.

I wish I could stay and watch, but the cart clatters onward.

When we reach the dock, dozens of men mill about in puddles of light emanating from lanterns hung from tall poles. Some men aren't wearing shoes or shirts while others wear only simple vests to cover their chests. They look up as the cart shudders to a stop before the gangplank.

Gravel threatens to poke through my thin slippers when I hop off, doing so before the driver can panic about having to help me down.

Aris's ship is smaller than I expected. Much smaller than any ship in the Royal Armada. Barnacles creep their way up the waterline of the ship, and the figurehead at the front doesn't make me feel any better. It's a wooden swan with its wings stretching back in flight. Several of the feathers have broken off, making the swan look uneven.

I scan the crowd looking for Aris, but what I see instead is a man in a blue coat leaning on the railing of the upper deck. The wind tugs his disheveled blond hair away from his face, and I notice he's roughly my age.

He's rubbing something small, a coin maybe, between his fingers. Lantern light glints off it. A flash of gold. I stiffen. It was just a reflection, I tell myself. It's probably nothing more than a copper coin or even a button.

As his fingers continue their slow circles, he does nothing to conceal the fact he's watching me. It's an odd feeling. Most people see me and quickly look away in horror, but my cloak must work better than expected.

After a few moments, he tucks whatever he was holding in his pocket and pushes off the railing, disappearing from view. I continue to stare at the spot until a voice sounds behind me.

"Look what we got here," a man says. He wipes his brow with his thin arm and drops a large sack of flour onto a pile of similar bags.

Another man whistles.

I turn to find two identical men looking at me.

"I saw her first," the man by the bags says.

"Doesn't mean she'll like you better," the second one replies.

The men are skinny and aren't much taller than I am, but they have several years on me. Both have ears that stick a little too far out from their heads and dark hair that spikes up at impossible angles. When they smile, their wide grins seem to balance out their faces.

I'm not used to so much attention. My first instinct is to curl inward, but I don't. These men aren't making fun of me. They don't even know who I am. I hope.

"Are you going to be joining us?" the man by the pile asks. He saunters closer and smiles. I pull my hood farther down.

"It's bad luck to have a woman aboard," another man says as he spits at my feet. I step back, disgusted. His nearly bald head reflects the morning sun as he turns away from me. The small tufts of hair forming a semicircle around the bottom half of his scalp are gray around the edges, but even though he's older, his arms still bulge with muscles earned from heaving barrels and supplies around the ship.

"Quiet, Brus," the second twin says.

"Yeah, quiet," the first twin repeats, turning back to face me. He tries to catch a glimpse under my hood. I duck my face to the side in a motion I pray he'll mistake as shyness. "Brus doesn't mean any disrespect. It's just the last time we had a woman on board, well . . ." He trails off. He smiles and leans closer. One tooth is missing from the bottom row of his teeth and his breath reeks of alcohol. "I'm Phipps."

He holds out a calloused hand.

I drop a quick curtsy instead of offering my hand in return. "Nice to meet you," I say, hoping he doesn't notice I haven't given my name. I keep my head bowed until he speaks again.

"The pleasure is mine."

I risk a glance upward.

One gold hoop earring dangles from his earlobe.

Sweat trickles down my spine. I've forgotten how many places gold can hide. Shoe buckles, rings, and even teeth become potential hazards.

I start to back away. A hand comes down on my shoulder, and I jump.

"I don't blame you for trying to get away. He's always smelled bad," the second twin says. "I'm Thipps, his better half."

"That's not true at all," Phipps complains.

Thipps ignores his brother and smiles, and from my close proximity I spot one gold tooth right under his large front ones.

I try to scramble away from his grip. He looks hurt when I duck away.

"Ha," Phipps laughs. "Seems you don't smell any better."

"Meeting the crew, I see," Aris says, coming up behind me.

Despite the gold all around, I relax at the sound of his voice and turn to face him. He's silhouetted against the sky, and sunrays break over his head like a crown. It's obvious that a real crown would sit just as nicely.

Today he's wearing a green jacket adorned with thick silver appliques, which makes him stand out among the drab and dirty clothes worn by the sailors. Looking at my own dress, I realize we match.

"I was beginning to think you'd changed your mind," he adds, his tone light. "Welcome to the *Swanflight*." He gestures wide toward the rest of the main deck.

"*Swanflight?*" I fight against the image of stone swans spewing out water, of my father coming toward me.

"It's the name of the ship," he clarifies. "But don't worry. I've made sure there aren't any one-legged swans onboard." He winks, and just like that, my anxiety is gone. My stomach still feels jittery, just not for the reason it had been before.

"Don't let Phipps and Thipps bother you." He waves his hand dismissively at each twin as he names them. "They're harmless." He leans down and whispers, "The only way to tell them apart is by looking at their teeth. One's got a gold tooth and one doesn't. The problem is, I can never remember which one has the tooth."

"I heard that," one of the twins shouts. "You can tell us apart because I tie ropes better than Phipps. And I raise a sail faster too."

"That's not true," Phipps cuts in.

Aris laughs and shakes his head. He bends close to me. "Just never enter into any bets with those two. They'll win every time.

I can't count how much I've lost to them over the years." He says it like he doesn't care. I guess when you have as much money as he does, it really doesn't matter. "One time I had to climb up to the crow's nest naked and sing an ode to Poseidon after losing at a game of Drown the Cup."

I blush at his words.

He holds his hands up defensively. "I've always been a man of my word, so I had to go through with it. It's a good thing I've got a good voice, though," he adds. "Otherwise, I'm sure Poseidon would've sunk us right there."

I can't help but laugh as he draws me aboard, and I don't look back as my feet leave the dock.

Ropes coil around tall poles and pegs along the deck while gathered sails hang like curtains from the masts. Various sized crates are strapped down along the outer edge of the deck. I run my gloved fingers over the ropes holding them in place. I can't believe I'm actually on a real ship.

Farther down the deck, stairs lead up to another deck, which contains the helm. Below it is a door leading deeper into the ship. The whole place smells of fish.

I want to run along naming every part of the ship I know, explore the lower decks, and stand at the helm and pretend I'm leading the ship out of the harbor.

Aris clasps sailors on their shoulders and cheerily greets them as we pass.

"This is our fine captain, Royce Denes." Aris gestures to an approaching man.

"You're not the captain?" I ask Aris.

"No, I leave all the navigating to him. I'm just the financier."

When the captain reaches us, I realize he's the man in the

blue coat I saw watching me. I should've realized that most captains wear blue as a sign of their rank. Even the captains in the Armada do.

He's as tall as Aris, but not as muscular. Up close, his hair is even wilder. Loose strands hang over his forehead, falling just short of covering his eyebrows. It's the haircut of a man who'd been a long time at sea.

Royce's name sounds vaguely familiar, and I wonder if he is the son of a lesser nobleman. There are far too many families to know them all by name. Or more precisely, if I'd been a proper princess, I would've been trained to recite them. But I am not a proper princess. Not by a long stretch.

"Royce, this is Kora." Aris keeps his voice low, so none of the other sailors will hear. But he doesn't tell the captain I'm a princess, for which I'm relieved.

I worry my name will be a dead giveaway, but Royce doesn't react. I guess there must've been enough parents who named their daughters after me before I was cursed for it not to raise his suspicions.

But I worry I won't be able to keep my secret for long, that if the captain knew who I was before we left port, he would leave me and my curse behind.

"A pleasure to meet you, my lady." Royce bows, but the motion is forced, and I can immediately tell he has none of Aris's charm. His gaze is directed at me, but it's like he's looking through me to monitor his crew on the docks below. Unlike most of the men we passed, he doesn't squint to see what's concealed beneath my hood. I notice his eyes are a deep blue, so deep that I might be looking through them to the ocean beyond.

But it's not his eyes I fixate on. It's his blue captain's jacket. Gold buttons run in two lines down the front. Golden threads weave a wide web of loops over his shoulders. Even his cufflinks are gold.

The sight of it overwhelms me, and I take a few jagged steps backward toward the gangplank before my legs go rigid. I never realized until now how much Pheus has done to protect me from gold by keeping it out of the castle.

Aris might understand my having some sort of mental connection to the cursed gold, but how would he react if he found out what I could do?

I glance down the gangplank, wondering if it isn't too late to flee, but Phipps or Thipps is rolling a barrel up and complaining under his breath how this one is so much heavier than all the rest.

I'm trapped. It's like I can feel a golden noose tightening around my throat, cutting off my air supply. I shift my gaze toward the sea. I've always loved looking at the ocean from my balcony. It reminds me of my mother.

Tension drains from my body as I watch the even waves. Thoughts of the gold recede slightly, at least enough for me to remember why I can't turn back.

"Aren't you awfully young to be a captain?" I ask Royce, hoping he doesn't take offense.

Royce clears his throat, but Aris answers, "He might be young, but he's better than any older captain who lived through the Orfland Wars."

"Not many captains *did* live through the Wars," Royce says quietly.

"I see," I say, not knowing what else I can add. I eye Royce, careful to keep my eyes from drifting to the gold. He must be very lucky if he survived. "When do we set sail, Captain?" I ask.

"We're loading the last of the supplies now," Royce says, and this time, he doesn't add a *my lady*. He's nothing like the dashing, romantic captains I've read about. I bet that even if he found out I was royalty, he'd still treat me with the same curtness. It's a sobering reminder that I have no authority at sea.

"The captain has been good enough to give up his quarters for you to use," Aris says to make conversation, since Royce certainly isn't going to. "I wanted you to have the best cabin. It won't be like anything you're used to, but I've already taken all the necessary actions to ensure that it is as comfortable as possible."

"Thank you," I say. As I do, there's a great scraping noise as the gangplank is pulled onto the ship.

"Excuse me," Royce says. He moves toward where Phipps and Thipps are dragging up the gangplank and begins shouting that if they scrape the deck, they'll be made cabin boys for the voyage.

"Perhaps you'd like to watch us cast off with me?" Aris offers me his arm.

We head toward the rear of the ship and lean against the wood railing. When the ship pulls slowly away from the dock, several ropes slither off the dock and into the water. Sailors pull them up, winding them around various pegs.

As we leave the harbor, I watch the palace fade into the distance. It doesn't look like I thought it would—the walls don't lean inward as they seem to do when I'm trapped inside.

"Are you going to miss it?" Aris says.

I tear my eyes away from the retreating town. Only the palace towers are visible now as the foggy morning swallows the town.

"I guess I will." I've never been far enough away to miss anything.

The sea stretches out around us, fading from gentle blues to deeper, darker colors. A light breeze sprays us with a salty mist and lifts aloft the birds that fly in and out of crevices on the cliffs that border the harbor. Their shrill calls fill the air as some swoop toward us, rising and dipping in time with the ship.

I turn toward the bow, where the sun has started to peek above the sea. Sunrise has always been my favorite time of day, and past the horizon, the rising sun nestles in a cloudy haze of oranges and pinks.

There's an old saying that a pink sky in the morning means rough seas ahead, but for the first time in my life, with Aris at my side, I actually feel ready to face whatever dangers come my way.

CHAPTER 6

Aris leans over the railing as a pod of dolphins appears in our wake. "Some people say Triton sends dolphins as a sign of a good journey ahead."

I can't help the smile that slides across my face. I've never heard that before, and I'm fairly certain Aris made it up in an attempt to calm my nerves. I keep tugging at my sleeves and gloves. I cast a glance over my shoulder every few seconds to make sure Royce and his gold buttons haven't moved any closer.

"I hope you're right," I say. We'll need a smooth journey. And a fast one. Will my father last a week? A month? Two?

Aris must sense my apprehension because his voice takes on the jovialness it held when I first saw him. He switches position so that his back leans against the railing and his elbows are propped out on either side. He flicks hair away from his eyes. "Did I ever tell you about the time I used nothing more than a conch shell to fight off four men who accused me of cheating at cards?"

I give him a skeptical look.

"Really," he says. "We were on one of the small Rolliginian Islands, I can't even remember which one. It was in the island's only tavern, and every table had these ridiculously large conch shells as centerpieces." He stretches his hands out in front of his stomach to show how large the conch was.

Before he can continue the story, another voice cuts between us.

"We're clear of the harbor," Royce says.

I turn to find him standing with his arms clasped behind his back.

"Let's discuss what direction we need to head." Royce motions for us to follow him and then sets off without waiting to see if we do.

But I don't want to. Not when it means being so close to gold again and having to tell someone else how I can find it. Sadly, I have no choice.

Royce leads us to a room right under the helm. The air is stale, but at least it doesn't smell like fish. A small desk occupies one portion of the room, and across from it are two chairs with worn leather cushions. Several shelves run the length of the room and are laden with books and journals whose tattered covers are too worn to read from this distance. Thin wood beams run across the bookshelves, preventing the books from falling while the ship is in motion. At the far end of the room is a large window looking out the back of the ship. Underneath it is a rumpled bed with my trunk shoved against the foot. So I guess this is my new room.

Beneath one set of shelves opposite the bed is a mirror. I haven't kept one of those in my room since being turned back. It's bolted into the wall, so there's no chance I can take it down.

I turn and catch my reflection as I move farther into the room. One flash of gold. I look away.

Royce shuts the door. "We're about to hit open water, and I need to know which direction to take." he says. "Aris tells me you have the map for this voyage." He waits.

My throat is dry. I've never trusted men who wear gold. A

few had tried after it was banned from the palace, and even after they were forced to take it off, I felt uneasy around them. They always seemed to be looking to confirm their own importance, to show how important wealth was to them. And I've seen firsthand what a want for wealth could do to a man.

But if Aris trusts Royce, I suppose I must.

I try to think of what to say, of how to explain how I know where we're going without sounding crazy. Something tells me he won't simply accept me pointing in a direction and telling him to go that way.

"May I see the map?" The annoyance in his voice is clear.

Seconds tick away.

"There is no map," I finally blurt out.

"What?" Royce turns toward Aris. "What's going on here? If you're leading me on another one of your wild goose chases, then I'm heading back to the dock right now. Last time we didn't have a map, we ended up in the Straits of Temperance, and I'm sure you remember what happened then."

"She's the map." Aris points to me.

"I can find the gold," I say with as much authority as I can muster.

"Gold?" He turns to Aris, clearly confused.

"Come on, it'll be just like old times. Remember the time we sailed out to that little island in the middle of your lake looking for treasure and swung from vines and found that snake . . ."

"We're not kids anymore. I don't have time to sail off searching for treasure that doesn't exist," Royce snaps.

"So it's a little more complicated than I made it seem," Aris says with a shrug. "It's nothing you can't handle."

"You said it would be a simple journey, a journey to find some girl's father on a merchant ship because his wife is dying. You didn't say anything about gold."

I turn to Aris, confused.

Aris looks apologetically at me and clears his throat, but Royce cuts him off. "My ship is in need of repairs. Whatever gold you're after will have to wait."

"It's a matter of life and death," Aris says.

"Whose life?" Royce asks.

"The king's," I supply.

There's a beat of silence, I think Royce may finally relent and start listening, but instead, he has the opposite reaction.

Royce's eyes snap upward like he's pleading with Poseidon himself. "No." He marches toward the door.

Aris matches him stride for stride and slams his arm against the door before Royce can storm out.

Royce eyes Aris's arm as if he's trying to decide if it's worth the fight.

"You know I don't work for *him*," Royce spits. "He has an armada at his disposal. And despite the fact I've never once seen those ships sail to fight the pirates plaguing the coast, his fleet is actually meant for things like this. Let them help with whatever this gold problem is. I have no desire to fill the king's coffers."

I'm stunned by his reaction. "You can't deny aid to the king."

"What do you think he did during the Orfland Wars, hmm?" Royce asks, his voice hard. "His people were dying, and he stayed locked up safe and sound in his precious palace. I owe that man nothing."

I want to defend my father, to explain why he couldn't be in the front lines. But I don't—part of me knows the curse, and everything that followed, stemmed from my father's greed. "Please," I say. "We need your help."

Royce's eyes flick to me. "I doubt it."

My hands go to my hood. I hesitate. But I can't imagine what having to sail back to the harbor and outfitting another ship would do to my father's health.

We need all the time we can get.

I lower my hood, and Royce's eyes follow the movement.

He gasps. "It's not possible." His eyes have gone wide. His mouth opens and closes a few times, like he's trying to work out what to say.

"I'm Princess Kora," I say, "and my father's gold has been stolen. His *enchanted* gold, which he needs to survive. We need to get it back as quickly as possible. The Royal Armada would have taken too long to supply, so Aris offered the use of his ship."

Royce's eyes narrow and swing to Aris. He looks shocked, like he's been betrayed. "Is this some kind of trick?" He's pale, as if he's seen a ghost. "Did you paint a girl gold just to fool me? Everyone knows the only thing Midas keeps locked up tighter than his gold is his daughter."

"It's not a joke," I plead. "I really am the princess."

"Who took the gold?" Royce asks. His voice sounds even colder than before.

"I don't know. But I can find out." Desperate, I clamp my eyes shut. The aura of the cursed objects overwhelms me— either we're getting closer, or I'm getting better. I can just make out the room the gold is in from the light it gives off. All the items are stacked in a corner on a wood floor. A sheet has been thrown over them.

I return to myself, shaking. I've never pictured the gold or its location that clearly before. And I don't even know if what I've seen is enough to go on.

"You don't know who took it, or how many men we're going to be facing, or even if we're sailing right into a trap?" Royce asks.

"No . . ." I admit.

He cuts me off. "You don't know, and yet you expect my men to fight for you, to die for you?"

"I expect them to fight for their king," I say. I realize too late it's the wrong thing to say.

Life comes back into Royce's face as his cheeks redden. "A king that's done nothing for his people these past ten years? No, thank you. I've tried fighting for him before, and it didn't turn out so well for me."

"Royce," Aris says, trying to step between us.

"Stay out of this, Wystlinos. You're the one who got me into this mess. I agreed to take you out to a merchant ship, a ship that would be easy to catch and deal with."

"You were willing to help a girl help her father," I say, fighting to find anything to keep us from losing more time. "That's still the case here."

"Going after a merchant isn't the same as going after a thief," he shoots back.

"No," I concede, "but Aris told me how his crew has taken on pirates and cutthroats before."

Royce doesn't look convinced, so I say the only other thing I can think of. The thing I know I'll regret. "You'll be paid."

That gets his attention. "How much?"

"Enough to repair your ship and pay your crew for their services," I say. Already my stomach is starting to churn along with the ocean beneath us. I can't take that much money from the treasury.

In fact, there's only one way I know of to get enough to pay him off. The thing I promised I'd never do—use my abilities to create gold.

I've never been good at reading people, primarily because most people won't get close enough to let me study their faces, but Royce seems even more difficult than I imagine most are. His stare gives nothing away.

"Please," I beg in one final attempt, "my father's life and the welfare of the kingdom depend on us getting that gold back."

Royce studies me, weighing me with his eyes. "I'll take your offer to my crew, but I'll make no guarantees," he says curtly and leaves.

I wonder if he'll come back or if he's just ordering the ship to turn around.

"I'm sorry about Royce," Aris says, staring at the door. "Bringing me to the palace was his final payment for buying the *Swanflight* from me to start his own shipping business." He stares out the window. "I should have told him everything, but I was afraid he wouldn't help us. As I'm sure you noticed, he has no love for your father."

"Why?"

Aris sighs. "Do you remember hearing about the incident with the Orfland Treaty?"

I think for a moment before the realization hits me. *That's* where I'd heard his name before. Everyone had been talking about the young captain who'd lost the treaty, the one who could have stopped the war weeks sooner. "That was him?"

Aris slowly nods his head. "And me. I was on that ship too, carrying the treaty to Orfland. That's the document the pirates stole from me that I mentioned in the rose garden. I didn't want to tell you because I was afraid of what you'd think of me."

"What do you mean?" I ask.

Aris sighs again. "We weren't far from Port Tamur when we picked up a woman floating in the water. I urged Royce to lock her up, but he wouldn't. That night, we awoke to the sound of cannon fire. A ship had snuck up in the darkness. Just as the men were rousing themselves for a counter attack, the bottom blew out of our ship. Turns out the woman was one of the pirates, the ones I told you about back at the palace. She drugged the lookout and used one of our own barrels of oil to blow the ship in half." He shook his head. "Royce and I and a few others made it out, but the ship was destroyed, and the treaty papers were lost. We were lucky the currents took us to Port Tamur."

"I thought you said you fought the pirates."

"We did. After we reached Port Tamur, I bought another ship, this ship, and went after them. I gave the death blow to the pirate captain myself. After we got back, though, Royce wasn't the same. He lost all credibility, and they kicked him out of the armada."

I can see why, and I can see why Aris wouldn't want anyone knowing about his involvement as well. That lost treaty almost cost us an end to the Orfland Wars. It took months to get a second copy through, and during that time, rumors swirled about what had happened to the first treaty.

"But if anyone can get your gold back, it's him. I've never known a better sailor or swordsman." Aris moves closer to the window so that sunlight falls on his face, and he smiles at me, the same confident smile he wore in the palace. "Besides, I wouldn't be here if it hadn't been for that incident. I first met your uncle when he was investigating what happened to the treaty. Somehow, he knew the truth about my father's death and encouraged me to come visit you. He thought we might get along."

Without thinking about it, I move to stand beside Aris. Sunlight hits my face and sends a glint around the room, and he winces as it passes across his eyes.

I duck my face. "I'm sorry."

Aris lifts his hand to my cheek and lightly touches my skin. My pulse quickens as his fingers trail along it.

"Don't ever apologize for being what you are." His smile broadens. A strand of dark hair falls across his gray eyes.

I have the strange urge to sweep it back.

But before I can, the door crashes open.

I reach for my hood but stop when I see it's only Royce.

Aris drops his hand from my cheek, and we take a few hurried steps away from each other.

Royce clears his throat. "My men don't want to help a king who lets pirates raid the coast while he sits locked away in his palace with his gold. But"—he pauses—"lucky for you, I need the money to repair my ship. So I agree to accept your offer."

Relief floods through me. "Thank you, Captain."

Aris finds my hand and squeezes it.

"I'm still going to need to know how we find the gold, Princess," Royce says, obviously not caring about our tender moment.

"Of course, and call me Kora, please." I say, trying to remove some of the tension between us.

He doesn't respond, so I focus on finding the tapestry. My mind returns to the room I saw earlier, and I struggle to find where it is in relation to our ship.

Finally, I point to the far wall. "That way."

"Are you sure?"

"Trust her, Royce," Aris says.

Royce studies both of us and nods.

I exhale. I thought he would demand an explanation for my abilities. I guess as long as he gets paid, he doesn't care.

He walks back toward the door before turning back. "I'll expect an update every hour in case they change direction."

I swallow. Of course, I'll have to continually check on the gold. Continually let it into my mind. I take a calming breath and try not to think about what effect that might have.

Royce swings the door open but jerks to a stop.

Phipps, I think, and Brus—the one who spit at me on the dock—are outside holding a hooded figure between them. I pull up my own hood and stuff my braid inside so the men can't see my skin at the same time they pull back the hood of their captive. A mass of auburn curls explodes.

It's Hettie.

〉〉〉〉〉〉〉〉◉〈〈〈〈〈〈〈〈

CHAPTER 7

I let out a groan at the same time Hettie does.

"Found this one hiding in a barrel, Captain," Phipps says. He shoves Hettie into the room. She whimpers and clutches her stomach.

"I don't want no trouble for disobeying, Captain," Brus says. "I was all for throwing the girl overboard right away."

"But," Phipps cuts in, "I thought you might want to take a look at this one."

"Do you know the punishment for stowing away?" Royce asks. "I have every right to throw you overboard. Convince me why I shouldn't." He waits, poised like a cat ready to pounce.

When Hettie doesn't answer, Royce strides over and stands menacingly above her. "Who are you?"

Hettie moans in response.

"She's my cousin." I push past him, careful to steer clear of the gold on his jacket, and help her stand upright. "Hettie," I whisper and glance at Royce to make sure he and his buttons haven't come any closer. "What are you doing here?"

"You didn't think I was going to let you have all the fun without me, did you?" Her face is pale and her fingers clammy.

"Get her some air," Royce says dismissively. "She's seasick."

Phipps scoops his arms beneath Hettie's and helps her out

of the room. Brus follows them with a scowl. I'm pretty sure he mumbles something about two women on board bringing twice the bad luck.

Royce whirls to face me as soon as the door clicks shut. "What's she doing here?" His eyes have gone from sea blue to sky blue. But it's not a calm sky; they're the color right before a storm.

"I have no idea. No one even told her I was leaving." What could have possessed Hettie to do something so dangerous?

"I don't . . ." He pauses and clenches his fists. "I don't like having stowaways on my ship, Kora." He pronounces my name like a curse.

"I never thought she'd follow me like that," I say. Hettie is meant for the palace world, meant to have people waiting on her hand and foot—because if they didn't, I doubt she'd last more than a day. What will Uncle Pheus do when he finds her missing?

"We could take her back now," Aris suggests when he sees the anguish on my face. "We'd only lose a few hours."

"No," I grumble. I know if we take her back, Royce won't set sail again. We'd also lose too much time. I soften my tone. "She can share my cabin." The bed tucked against the far side of the room is just wide enough for two, but it's going to be tight. And Hettie tends to kick in her sleep. Or at least she did when we were children sneaking into each other's rooms at night after days spent playing in the garden.

Royce frowns, but he doesn't argue. "I recommend you stay down here out of . . ." He clears his throat. "Out of the sun, while I have a few words with Aris."

Royce disappears through the door without another word. The movement has such a note of authority. It says he'll brook no disapproval, no questioning of his commands. I make a note to tell Uncle Pheus about this tactic so he can use it in negotiations.

"I'll talk to him," Aris says. "He'll lighten up." He has the decency to bow and flash a smile before shutting the door softly on his way out. "And I'll check on that cousin of yours too."

I feel a pang of guilt, knowing I should be the one worrying about Hettie, but my head is pounding from the exercise of searching for the gold and dealing with Royce. I promise myself I'll find her after I close my eyes for a few moments. I flop down on the bed, which smells of sweat and the sea. I press my palms to my eyes. My head is still pounding. I try to relax my mind, to let my thoughts float away with the rhythm of the sea. My breathing quiets.

Then, I'm asleep. Arms encircle me, cutting off my air supply. I know what comes next—the dream, the nightmare, is a familiar one.

Gold crashes against my body. It floods my mouth, weighing me down. I sink into the mattress. I try to fight it off, but my arms won't move. I try screaming, but my mouth is frozen, my tongue too heavy to lift.

Gold fills my senses until I can't tell if there are any human parts left of me. Then, with a flash, my vision clears. I'm standing in front of the golden tapestry. It lays jumbled with the other gold objects in the room with the wooden floor I'd seen earlier. Maps hang on the walls. Black curtains block the windows over the bed and table. A man stands over the table holding up a round object and a knife.

He's so gaunt that I'm not sure if I am looking at a human or merely a skeleton. His completely shaved head accentuates the illusion. As do his cheekbones, which stretch high up his face, as if they're trying to get away from his thin chin. His eyes recede behind his other features, and his pale skin combined with his dark clothes makes him look even more like a living set of bones.

As he casts his eyes down over the object, a black tattooed skull is visible on each eyelid. He hums while he saws the knife toward the tabletop. It takes me a moment to realize what he's holding.

A severed human head.

He's cutting off the flesh and tossing it into a bucket at his feet.

Next to the head is a helmet. And not just any helmet—one of a Lagonian guard.

I gasp.

The skeletal man looks up. His eyes pierce through me before going wide.

"It's you," he breathes.

Just like that, the vision vanishes, but the feeling of the gold doesn't. It burns my skin. I scream and claw at it, trying to get free.

My hand strikes something else.

"Kora, calm down," a voice shouts.

My eyes snap open. It's Aris. His hands grip my arms, trying to prevent me from clawing at my skin again. Gouges from my nails run down both our arms.

He relaxes his grip when he sees that I've come to. "What happened?"

I'm too shocked to speak. The image of the man carving into that head sends my stomach spinning.

Aris sits on the bed next to me and wraps his arm around my shoulders, drawing me closer to the warmth of his body. "Was it a nightmare?"

I shake my head slowly and look at the claw marks on my arms. Finally, I find my voice. "No, I think it was a vision."

I shudder to think that the more I search out the gold, the more my connection to it grows. How long will it be until the gold steals my every thought, and I end up like my father?

"What kind of vision?" Aris asks. He rubs a hand up and down my arm.

I stare at my hands. "I saw the gold. And a man. He was tall and slender, and he had skulls tattooed on his eyelids. He was . . ." I trail off before I can describe what he was doing.

Aris's arm stops. He looks down at me, panic in his eyes. "A man with skulls tattooed on his eyelids? You're sure?"

I nod. "He took the gold."

"Are you sure it wasn't just a dream?" Aris asks. There's desperation in his voice that I don't understand.

I want it to be a dream, even though it wasn't. But I don't want to argue with Aris.

"It must have been a dream," Aris says resolutely. "The man you're talking about was Raiktor Hypatos, but everyone called him Captain Skulls because of his sick obsession . . ." He trails off when he sees the look of disgust on my face. "He was the pirate who attacked Royce and me and stole the treaty. But I killed him."

"Could he have survived somehow?" I ask.

"Pray that he didn't." Aris stares off into the distance, as though remembering his encounter. "I've never heard of anyone crueler than him. As you may know, he collected the skulls of his victims." He rubs his neck absently, like he's imagining losing his own head. "His men got paid based on how many heads they brought him. If they broke one of his skulls, their own head was forfeit as a replacement. I've even heard sailors say that if a skull broke because the ship rolled during a storm, the man at the helm got blamed."

I swallow. "If he is alive, you've faced him once and won; we can defeat him again." My words are shaky, and it's not only from the vision.

"Of course." Aris tries to muster a smile, but it's clear my vision has rattled him as much as it has me. He gives my shoulder one last squeeze. "Try to get some rest." He eases off the bed and turns to leave, but then turns back. "I wouldn't tell anyone about this vision. It will scare the men and might cause Royce to reconsider taking us after the gold. The crew won't look kindly on facing a pirate captain they all thought was long dead."

I nod, trying to mask the fear creeping up inside me. I wrap my arms around myself for warmth.

Aris must sense my discomfort because he hesitates. He pulls a small book from his pocket and slowly approaches me. "I brought this. I don't even know why I brought this." He runs his fingers through his hair. "I just— I thought it would be easier this way." He holds it out to me.

I run my hands over the cracked leather and flip through the pages. It's clearly seen many days at sea. Some of the pages no longer lay flat, and some are missing. Blotches stain the edges where ink has bled across the paper after getting wet. "What is it?"

"It's the journal I started the day after my father's accident."

My eyes fly up to his.

"I don't want it to scare you," he adds quickly. "I know it's a lot to take in." He pauses, sucking in a deep, uneven breath. "I tend to make light of situations, and I'm not always good at talking about everything that happened. But I want you to understand, to know who I am. I guess what I'm trying to say is that I hope you will."

"Thank you." I hold the journal against my chest. He's given me such a large part of himself, something I'm sure he's always kept hidden.

Aris won't meet my gaze. "I hope you'll keep it out of sight. Some of the crew wouldn't understand if it fell into their hands. Most of them don't even know how my father died."

"Of course," I say.

He offers me a strained smile. "Well, I should go invent some excuse for Royce as to why you screamed before he comes down here himself."

I can't help opening the journal as soon as the door shuts behind him.

❀ ❀ ❀

I dreamt of my father last night. A cold dream that left me shivering when I woke.

At first, there is only darkness. The kind that presses so hard against you, you wonder if anything else exists anymore. Then, small lights appear. They fall from the sky like stars. But they aren't lights. They're coins. One by one, they clink into place. A thin layer at first.

That's when my father arrives. He's trying to tell me something, but I can't hear him over the clinking of the coins. They bury him up to his knees. But he's not concerned. He wanted this.

As the pile around him grows higher, he becomes worried.

Then, the screaming starts. The coins are up to his chest. He reaches out to me. I run toward him, but there are too many coins raining down. They pelt me.

Still, I struggle forward. Somewhere behind me, my mother is crying. She's trusting me to save him.

I make it to the pile, but it's up to his eyes. They plead with me.

I rip at the coins. I knock away handful after handful. I dig until my palms bleed and fingers blister.

The pile swallows his head.

I leap onto the pile. Coins bite into my knees. I swoop away armfuls.

His head comes free. I dig faster, spurred on by my success, unburying him to his neck. I heave him upward.

"I've got you," I say.

His head rolls back. His eyes shoot open. They look straight through me.

"You failed me," he says.

And I can't move as the coins bury both of us, and my mother continues to cry.

❀ ❀ ❀

I slam the journal shut. I pull my braid over my shoulder and tug the end of it.

Aris said he didn't want the journal to scare me. If I'd read it without meeting him, I would've imagined that the owner of these dreams would be just as lost and alone as I feel.

But somehow he's found a way past that, found a way to

be the happy, confident man who stood in front of the court yesterday.

I run my hand down the front cover of the journal. He was right. I do need this. Because it doesn't scare me. It gives me hope.

CHAPTER 8

꙳꙳꙳꙳꙳꙳꙳꙳@꙳꙳꙳꙳꙳꙳꙳꙳

Hettie staggers into the room, and I hastily shove Aris's journal under the covers. I'd just been planning to go look for her.

Her face is green, and every time the ship dips, she grips her stomach in an attempt to hold everything in. She collapses onto the bed without a word. A moment later her head shoots up. "The air is so stuffy down here. It smells like a sweaty man." She shoves her face into one of the pillows and then lifts it up right away. "Ugh. That smells too. How am I supposed to sleep in here?"

"You weren't," I say.

"Can't the pillows be washed?"

I sigh. "You can wash the pillows if you want."

"Me?" Hettie says, her voice rising several octaves. "I would never, and nor will I sleep in here with these." Hettie throws the pillows on the floor and crosses her arms. She pouts. She always pouts when something's not going her way.

Heat rises in my cheeks. I snatch a pillow from the floor and throw it at her. It hits her square in the jaw and knocks her off the bed.

"How dare you," Hettie screeches, clawing her way back onto the mattress.

"No one asked you to come," I shout back.

"No one asks me to do anything."

The insult forming on my tongue fizzles out.

Of course I hadn't invited her. This very argument is proof of why I didn't want her around. It just never struck me that Hettie was as trapped in the palace as I was.

She hugs a pillow to her chest.

"Hettie"—I soften my tone—"I'm sorry."

"You should be. It's all your fault I'm here anyway." She tries to hide the fact that she's crying by brushing the end of her sleeve across her eyes. "You're the one who told me all those stories about far-off places. You made it sound like leaving the palace was going to be the best thing that ever happened to me. It's the worst. The worst! Now, I'm stuck on a boat that stinks of rotting fish and sleeping on pillows that smell like the men who clean out the stables."

"This isn't one of my adventure stories," I say. "You know what'll happen to my father if we don't get the gold back."

Hettie frowns. "I know that. I just didn't want you going off alone. I'm your only friend"—she grimaces—"your only sort-of friend, and I thought I should be the one to go with you. And someone's going to have to carry that gold since you can't touch it." She suddenly straightens her shoulders, refusing to acknowledge she'd had a moment of weakness. "I bet you didn't think about that. I bet you're glad I came along now."

I'm surprised she even had time to spare me a thought in her mad rush out of the palace, and I'm actually a little bit touched.

But then Hettie goes and ruins any goodwill I feel toward her. "Besides, how was I ever supposed to find a man with you scaring all the suitors away?"

I roll my eyes.

"It's true. Do you think Duke Wystlinos even gave me a passing glance? What about any of the other suitors? As soon as they realized you didn't want them or you scared them away, *poof.*" She fans out her hands. "They were gone."

I can't fathom which suitor Hettie had her eye on. It couldn't have been Duke Polmey's oldest son. He was bald and had teeth sharper than cutting knives. The merchant's son, Tyoul, couldn't even eat his food with his mouth closed.

I cycle through the suitors, eventually landing on Aris. He's handsome, dashing, adventurous, and has the most understanding spirit of anyone I've ever met. Who else would calm you down after a vision of cursed gold causes you to claw your own skin off?

"You'll find someone," I say.

"That's easy to say when you have men flocking to you."

"I don't want that. I never did."

"Then what do you want?" she snaps.

I find myself at a loss for words. It's been so long since anyone's asked me that. Actually, I can't remember anyone ever asking me that. Perhaps people did before I was cursed. Maybe they asked me if I wanted honey-drizzled tulumba or toasted almond tarts for dessert. Maybe they asked me if I wanted a blue dress or a pink one. Maybe they even asked me what I thought about ruling Lagonia someday.

My gaze drifts toward the top deck in a movement I realize is not unlike my father's glance toward the tower. He always looked for the gold, the thing he wanted most in the world, and in that moment, what I want most is up there, walking around. Because being with Aris puts images in my head that I haven't dared to think about in years. Aris wouldn't make me hide. He's the one who helped bring me out from under my veil. Together, we'd be a team. Slowly, we would show the world that you could survive a curse.

Hettie's impatience saves me from having to answer her question out loud. "At least I know what I want. And right now, I want to eat something. How do we get servants to bring us food?"

"If you're seasick, eating's probably not the best idea," I venture.

She shoots me a glare. "I've already thrown up everything I ate, and now I'm starving. Besides, eating *always* settles my stomach."

In truth, Hettie always gets grumpy when she doesn't eat regularly, but I can't decide which would be worse: to hear her complain about her empty stomach or to hear her complain when she inevitably gets sick after eating. I decide to put off the complaining as long as possible.

"There aren't any servants to bring you food here. You'll have to go find some."

Hettie rolls her eyes and lets out an exaggerated sigh.

Sometimes I think she would've done better growing up on the farm our fathers shared before my father became king, before the Great Oracle ever made that accursed prophecy.

Still pouting, Hettie slides off the bed. "At least I know where they keep the supplies."

I dash after her, pulling on my cloak as I go. If she's determined to get something, there's no telling who she'll push out of the way to get it.

She ends up leading us to a dark room deep within the ship. The only light coming in is from the small staircase leading down into it. Barrels are stacked atop one another, and yards of sail lay folded in the corners. I swear I can hear scurrying and rustling.

It smells like rotting wood, and my feet squish into the floor as wet planks bend beneath me. No wonder Royce said he needed money to repair his ship. I'm just waiting for the whole thing to give way.

Hettie eases into the room. "I think those are the food stores over there." The way she says it indicates she wants me to go investigate.

There's a rustle from deeper in the room. This time it's unmistakable. There is something else alive down here.

I shake my head. There's nothing that could convince me to go any farther.

Hettie takes a tentative step forward.

A shadow rises in the middle of the room.

Hettie screams and stumbles backward, hiding behind me and shoving me forward in the process.

The shadow rises higher and higher and higher. It's far too big for a rat. Or a mouse.

A figure emerges from between several barrels.

As it steps forward into the light, the figure becomes a man with deeply tanned skin. At first, I assume he's bald, but as he turns slightly, I notice his head is completely shaved except for a long black ponytail in the back. His lack of hair makes him look older than he is despite a surprisingly youthful face. He's wearing loose red pants and no shirt, his taut chest muscles on full display. So is a necklace with several sharks' teeth.

Hettie gapes, open-mouthed.

He stops when he sees us, holding a half-gnawed pickle in one hand. "Rhat," he says.

"Rats?" Hettie shrieks. She jumps onto the nearest barrel.

The man laughs. "No, that's my name. Rhat." He drags the syllable out. "It's short for Rhatan. Captain would never allow rats on his ship."

There's another rustling from behind him that says otherwise.

"Then what is that?" Hettie squeals. Her hair is sticking out more than usual, like even it is frightened by the noise. Or maybe it's simply from the humid air below deck.

Rhat laughs and picks up a big cloth-covered square. With a flourish, he removes the cloth to reveal five pigeons in a cage. "Messenger pigeons," he says.

The birds coo. One shoves its head under its wings, preening itself.

"Oh," Hettie says. She daintily steps down off the barrel as if she's descending a grand staircase and fixes her skirts. "I knew that."

"They like the cooler temperatures down here. It's too hot for them up on deck, being in the sun all day." He's about to put the cover back on when he pauses. "I could've sworn there were six in here this morning." He scans the rafters as though one might have escaped. "Captain must've already sent a message," he mumbles to himself before repositioning the cloth and setting the cage atop one of the barrels.

"Now then," he says, "are you ladies lost? I know a big ship like this one can be confusing. If you're looking for the deck, it's up you want to go. Not down. I've never found that you can go up by going down." His words jumble out, and he stares at Hettie the entire time he says them.

She nudges me from behind. "Tell him we're hungry," she whispers.

I turn and stare at her. She's never had a problem telling anyone what to do.

"You tell him." I shove her forward.

She stands there a moment but recovers quickly and begins batting her eyelashes. "Um, is there anything to eat?" She gently sways back and forth as she speaks. Rhat's eyes follow the slight movement like he's been put under a spell.

For a moment, I stand in awe. Is Hettie . . . flirting? With a sailor?

Rhat manages to quit gawking and produces another pickle. "Here you go."

All Hettie's charm vanishes. "You expect me to eat that? It looks like a sea slug."

"It's really quite delicious." Rhat takes another bite of his pickle. A thin line of juice runs down his chin. "We always get a large supply anytime we pass near the Halpen coast."

Hettie's mouth goes slack. Her hand goes to her own chin as though she can feel the juice too. "I think I've lost my appetite, unless you have something else back there."

"Nothing until dinner. We have to ration food. Well, except for the pickles. We've got plenty of barrels of those."

Thankfully Rhat is tactful enough not to mention that we'd have another barrel of food if one hadn't been occupied by a stowaway.

"Fine, give me the pickle. It probably tastes awful." Hettie grabs the offering and bites into it with a loud crunch.

Rhat smiles. "Want another one for later?"

"No," Hettie says. "I just needed something to last me until dinner. And this barely counts as edible."

I groan. Despite the fact some of Hettie's tutors stuck around, she still managed to miss the lesson on how to be gracious.

"Thank you," I say to Rhat. "Maybe we'll go back to the deck for a little while." After taking a few bites, Hettie is starting to turn as green as the pickle she's holding.

"Are you sure?" Rhat asks. "We could stay here, and I could tell you about the Polliosaian Islands. That's where I'm from." He gazes at Hettie. "It's famous for pearls. Pearls prettier than anything you've ever seen. I used to be a pearl diver up until . . ."

Hettie clutches her stomach.

Rhat cuts off. "Are you okay?"

Her eyes have gone glassy. I drag her from the galley. Her hand goes to her mouth, and I know we don't have long until that pickle makes a reappearance.

I make a wrong turn.

"This way," Rhat says. He scoops Hettie into his arms and barges up to the top deck, setting her down by the railing.

"It smells like fish up here," Hettie moans.

The smell isn't nearly as strong as when I first set foot on the ship. The ocean breeze has done a nice job of whipping away the scent.

"Look at the horizon," Rhat instructs.

Hettie weakly nods.

"What's all this about?" Royce says, coming up behind us. His voice is accusatory, like the three of us gathered together must mean we're planning a mutiny.

I go cold at his approach, but thankfully he's removed his coat and now wears a loose shirt instead. I hate that I never hear him coming. It may have something to do with the fact that no one in the palace dares approach me—I'm not used to listening for footsteps.

"Just seasickness, Captain," Rhat says, answering Royce's question.

"I see." He relaxes slightly, though that's like saying the silver suits of armor in the palace halls relax. He still seems suspicious.

"The breeze is better on the other side of the ship. It might help settle her stomach," Royce says to Rhat, an attempt to be civil. Or maybe an attempt to get us out of his way. "Take her over there and then take over the helm."

"I'm right here," Hettie croaks. She lifts her head in a look of pure defiance that's only marred by the saliva rolling down her chin. "Don't talk about me as if I'm not here."

Royce raises an eyebrow at her.

"Aye, Captain," Rhat says. He edges Hettie away from the railing. I move to follow, but Royce puts an arm out to stop me.

I jerk to a stop before I collide with it. I can't help myself. The last time I saw him, he had on so much gold.

"Looks like you haven't gotten your sea legs either," he says.

I glare at him. "My mother came from Sunisa. I have the sea in my veins." And it's true; I feel more alive in the sea breeze than I did during any of the years spent at the palace.

The lapping of the water beneath my feet calls to my blood in a way different from the gold. It isn't the greedy call to come closer. It's a gentle sigh that fills my body with each breath. Instead of threatening to harden me in place, the ocean offers a chance at new memories and freedom. A chance I want more than anything.

"You may have Sunisan blood, but that doesn't mean you're immune to seasickness. They're both Sunisan"—he nods to where Phipps and Thipps are racing up the rigging toward the crow's nest and shouting about how the last one there has to take first watch that night—"and they were both sick for a week their first few journeys aboard."

His superiority grates against me.

I straighten. "I may not have had much opportunity to sail, but clearly I'm suffering no ill effects."

He transfers his gaze to the horizon. "I think all monarchs should travel, see the way other countries do things. If they see how others live, they may not be so quick to ask for things they don't need."

I stiffen. "If you're referring to The Touch, you don't know what you're talking about." My father wanted gold because he knew war was on the horizon. He wanted to protect his people, to provide for them. Never mind it was his fault the treasury had been depleted in the first place from too many parties thrown at the palace.

"I know what curses can do to people," he replies. His eyes switch back to me.

"You don't know anything about my curse."

"Then tell me."

I scoff—I'm not falling for that one.

"Or don't." He seems disappointed whenever I don't reveal my most closely guarded secrets. He leans on the railing, strangling his hands around it.

I'm pretty sure our conversation has ended. I turn to leave, but his words call me back.

"I need you to check on the gold."

That's the last thing I want to do. Searching for the gold means letting Captain Skulls back in. After my experience in the cabin, his world is not one I am eager to reenter. Especially out here, where everyone will see my reaction. Though if I refuse, Royce will ask why. And I can't tell him about the vision.

I swallow.

Royce looks at me expectantly. "The gold," he prompts.

I decide the fastest way to make him go away is to give him what he wants.

I snap my eyes shut. I find the golden aura. I toss it away as soon as I do, but I hear an echoing laugh. A laugh I can only imagine belongs to Captain Skulls.

I jerk backward to get away from the sound and a hand grabs me. My eyes pop open. It takes me a moment to realize that the hand belongs to Royce.

I shake him off and steady myself on the railing. "The gold's still on the same course."

It's unsettling how quickly he reached out to help me. Maybe he really isn't afraid of me. And that is terrifying. Because the only people I've ever met who at least pretended not to fear me were after my father's money.

"You look flushed," he says. He eyes my cloak and gloves, as if suggesting I remove them.

I get the eerie feeling that he's testing me, that he's still trying to get me to expose my power. I wrap my arms around my chest and recoil from him before he can reach for my hood or my hands. "Your ship is dirty, and I'd rather keep them on." I stumble over the words, barely managing to force my arms back down to my sides.

He stares at me with curiosity, and I fear I've somehow confirmed his suspicions.

He moves closer. "I've just heard rumors . . ."

Heat rises in my face. Of course he's heard rumors. Everyone's heard them.

All the anger that's been hiding inside me from every backward glance, every platter shattered by servants distracted by my presence, every gaze my father avoids when I look his way, every moment people scoot away from me in fear bubbles to the surface. "I'm not the only one aboard this ship with rumors about them," I spit.

To my astonishment, Royce pulls back like I've struck him. His eyes harden, then burn as they take in every inch of skin visible beneath my hood. "I wouldn't bring that up again." His voice is so calm. So controlled. So cold.

"There you two are." Aris's voice cuts through the air.

Royce's face sours for just a moment before he quickly straightens and backs several steps away.

"Everything all right here?" Aris asks. His eyes swing between Royce's unemotional face and my flaming one.

"I'm sure it will be," Royce replies in a cool tone, his eyes never leaving my face.

I swallow whatever reply was forming in my mouth. I doubt Aris, with his easy laugh and welcoming smile, has any idea how dark his friend has become.

If Aris suspects anything, he plays it off with another wide smile. "Well, then you won't mind if I borrow Kora." He reaches for my arm before Royce can reply.

I let him pull me away, but I can't help looking back just once.

Royce's face is still stoic, but his eyes are bright. The burning fire has faded to glowing embers, embers I'm sure could reignite at any moment.

Aris leads me down the deck. He smiles gently. "I know things got off to a bumpy start on board, and I know this journey must be full of fear and pain for you. It's certainly not the way you were hoping to explore the world. But we will get your father's treasure back. And then we will have a real adventure." He takes my hand in his. A tingling sensation runs up my arm. Unlike the gold, which always threatens to stop my heart, this feeling makes it beat faster. It makes me come alive.

"And," he continues, "the first thing you need is a smile on your face."

I try to offer him one, but we can both tell it's forced. My encounter with Royce left me shaken in a way I've never felt before—no one has even spoken to me like that. I can't decide if I should tell Aris, but I don't want to taint that friendship for him, not when I know he has so few happy memories. I decide against it, instead bolstering my smile until I feel real happiness creep through me, becoming more powerful the longer I look into his gray eyes.

They're soft and kind. They take on the reflection of the water around us, turning them a beautiful shade of gray-blue. There's a brightness to them as well that seems to spill out into all aspects of his personality.

He can't keep a silly grin off his face. "I knew you'd need a little help." He cups my chin, then leans closer, and for a moment I think he's going to kiss me.

Instead, he says, "That's why I thought you'd like to dance." He tilts my head until I can see several of the crew bringing out what I suppose pass for instruments. Thipps holds an accordion that wheezes when it opens and closes. Another sailor has a fiddle. "The men always think dancing on the first day appeases Triton and makes for a safer journey because if Triton's happy then Poseidon must be. They hope that starting things out on the right foot will carry happiness into the days that lie ahead."

Aris's enthusiasm makes me want to say yes, but flashes of Lord Libton, one of my suitors, hightailing it from the dance floor fill my mind. And there's the fact I can't dance.

I shake my head.

Aris's smile falters.

My heart drops. He's going to think I don't like him or that I'm ungrateful after all he's done for me. I cast around for what I can say, how I can explain.

"Aris . . ." I start.

"No, I understand." He clears his throat, taking my rejection in stride. "It's only that I think it would be good for you." His eyes search out mine. "The happiest I've ever been was when I was honored by a local tribe on the smallest of the Polliosaian Islands for saving several of their fishermen who'd been swept out to sea. They threw a great feast and wanted me to dance. I refused because I had no clue how to dance like they did, but do you know what their king said to me? He said, 'In order to enjoy the dance, you don't have to know all the steps. You just have to be part of it.'" He looks pointedly at me.

Before I can reply, the music strikes up, and a makeshift dance floor is cleared around the main mast.

Thipps has climbed into the rigging and dangles over all of us. The other musicians have situated themselves on various barrels.

Hettie must've gone back downstairs, as I don't see her on deck. I hope she's feeling better, but I also don't want to be in the cabin with her if she's going to be sick. That probably makes me a terrible cousin, but I try not to dwell on my guilt.

Slowly, other sailors abandon their tasks and take up positions around the musicians. Phipps lounges on a nearby barrel but begins slapping his knee and rising as the tune starts picking up speed. He's the first one to meander onto the dance floor, where he kicks up his legs and spins in circles.

It isn't a dance I recognize, but it's enthralling because he looks so utterly free. He links arms with another sailor and spins around. Several men hoot and holler. Only Brus sits off to one side with his arms crossed. He keeps shooting me glares when he thinks I'm not looking. I ignore him.

Eventually I forget about Brus and everything else, the music loosening the tension I hadn't known I'd been carrying in my shoulders. Everyone claps along in time with the music, and I join in. I find I can't help but hope that Aris will ask me to dance once more because he may be right . . . it appears I need this. Don't I deserve to feel happy? Free?

And as though the universe is making up for my curse all at once, I get my wish. Aris smiles before extending an arm and pulling me onto the dance floor. The men hoot louder. I catch snippets of Thipps and Phipps arguing about who'll dance with me next.

After a moment to catch the tempo, Aris loops one arm around my waist and takes my hand with his free one. We twirl across the deck like two untouchable stars twinkling as sunlight glints off the sea around us.

A laugh escapes my lips and is taken by the breeze running over the ship. I can barely feel Aris's arm against my back, and yet it's there, constant, reassuring, always guiding. I forget about my skin, my gloves, my cloak, my need for anonymity. I lose myself in the moment, happy and free.

We sweep across the deck as the melody heightens. We spin faster and faster. I close my eyes and let the song cast its web over me, knowing that if I stumble, Aris is there.

The music reaches a crescendo. Aris pulls me close. My heart leaps forward in my chest. A grin spreads across his face. He lets me slip backward, leaning with me and catching me in a dip.

His chest touches mine, his face inches away. His eyes have taken on a new energy. His gaze shifts to my lips. We stay frozen in that moment, both breathing hard. He makes the slightest movement forward. I respond. Before our lips meet, a voice cries out from the crowd.

"Demon!"

The moment shatters. Everything shatters. I didn't realize the music had stopped and that the deck had fallen into silence.

"Demon!" the voice cries with more urgency.

Aris quickly pulls me up. A breeze rustles my hair. My hand snaps to my hood, but it's pooled around my neck, exposing my skin, exposing me.

"Throw her overboard," Brus cries. He looks to his fellow sailors for support.

"Triton take us all," one man curses. Or maybe he meant it as a prayer.

"I'll take care of this," Aris soothes. He tries to hide me behind him, while also putting his arms up in a gesture of peace.

"What's going on?" Royce pushes into the circle. He takes in my fallen hood, and I see understanding click into place on his features.

But to my surprise, Royce doesn't leap to Brus's side. "Calm down, Brus," he says. "This is King Midas's daughter, and she's not going to hurt anyone." He shoots me a look as though to say, *Don't make any sudden movements.* "She holds the purse strings for this journey."

"She's gotten to the captain too," Brus shouts. "We've got to get her off the ship before she ensnares the rest of us with her magic."

I open my mouth to protest that I won't be ensnaring anyone, but I decide it's better not to draw the men's attention back to myself now that Royce has it.

Several men grumble and whisper among themselves.

"Look at her," Brus pleads. "She's cursed. She'll curse us all."

"Go back to your duties," Royce says, and for once, I'm thankful for his gruff tone. "There'll be no more dancing."

The men stand there for a moment, and I can't decide if they'll obey him or not. After a few more heartbeats, the men slowly disperse.

Brus gives me a long glare as he stalks off.

I exhale. But it's not over yet.

"Royce." Aris steps forward, breathing hard. "Are you really going to let him get away with that?"

If I thought Royce's eyes held unkindness when they looked

at me, they hold pure hatred when they turn on Aris. "Watch yourself, Aris."

Aris steps forward. "Kora's life is more valuable than you'll ever know. And if you can't keep your crew in check, then I'll be forced to."

"I know how valuable she is," Royce snaps. "Make no mistake about that." His words cascade like ice over my body. I shiver.

The two men stare at each other for a moment. I sense they might come to blows right there, which I'm pretty sure will end the thinly veiled cooperation toward a common goal that we have now.

As much as I'd like to see the smugness knocked out of Royce, I still need him. I place my arm on Aris's. He startles, seeming to remember I'm there for the first time.

"I suggest you two head downstairs and stay there while I try and clear this up with the crew," Royce says. Then he charges off in the direction the men went.

Aris stares after him with a look sharper than a sword blade.

"It's all right." I put my hand on his arm to get his attention. The situation could have been much worse.

Aris exhales. "It's not all right. You could have been hurt." He swallows.

"I wasn't," I say.

"I won't let anything like that happen again," he vows. "I want you to feel safe."

"I do," I tell him. It's true—I feel safe when I'm with him, and I never want that feeling to go away.

CHAPTER 10

꙳꙳꙳꙳꙳꙳꙳꙳꙳◎꙳꙳꙳꙳꙳꙳꙳꙳꙳

Hettie and I spend the entire next day cramped inside the cabin. My only respite is when Aris stops by after a shift keeping an eye on Brus and the other sailors.

We pass the time playing Seascapes on an old board I found in Royce's cabin.

I used to love playing with my father. We'd race to maneuver some of our little carved ships along our respective sides so the other couldn't invade before sending the rest out to battle across the board. When I was younger, I always used to focus solely on defending my coast. Only under my father's coaching did I finally learn enough strategy to fight my way to a win.

Aris wins the first three times we play. He always seems to know just when to move a ship to avoid an attack or when to shoot his across the board to attack mine. His strategies always change from game to game. I can never tell when he'll attack and when he'll race back to guard one of his ports.

Each game leaves me breathless as I inevitably race to keep my last ship from his grasp long after I already know I've lost.

I smile up at him each time we collect our pieces after a finished game. Watching him play reminds me of watching Uncle

Pheus play against my father when I was a child. No wonder Uncle Pheus likes Aris so much. They're both able to see in advance how one move could affect all the other pieces.

Even Hettie, who used to play far more often with her father, only comes close to beating Aris once. And I love that he doesn't let me win. He challenges me, forces me to think like him in order to stay alive.

When we tire of Seascapes, Aris distracts me by telling me tales from his travels.

He tells me about the time he was nearly trampled by camels in Kalakhosia but was nursed back to health by the sultan's daughter. He recounts how he climbed to the top of the Iglanic Volcano by himself simply because the locals didn't think a foreigner could. He tells me about the time he dug for diamonds in Lutina and found one nearly as big as his thumbnail, but his companions attacked him in his sleep, stealing it. He was lucky to make it out alive.

That's how most of his stories end, with him being lucky to be alive. And I love them. They remind me of how much living a person can do outside the walls of the palace. It's like having one of my storybooks come to life in front of me, but all too soon Aris rises from his chair and says he better give Royce an update on the gold's direction.

After Aris leaves, the only other person brave enough to venture down to our cabin is Rhat. Or more precisely, he's the only one allowed after Phipps and Thipps got in a fight about who could bring us breakfast this morning because they both wanted to see if I turned into a golden statue in my sleep.

When Rhat brings dinner, he makes a big show of placing Hettie's right in front of her at the desk. If I'm not mistaken, the pile of peas and hard roll are meant to be the eyes on a face completed by a thin strip of salted pork acting as the mouth.

I glance at my plate. The peas have rolled all over the place.

Hettie doesn't even look up from the piece of rope she pulled from who knows where. She's been trying for the last hour to imitate the spiraled knot already tied into the top portion.

"I also brought you this," Rhat says in an attempt to gain her attention. He slaps a pickle onto Hettie's plate. I'm not sure if it's meant to be a nose or if that was the only open spot. Green juice oozes out and begins to stain the bottom of the roll.

Hettie drops the rope. "Now it's ruined the bread." She shoves the plate away.

I suppress a groan.

Rhat shoves the plate back. "No, it makes it taste better. Trust me, you won't want honey anymore after dipping it in pickle juice."

Hettie's mouth hangs open in disgust.

"See." Rhat breaks off a chunk and shoves it into her gaping mouth before she can protest. She smacks it around a few times looking for something to spit it out in. The more she smacks, the less agitated her face looks. Her cheeks relax, and she actually swallows.

I take a bite of my own roll. It's a little bland, but palatable.

Rhat beams at Hettie. "I knew you'd like it."

"I didn't say I liked it," Hettie snaps.

"You didn't spit it out," he supplies.

"I didn't want to be rude." Hettie turns up her nose but takes another bite.

Rhat smiles knowingly. "I could teach you how to tie that rope too, if you wanted."

Hettie takes another bite out of her roll and looks Rhat up and down. He's certainly a far cry from the men who frequent the palace, but Hettie seems desperate for any attention. She tosses the rope toward him. "Fine."

Rhat spends the next hour guiding Hettie's hands through twists and turns to make different knots with the rope, all the while regaling her with stories about his home island. I can't tell what he's making up to impress her and what's actually true. For her part, Hettie is eating it all up faster than the food she'd stuffed down. Once she tires of the knots, she sits with her elbows on the desk and her chin in her hands. She asks him question after question about every island he's seen.

It's only when the ship pitches further to the side and her empty plate clatters to the floor that Rhat rises. "Looks like we're in for a bit of rough weather."

Hettie pulls back from the table and her hand goes to her stomach. "How rough?"

I can tell she's already worried about dinner making a reappearance after she'd barely gotten over her seasickness.

"Just a storm," Rhat says. "It's nothing this old ship can't handle, but I should probably go help fasten down the sails. Is there anything else you need?"

Hettie sits back in her chair. "I could use some water."

Rhat leaps to obey.

In fact, though the ship continues to tilt more and more to each side, he spends the next ten minutes going back and forth fetching things for Hettie: another pickle, a softer pillow, a blanket that doesn't scratch so much. Each time he arrives with a bright smile on his face like he's returned triumphant from some dangerous quest.

"Anything else?" he asks again after arriving with a pair of warm socks, since Hettie didn't bring any. I bite my tongue before I can blurt out that, technically, she didn't bring anything.

"No," Hettie says. "Thank you," she adds, and I nearly choke. Hettie being polite? That's something you don't see every day.

"My room's just down the hall if you need anything," Rhat replies, "but I wouldn't recommend leaving the cabin with that storm rolling in." He strolls backward toward the door, nearly tripping over the edge of my trunk. He recovers nicely, his face showing the barest hint of a blush.

I decide I like him. Anyone who can put up with Hettie must have a kind spirit. Though I don't know what that says about me.

"Good night then," he says, closing the door behind him.

I notice Hettie staring at the door a moment longer than necessary. She catches me watching her and glares at me. Without a word, she climbs over me and takes the side of the bed next to the wall.

Great. Now if someone's going to roll out of bed, it's going to be me. And that's if Hettie doesn't kick me out of it first.

But the storm has me too unsettled to sleep, so once I hear Hettie's breathing settle, I pull out Aris's journal again.

※ ※ ※

How are you supposed to overcome a curse that isn't yours? Does it taint me as I stand here? Will I be the same as my father? Is it already too late? Are all sons destined to repeat their father's mistakes?

I've put out to sea in the hope I can avoid it. I don't need the manor life anymore. My mother can't stand the sight of me. I remind her too much of my father. It's my eyes, she says. If only I didn't have his eyes.

Now that I am away, I've found the sea has given me respite. Its waves crash endlessly against the hull. They're the only thing that helps me sleep, that chases the nightmares away.

I cross from ocean to ocean and back again just to keep those nightmares away. Every time I sleep on land, the dreams come back.

On the darker nights, I set a course for Lagonia, toward the only person who might understand. But if she's been locked away, she's probably no better off than me.

And yet I still fight the urge every time we near that coast to pull in and march up to the palace and demand to see her for myself.

Maybe she's found a way to keep the nightmares away permanently. Maybe she's found a way to overcome it all.

❁ ❁ ❁

Hettie rolls over, knocking into me. I quickly close the journal and shove it under my pillow. Thankfully, Hettie doesn't wake, and I blow out the candle and snuggle down farther beneath the covers, reveling in the fact that Aris has been thinking about me. He doesn't see me as a curse, but as someone strong enough to help him.

Though the moment my head hits the pillow, thoughts of Aris are replaced with Captain Skulls. If I close my eyes, will I see him in my dreams again? My stomach churns. I'd slept fitfully last night, nightmares waking me more often than they had at the palace.

Above my head, rain pelts the window. Tendrils of wind scrape across the glass looking for a way in. The ship pitches, causing Hettie to roll back into me, but I'm glad she's here for once. Constantly shoving her back to her side of the bed keeps me awake.

The books on the shelf whisper back and forth.

The ship dips again and Hettie crashes full force against me. The blow sends me spiraling off the edge of the bed, and I land on the wood with a thump. Hettie doesn't even wake up. She rolls back to her side as the ship tilts in the opposite direction.

When I make it to my feet, lightning illuminates her sleeping form. In the few moments of my absence, she's taken over the bed, lying spread-eagle in the middle. I sigh and contemplate shoving her once more. But I'm too tired for that fight.

And if I wake her up, I'll never hear the end of it tomorrow.

I decide air is what I need after being stuck in the stuffy cabin all day. I know Rhat said not to leave the cabin, but nothing too bad can happen if I only step outside our door.

I slip into the darkened hallway. Either the lanterns haven't been lit or the bursts of wind let in by sailors going in and out to the deck have extinguished them. I decide it's the second reason when the ship jolts, causing a small puddle of water to trickle over my feet.

At least it's cool here. And quiet. I relax against the wall.

I rub my side, where Hettie's already kicked me twice. There'll be bruises in the morning. They'll probably be as deep purple-gold as the circles under my eyes will be if I don't find a way to sleep.

I rub my neck.

The water running over my feet has gone from comforting to cold. I'm about to head back into the room and force Hettie to move when I notice a light down the hallway and hear hushed voices.

I can only imagine they're talking about me. What else on this ship is worth talking about in the dark in the middle of the night?

I creep closer to the shaft of light, careful to spread my weight out so any sharp dips don't send me crashing into the wall and give away my presence.

The hallway on the other side of the door is darker than where I'm standing. It'd be easier to hide in, but I can't risk darting past the door.

I stay well back from the door and peer forward. I can only make out the back of one of the men inside. It's Rhat. I can tell by his hair.

I relax. I bet he's mooning over Hettie. That I don't need to hear. I almost turn back, but Royce's voice freezes me in place.

". . . part of the plan all along."

I catch sight of his hands through the crack in the door. He's weighing a coin in his hand. A gold coin. It must be what he was rubbing between his fingers when I first saw him.

"Get her out of the palace and see what she can do."

"It's so risky," Rhat replies. "You don't know why she was locked up. Killing her would be the easier option."

My heart stops.

"Unless the rumors are true," Royce says. He tosses the coin back and forth between his palms as he continues. "The princess would be worth more alive then."

I clench my hand over my mouth to stifle a gasp. My shoulder knocks against the wall as the ship drops beneath me.

The coin stills in Royce's hands. Rhat turns his head halfway toward the noise, but stops when he hears nothing more.

I'm surprised he can't hear my heart thudding against my

ribs. It's all I can hear. I don't know how much longer it has left to beat. Not long if Royce decides I'm not worth keeping alive.

I scan the hallway. Not only is it too dark to see the doorways that line it, but I don't know which one is Aris's. I can't risk barging in on another group of sailors, of Royce's men.

I fight the urge to flee to my room, but this isn't a dream. The danger won't disappear come morning. I quiet my breathing. If I'm going to figure a way out of this, then I'll need to know what they're planning.

I've missed part of the conversation.

"There's always ransom," Rhat says almost gleefully.

Royce scoffs. "There hasn't been money in years." He moves some heavy object I can't see.

Would Uncle Pheus even pay the ransom if we did have it? He can't. As much as he may care for me, I'm no use to anyone there.

"What do we do with Aris? We can't risk him getting back to Lagonia." Rhat pauses. "I know he was your friend once."

"Was," Royce replies. It's the most chilling word I've ever heard. "All that's left are the usual choices."

Somewhere to my left, a floorboard creaks. My head snaps in that direction, but it's impossible to see anything in the dark.

I'm not the only one who heard it. Once again, Rhat's head cocks toward the door. One more sound and I know he'll come out to investigate.

I hold my breath.

Silence.

The conversation continues.

"Murder or being marooned on an island?" Rhat shakes his head. "That's not much of a choice."

"He didn't leave us a choice once he brought her aboard, but we'll deal with that when he becomes a problem. I want to figure out how he's . . ."

Creak.

This time the noise is too loud to be ignored.

Inside the room, chairs screech across the floor, and then I'm running. Heavy footfalls pound after me.

I take off down the corridor and blindly race toward my room, praying the darkness conceals me. But with my skin glistening ever so softly, I know I'm visible to whoever's behind me.

The ship heaves, and I crash into the wall. The railing digs into my back. As the ship rolls back to the other side, I'm thrown again. I wind up on my knees with water seeping through my nightgown.

The footfalls grow closer. My heart feels like it might beat out of my chest.

I stumble toward my door and throw it open, rushing inside. Half woken by the noise, Hettie snorts and rolls over.

I ignore her, heaving my weight against the door and sliding the bolt into place. The wood bites into my palms braced against it.

One set of footsteps goes past my room.

Another stops outside.

I hold my breath.

The boots scuff closer. I close my eyes, willing my heart to slow down.

Finally, the shoes scrape back the way they came.

I exhale. I lean back against the wood. My head throbs, and it won't be long until the bruises I acquired tripping down the hall do the same.

CHAPTER 11

I change into dry clothes and slide into bed next to Hettie. How am I going to tell her about Rhat? Or worse, Royce? How will we get off the ship? I'd seen some longboats lashed to the deck. I could wake Hettie, find Aris, and we could make a run for it. I'm just about to reach for her when the ship lurches again, sending Hettie spiraling into my side.

The storm.

I'd forgotten about the storm. We can't take a small boat out in this. We'd drown for sure.

We'll have to wait until tomorrow night.

But then another thought crushes me. What about the gold? How many days will we lose floating in the ocean? How will we get another ship?

I gently shake Hettie awake.

She nearly smacks me in the face as she sits up, bewildered. "Are we sinking?" She blinks, frantically looking around for signs of water flooding the cabin.

"No." I sigh. "But we need to get off this boat." I explain what I overheard.

Hettie lets out a low whistle and sinks back against the wall when I'm done. "Are you sure that's what you heard? Maybe you dreamed it." There's a hint of desperation in her voice.

"I didn't dream up my sopping nightgown over there," I say.

Hettie looks visibly shaken. "And you're sure you heard Rhat talking with Royce?"

I nod.

"I just don't believe it." She runs her hands through her hair. "How could they do that?"

"There are a lot of greedy people in the world," I reply.

Hettie crosses her arms over her chest. "Maybe I should try to get closer to Rhat, to find out for sure."

I shake my head, wondering if she is more worried about losing her flirtation with Rhat or losing me. "That's too dangerous. Besides, we need to get off this boat as soon as possible."

Hettie looks out the window at the rain pouring down. "Well, we're not going anywhere tonight."

"I know," I say. "I'll talk to Aris in the morning, and we'll figure something out."

"Aris?" Hettie's eyebrows shoot up.

I blush. "Duke Wystlinos."

Hettie smirks. Even in the midst of a crisis, she can't let the latest gossip go. "Well, then the best thing we can do is get some sleep so we can think straight in the morning, when you and *Aris* and I need to come up with a plan."

I ignore her tone and nod, but I doubt I'll sleep much.

❧ ❧ ❧

I rise before Hettie. I don't bother pulling on a cloak after I slip on an airy pink dress. It's pointless now.

I wait until I hear multiple sets of footsteps above me before venturing out of the cabin. I pray I can find Aris before I run into Royce or Rhat or Brus.

Warm air hits me above deck. The sea has long since calmed, returning to its glassy appearance. A few spindly clouds puff across the sky, and it'd almost be an ideal setting if the ship in front of me wasn't such a mess.

Gaps in the railing mark the departure spots of whatever got washed overboard. Fabric shreds hang limply from several of the sails, and ropes strangle poles or lay lifeless on the deck. Even the crow's nest sits slightly askew atop its perch.

I'm not in much better shape myself. Not only do bruises taint my arms and race down my knees, but my back feels as stiff as the mast. Or at least as stiff as the mast was yesterday, before the storm hit it. Now I'm not sure if it's off kilter or if everything around it is.

Royce barks orders across the boat, and men scurry to obey. He disappears beneath deck before he sees me, and I breathe a sigh of relief. I stray a bit farther out onto the deck, searching for Aris, but he's nowhere to be found.

Then a voice calls, "Get her now."

Hands seize me.

I'm violently jerked sideways. Several bodies, all smelling as if they've baked too long in the sun, surround me. I try to scream. A dirty rag is shoved into my mouth. It tastes like sweat and wood.

"Don't touch her skin," someone calls.

Rough hands yank my arms nearly out of their sockets as I'm propelled across the deck. I kick and throw my elbows around, finally connecting with something. I hear a grunt before another hand tightens around me.

Two men, one on either side, pull me to the opposite side of the deck, where a large triangular portion of a sail dangles limply, acting as an effective curtain.

"Don't look her in the eye," a voice says. Brus. He appears before me just as the fallen sail conceals us from the rest of the deck.

"Maybe we should cut her hair off before we throw her over-board," another sailor says. Our progress toward the railing slows. "That's got to be worth something."

"Do you want to be cursed?" Brus says. "Stick to the plan."

I thrash around in my captor's grip, trying to scream, but it only comes out as a gurgle.

"See, she's trying to cast a spell on us," Brus says. "Throw her overboard. Let Poseidon deal with her."

Hands yank me upward, and the railing rears as my feet leave the deck. Waves crash against the side of the boat.

"Let her go." The dangling sail gets ripped away to reveal Royce.

My chest crashes into the railing as the men hesitate. If hands weren't holding me up, I'd be doubled over in pain.

"We've got to get the demon off the ship," Brus says, stepping forward. "That storm last night was unnatural."

Rhat, Thipps, Phipps, and a few other sailors gather behind Royce. They all have their swords drawn, facing my captors.

"Let her go," Royce says again.

"You should've told us she was cursed," Brus continues. "We didn't want to help her in the first place, and if we'd known what she was, we'd never have left Lagonia." He spits at Royce's feet before turning back to his men. "Throw her over before she curses us."

I brace for their rough hands, but Royce's next words stop them.

"She's more valuable to us alive."

The men eye each other.

"She's the only one who knows how to find that ship full of gold."

"Cursed gold," Brus shoots back.

"Her father is cursed," Royce says forcefully. "The gold is fine. And it could be ours." He lets that hang in the air before continuing. "We could be the richest men on Poseidon's ocean. Think about it. Many of you have families you haven't seen in years. This is your ticket home, your chance to have an easy life." Royce points at me. "She's promised us a large portion of the gold if we help her get it back."

I choke on the gag. I promised no such thing.

A light breeze pulls Royce's disheveled hair across his brow. It's the only thing about him that is not rigid, not poised to leap forward into action at the slightest movement by the men in front of him.

I don't breathe while the men stand there and look between themselves.

"Brus," a sailor prompts, "we could use that gold."

"What if she curses us?" Brus hisses.

"Maybe Captain's right. She would've already done it. I don't feel any different—do you?"

Brus's eyes drift toward me, but he's careful not to meet mine, probably thanks to that rumor I turn anyone I look at to gold. "She'll curse us for sure now. After all this."

I shake my head. I'm not sure if it helps.

Brus studies Royce and the sailors standing at the ready behind him. "How much gold?" he asks Royce.

"More than you can imagine," Royce says, his eyes gleaming and a smirk tugging at his lips. "We're going to be very rich men, but we've got to be in this fight together." He turns to the men around him, gesturing grandly. "One last fight, and then each of you can buy your own ship or your own island if you want. Don't like King Midas? That's fine. Start your own kingdom." He turns back to Brus. "What do you say, Brus? Are you ready to live like a king? Are you ready to be richer than King Midas himself?"

Brus flicks his hand, and I'm roughly shoved forward.

I collide with Royce. He steadies me with one hand without breaking eye contact with Brus. I yank out the rag. Grime coats my tongue.

"Good decision, Brus," he says.

"We'll see about that." Brus turns his head toward me but still not enough that our eyes meet. "Don't you ever look at me," he grunts as he shoves past Royce.

The hairs on the back of my neck rise.

"The rest of you get back to work," Royce shouts. "And if any of you so much as lay a finger on our golden girl from here on out, I'll put you in the brig."

The men slowly disperse across the deck. Several give me sidelong glances. Others still avoid my gaze.

Royce doesn't drop his arm from my shoulder until we stand alone.

I'm trembling, and I can't help it. And I hate that he sees it. I direct all my anger into my glare. He may have saved me, but he's no better than those men. He's simply more selfish than he is superstitious.

For someone like me, that's the worst thing a man can be.

"Check on the gold," he says. His voice is hard, unfeeling.

"I never promised you my father's gold, and if you think I'm just going to hand it over to you—" I start to say.

He shoves his face close to mine. "I don't care what you did or didn't promise. That gold is the only thing keeping you alive right now, Princess." He says my title like it's poison in his mouth. "So I suggest you try a little harder to find it."

I hate him. There are no other words for it.

"The gold," he prompts.

I ball my hands into fists and swallow down as much of my rage as I can. I'll have to save it for later. For when his guard is down.

I close my eyes and locate the golden aura as quickly as I can.

"It's headed west," I say curtly, pointing in the direction I sensed it. I just want to get away from him. Now that I've given him what he wants, I turn to go, but he calls me back.

"There's one more thing we need to talk about," he says.

I whip back toward him. "I've told you where the gold is. I doubt we have anything else to talk about."

"Sails."

"Sails?" I search my brain for why he would mention them to me.

"All of these sails were fastened down last night."

I have no idea why that matters so much. My confusion must show on my face.

"We closed and secured them," he says, "but somehow every one of them came undone. All the ropes holding them in place had a clean cut. No fraying." He eyes me.

I'm not sure what to say.

"Not to mention," he continues, "no storm does identical damage like this on each sail." He pulls on the fragment closest to us. The section is nearly as wide as my arm span and about a foot taller than me. Once he pulls it open, it takes on the ragged triangle shape I'd noticed when the men attacked.

I stare at the other sails. What I thought had been random shredding turns out to be nearly uniform shapes.

"Can you think of any reason why someone would want to sabotage our sails? Anyone who would want to slow us down?"

The way his eyes bore into me means he can only be thinking one thing. "You think I did it?"

"I heard someone moving around last night, and my room's only a short distance from yours. I thought I heard your door slam shut last night." He raises one eyebrow as though he's questioning me. But there's something deeper to his stare.

He's challenging me.

No, warning me. He knows I overheard his conversation with Rhat last night.

I ignore the implication of his words, refusing to confirm his suspicions. "Why would I want to slow us down? In case you've forgotten, my father's life is at stake. After that display, it's more likely your own men did it to force us to turn around, to get me off the ship."

No emotion crosses his face, no recognition of my accusation. "You wouldn't be the first monarch to wish their parents dead to speed up their own path to the throne."

I gasp.

"Everything all right over here?" Aris says, coming up beside us. "It looks like I slept through a pretty bad storm." He looks calm and refreshed in a bright blue jacket. Without gold embellishments, I note with relief.

His relaxed stance is the most obvious difference between

him and Royce, and it's hard to imagine they were ever friends. Aris is everything Royce is not.

"It's nothing," Royce says at the same time I say, "Brus and a few soldiers tried to throw me overboard."

Aris goes rigid. He clenches his hands into fists. "You call that nothing?"

"It's been handled," Royce snaps back.

"Handled how?" Aris holds his hands out questioningly. "Did you throw those men overboard? Did you lock them in the brig? Or are they still waltzing about plotting the demise of the princess?"

"They won't do it again," Royce says.

It's the wrong thing to say. Aris's face darkens.

Aris might win a fight against Royce, but he can't beat the whole crew.

"I'm fine," I say to appease him.

"Stay out of this, Kora," Aris snaps.

I wince. His admonishment hurts, but I know he's only doing it to protect me. I put my hand on his arm.

He shakes me off. "Not now." His voice is gruff, unforgiving.

I take a few steps back, shaken by this side of him. He doesn't know Royce is already plotting against us and would probably welcome any excuse to eliminate him now. It's a miracle we haven't been thrown in the brig already. And if we're going to keep it that way, I have to stop him before he ruins every chance we have of getting off this ship.

I rush forward and step between him and Royce. "Please."

Aris glances down at me with fire in his eyes. He's breathing heavily through flared nostrils. He looks like he's about to snap at me again but doesn't. His eyes fixate on Royce, who is leaning against the railing looking as collected as ever.

"Really, I'm fine," I say. "Besides, we have bigger problems."

Aris's jaw stays clenched as he finally rips his eyes away from Royce. "What problems?"

"The sails."

Royce pulls on the tattered sail once more. "As you can see, the ship is in shambles. We're barely limping along. I told you she wouldn't last at sea and that I needed time to get supplies and make repairs. Now we'll have to stop somewhere and get what we need." His eyes flicker to me as he says it, measuring my reaction, looking for guilt.

As much as I hate the delay, this might be the best news I've received in days. Tension drains from my shoulders. Stopping means land. Land means a chance to escape this horrid boat and its captain. I only need to keep Royce and Aris on civil terms until we reach it.

"Where exactly do you propose we stop, *Captain*?" Aris spits out.

Ignoring Aris's tone, Royce moves across the deck toward a barrel near the helm. A map is spread out across the top, and I recognize Lagonia along one edge.

"We'd lose less time if we stopped here." Royce points to a dot on the map that's been drawn in.

I notice he has the same gold coin from last night clasped in his other hand. His fingers glide across its smooth surface. The crown that should be embossed there has been rubbed down.

I suck in a breath. Is this his way of taunting me? Does he think handling gold around me will cause me to react? To show him what I can do?

I hold my ground, thankful for Aris's presence at my back.

I slide my hand into his, and he offers me a distracted smile. I force my gaze back to the map.

"There's no island there." I may not have had tutors that stuck around, but I can still name the islands and countries surrounding Lagonia thanks to my extensive reading. And there has never been an island there.

"The Island of Lost Souls," Aris says, leaning forward to get a better look at the map. "You want to take the princess of Lagonia to the Island of Lost Souls, the festering wound of Poseidon's ocean?"

"We have no choice," Royce says. "The thieves are heading in that direction anyway."

"Don't you have some spare sails in the hull?" Aris says.

"Only one. I've never seen a storm take out all the sails like that." There's an edge to his voice that I fear will set off Aris again. "We'll be lucky to make it to land as it is, so I'll gladly take the Island of Lost Souls over the alternative."

Aris glares at Royce. "We can't go there."

"It's there or back to Lagonia." Royce weighs the coin in his cupped palm. "We can't catch up to anything in this shape." He throws his arms wide and gestures to the ship once more. "And if we tried, the thieves could lead us days from port. If we hit another storm, we'd be done for. It's better to stop now and lose a few days than to sink in the middle of the ocean."

I lean forward to inspect the dot. It's easy to miss, but there's no way I'd forget such a name if I'd ever come across it in the books I'd read.

"What is the Island of Lost Souls?" I ask.

Both men turn to look at me.

"It's a hideout for pirates and thieves." Aris drops my hand to run his fingers through his hair. "A lawless place, a safe haven for anyone on the run. No self-respecting citizen would go there."

"No self-respecting citizen knows about it," Royce chimes in from across the table. "It's a miniscule island, but it does receive supplies on a regular basis. And it means continuing forward instead of turning around." He closes his fingers tight around the coin he's holding. I feel like his words cast just as strong a hold over me. He knows I'll never go back. Not without the gold.

Aris scoffs. "After what your own sailors just tried, you think it's a good idea to take her there? No—we're heading back to Lagonia."

As much as I want to agree with Aris, I can't. Because going back to Lagonia means losing at least another four days. Four days I can't afford. My only hope is to find another boat on the Island of Lost Souls.

"If it's faster than going back to Lagonia, then it's our only option," I say. I look away from Royce's closed fist.

Aris shakes his head. "Kora, you don't know what you're talking about, what you'd be getting into."

I duck my head, feeling as useless as when I attended a few council meetings where Uncle Pheus and visiting dignitaries discussed treaties and trade agreements I knew nothing about. Except I do know something about this. Something Aris doesn't. If he was aware of what I overheard last night, he'd be just as eager to get off the ship.

"We'll only be staying a few hours to resupply," I say, afraid to meet his eyes, afraid he'll be angry.

Aris sighs and takes my hand, drawing my gaze toward him. "It's not safe there." His eyes plead with me.

It's not safe here, I want to say.

I look to the waves. "We have to."

"It's settled then," Royce says from the other side of the barrel. He tucks the coin away.

"It's not settled, Royce." Aris leans on the rim toward Royce, his anger rising again.

"I'm still captain," Royce replies, matching Aris's position from the other side of the barrel. The wood groans under the weight of both men. "I asked you as a courtesy where you thought we should go, but I make the decisions." Royce eases away from the barrel. "We're going to the Island of Lost Souls."

CHAPTER 12

I manage to pull Aris away before he and Royce come to blows. I steer him toward a section of the ship mostly cleared of debris and therefore mostly devoid of sailors.

"I'm sorry." His shoulders slump as we turn to face each other at the edge of the ship. "I don't know why he would act that way. He hasn't been himself lately." He moves closer until one hand cups my cheek. "I shouldn't have fought with Royce that way. I just want you to be safe."

I put my hand on his arm. "I know, but I think it's part of a larger problem."

"What problem?" He drops his hand from my cheek and looks around the deck.

I recount what I overheard, focusing on Royce wanting to use me for my powers and marooning or killing him.

Tiny muscles contract around his jaw as he clenches it. He slams his fist against the railing. "I trusted him. We grew up fishing with one another, playing pranks on our siblings, competing to see who could climb to the top of the old oak the fastest. He was the one who carried me back to my house when I fell out of that tree and nearly broke my neck." His knuckles whiten as he grips the rail. "I let those memories get in the way of what everyone was telling me, of what was right in front of my face."

"I don't understand," I say, lowering my voice as Phipps and Thipps hoist a broken beam over their shoulders and carry it off, each one complaining that the other isn't carrying their fair share.

"I didn't want to tell you this before because I didn't think it could be true." He finally meets my gaze. "There have always been rumors about what happened when we lost the treaty. I'm sure you heard some of them yourself."

Toward the end of the wars, I'd overheard some noblemen say Royce Denes had only been promoted to captain because of his father's influence and that he wasn't qualified for such an important mission. And Aris had reminded me Royce was the one who'd lost the treaty, but beyond that, I hadn't heard any mumblings about the true cause of the mission's failure.

Aris sighs as he continues. "Only Royce and I knew the treaty was on board. How did Captain Skulls find out? And how could one small woman move a barrel full of oil all by herself in order to blow up the ship? Someone on board must have helped her."

"Royce," I breathe.

Aris drops his head. "He's been to the Island of Lost Souls before too. After months of searching, he traced the pirate woman there. I tried to tell him not to go, but he said he wanted to find out how they knew about the treaty.

"I went with him because I thought I could help prove his innocence. That was only a few weeks before I sailed to meet you." He chokes on the last word, on whatever realization he's made. "While on the island, we split up to search for the woman, and he could've met up with Skulls there, especially since he was trying to gather money for repairs. This could all be my fault.

I—I told Royce about you, about what I knew of your family, about why I wanted to meet you."

My body goes cold. I cling to the railing to stay anchored to the world as everything crumbles around me. Could Aris be responsible, even by accident, for the theft of my father's gold?

But how would Royce and Captain Skulls have known about the gold, about where to find it?

Archduke Ralton. The thought bolts through me. He easily could've shadowed my father or bribed a guard to figure out where the gold was.

"Do you think your uncle may have been the one to tell Royce and Captain Skulls where the gold was?" I ask.

Aris's eyes go wide as realization dawns in his face. "I knew he wasn't happy with the monarchy, but if I'd thought . . . if I'd known . . ." He trails off, shaking his head.

"You couldn't have known," I reply. "It's not your fault. Your uncle has probably been a part of this scheme from the beginning." He likely planned the whole thing.

"Kora, I have to warn you." His voice wavers. "My uncle may not only be after your kingdom. If he's working with Royce and Captain Skulls, he may be after you too." He takes a deep breath. "I know it might be difficult for you, but will you tell me what it is they could be after? There have been so many stories over the years, but perhaps if I know the truth, I can protect you."

I open my mouth to reply, but the words don't make it past my constricting throat. I'm paralyzed by the memory flooding back.

It happened a day or two after I was turned back from a statue, when I was seven. Alongside my father and uncle, I entered the tower room where they stored the gold. It was the first time I'd seen the other golden objects.

Everything was stacked on the table. A golden pheasant rested on the round gold platter my father had touched when throwing the feast celebrating The Touch. An embossed leaf design ran around the edge of the platter. Alongside the pheasant was the big carving knife he'd grasped. Its long, transformed blade gleamed. Next to those rested the single rose he'd plucked from the garden, its petals trapped in a perfect bloom. There were three coins that had previously been worth next to nothing but now carried their own hefty weight. Only the fish symbol stamped on each marked them as having originally been copper. I doubted any shopkeeper would see anything but the color and willingly accept it.

Two chalices, each with a rose border running around the lip, glimmered on the table. My father had ordered them made for my mother as a wedding gift, and they'd toasted their marriage with those cups.

Next to the chalices was a small golden tapestry no longer than my arm. It was rolled up, and I recall thinking it resembled a hollow log more than a piece of art. I never did find out what design it concealed. I'm not sure even my father knew.

At the end of the table was a golden necklace. My mother's necklace.

My father ran his fingers along the edge of the table. "What are we going to do, brother?" He turned to look at Pheus.

"The gold must be destroyed if you ever want the curse to fully end," Pheus said.

"Would it destroy me too?" my father replied. His gaze turned back to the golden objects. "Already, I can feel the gold taking over my thoughts. It's all I can think about. Waking, sleeping. At all times, it's there, waiting for me to let it take over."

Pheus laid a hand on my father's shoulder. "We'll find a way to end this. Together."

I wanted to offer some comfort, but I couldn't concentrate on their conversation. Being that close to the gold ignited something within me. It was almost as if the gold hummed softly, inviting me to come touch it. Just one touch wouldn't hurt.

But it did hurt.

I touched the necklace, which sat on a plump purple cushion. It looked like the one my mother wore in the portrait hanging in my father's room. I'd wanted to see what it would look like on me, to see if I could ever be as pretty as my mother despite my now-golden skin.

I never got to find out because the instant the gold grazed my skin, it absorbed into my body. The necklace dulled to silver.

I managed a sharp intake of breath before my insides turned to ice. The gold spun its web across my veins and down my bones, just like it had when my father hugged me in the garden. I flung my hands, trying to shake it off. I cried out.

My hand collided with something. It was the guard, roused by my cry. And the moment my skin touched his outstretched hand, the gold rushed from my body. It climbed over the guard, hardening him in place.

He'd become a statue.

His arms reached out for an invisible object. One leg was frozen backward. Golden eyes stared unblinking.

My father slumped against the wall with a groan. Pheus stood open-mouthed, looking back and forth between the guard and me. "What have you done?" he whispered.

"I didn't do it," I stuttered, unable to take my eyes from the guard's golden form. From my own distorted reflection gleaming back at me.

I reached out to my father and uncle.

Pheus moved away in terror, his eyes wide and his hands clasped to his chest.

I collapsed to the ground, horrified by what I had done. As I fell, my elbow crashed against the golden boot of the guard. Before I could even think my elbow should hurt, the gold careened back into my body, navigating its way toward my heart. All I'd done was touch it, and it had jumped right back into my body.

The guard sputtered back to life. Although his skin, thankfully, hadn't retained any of the gold coloring, the wild look in his eyes showed he hadn't escaped unscathed.

He stared at me. His breathing was as heavy as mine.

Before I could explain or apologize or form whatever words my brain was trying to produce, the man ran from the room.

Pheus tarried only a moment before cursing and chasing after him.

I did the only thing I could think of: I reached back and wound my tiny fingers around the necklace. My skin tingled as the gold passed through it, returning the necklace to its golden state.

Only my father remained in the room. I waited for him to speak, to explain or reassure. Even his anger would've been better than his silence. But he just stared at me like I was a monster. A monster he'd created.

I fled past him to the library.

When the door to the library creaked open hours later, I stuck my tear-stained face out from between shelves full of nautical books. I expected my father's form to grace the entryway.

It was Pheus.

He carried a golden candelabra in his hand and remained in

the doorway until I emerged. I waited for him to punish me. But what he said surprised me.

"Touch it," he said, placing the candelabra on the floor and backing away.

I shook my head.

"I need to know if it's all gold or just the objects your father turned." He crossed his arms and waited. "This will help me keep the people in the palace safe."

I didn't want to know what the powers could or couldn't do. I just wanted them to go away. I never wanted to touch gold again.

But Pheus wouldn't leave until I did.

I neared the candelabra.

I knelt a few feet away. I could feel the gentle heat of the candles wafting toward me as I leaned forward ever so slightly. I placed my hand over my heart for a moment, hoping it wasn't the last time I'd feel it beat.

I extended a trembling finger and touched the base. Gold drained from it into my body. The flames didn't even waver.

"Do you have the same power your father did?" Pheus pondered. His eyes took on a somber color in the candlelight.

I wanted to shout that I didn't have the same power; I had the same curse. But I couldn't answer. The gold was adhering to my insides, clinging to muscles and ripping down sinews, but it hadn't consumed me. I was still alive. Still breathing.

That didn't mean I could control it. The longer it pulsed through my body, the harder it got to contain. My head pounded. My muscles ached as the gold dug deeper into them, finding grooves and spaces I didn't know existed within my own body.

The metal spun through my mind. The room spun in response. Without thinking, I reached out an arm to steady myself against the ground. I didn't even feel the softness of the rug beneath me before it turned to gold. My body only felt the instant relief of the gold draining into the rug.

Pheus jumped when the rug beneath his feet hardened.

As I gathered myself, I began to realize that as I absorbed gold, anything I was already touching, like my clothes, remained untainted, but the next thing I touched instantly turned to gold. And the size of the object didn't matter. The amount of gold in a tiny necklace could turn an entire man into a statue. A candelabra's gold could cover a rug that spanned half the library.

Pheus had moved to the other side of the room by the door. His face was unreadable in the shadows. "Put it back."

I removed my hand from the rug and then plunged it back down again. The gold jumped back into my body.

I returned the candelabra to its golden state and was left shivering.

Pheus frowned and pursed his lips, as if he already understood the weight of my curse. "Now, I can make a full report to your father," he said. He moved toward the candelabra, but stopped before picking it up. He withdrew his hands and clasped them behind his back instead. "You must be very careful, Kora. For now, it would be best if you went back to your room."

Then he'd left to go tell my father about what my curse could do. I'd stayed in the library for hours trying to find a legend, a mixture of herbs, anything my young mind could think of that would fix it. I found nothing and had collapsed, crying and begging to the library rafters for Dionysus to return.

Later that night, I snuck toward my father's room. Maybe he and Pheus had found a way to cure us. Or maybe my father would just hold me and tell me it was going to be all right. I crept into his outer rooms. The fireplace was cold and unlit, but light spilled out of his bedroom chamber. I stood outside the cracked door and took a breath, praying that when I walked in and he saw me, he wouldn't make the same disgusted face I'd seen when he turned me to gold.

Whispered voices leaked out of the room.

"She can't control what she can do any more than you could," Uncle Pheus said. "Our only stroke of luck is that the guard she turned to gold ran down to the ocean and drowned himself. No one else can know. The people are superstitious. They'd revolt if they thought the curse was still alive, still active."

My heart clenched in my chest. I instinctively reached forward to steady myself and collided with the door, pushing it inward.

Uncle Pheus's eyes went wide at the intrusion. He stood next to my father's ornately carved wooden bed. My father lay among the silken blankets, looking drained and weak. He didn't smile. He didn't react. He only stared somewhere past me.

"Please." I staggered toward Pheus. He could fix anything. All the people in Lagonia went to him for advice. "Please," I said. "What can we do?"

He shook his head sadly. "I'm sorry, Kora. We're trying to find a cure, but I don't know if there's anything that can fix this."

My lower lip trembled. I stared at the ceiling as though I expected to find an answer hiding up there. "What about Dionysus?" I said. I'd found nothing about him in the library, and my earlier begging had failed. But someone had to know his whereabouts and how to bring him to the palace.

Pheus lowered his gaze. "Even if we could find him, I doubt he'd help us again. He deals in tricks and wordplay, always leaving chaos in his wake."

Guilt coursed through me faster than the gold had earlier. "I didn't know this was going to happen," I said. It was the only explanation I could offer.

Pheus nodded solemnly. "All we can do now is prevent it from ever happening again."

I swallowed. "I promise. I promise I'll never touch gold again." Even as I said the words, it didn't fill the emptiness I felt. I doubted anything ever would.

Pheus made it an easy promise to keep. All the gold objects disappeared from the palace. The candelabras were stripped bare. The gold plates were replaced with silver. The golden mirrors were taken away and sold. Even my father's crown was replaced with a silver replica. Only a few ornate carriages were left in case visiting dignitaries arrived and needed to be carted around. Pheus outlawed the wearing of gold in the palace. Silver became the highest currency in Lagonia. He passed it all off as my father not wanting gold around, but I knew it was all because of me. He was right to be scared of what I could do, of who I could hurt.

My father lost all the strength he'd gained over the previous days, and a man had died because of what I'd done.

I was a monster.

CHAPTER 13

〉〉〉〉〉〉〉〉〉◉〈〈〈〈〈〈〈〈〈

Aris looks down at me expectantly, waiting for me to tell him about the worst part of myself. But if I reveal my secret and he decides to abandon me here, I don't know what I'll do. The whole world would be against me again. Only this time, I know it will hurt worse. Much worse.

He grabs my hand and pulls me closer until our clasped hands are all that stand between us. "You're safe with me. You can tell me. You are not your curse, remember?"

I am not my curse. I repeat it over and over again. I close my eyes and let the words wrap around my mind, working their way through the wall built there by the gold. The one that says not to tell anyone. Not to admit the truth. Because that would make it real. And part of me still clings to the hope that it was a one-time thing. That it's never going to happen again.

Aris squeezes my hand, reminding me that he is real too. That what I feel every time I look at him—the uptick in my pulse, the blush in my cheeks—that is real. That is more powerful than any curse could ever be.

I close my eyes. "I can turn things to gold," I say. I release the words to the wind, to the world, quickly. Because now I can never get them back. "I first have to absorb gold from something else in order to do it."

"Okay."

I open my eyes. It's as simple as that. His face hasn't faltered. He hasn't run away. He hasn't presented me with a golden object and demanded to see a demonstration. He merely accepts it.

He runs his thumb down the back of my hand. Energy pulses between us as he continues the motion, rubbing away the last of the tower memory with his slow circles. I realize it's the first time I've been comforted. No one's ever told me who I am is okay.

I stare down at our clasped hands, willing him to never let go.

My heartbeat pounds through my body as his eyes slowly move down my face and land on my lips. One hand moves up to my cheek. He trails his thumb down my jawline, stopping at my chin to tilt it upward.

"Is there anything else?" he asks gently.

I shake my head. "You already know I can sense the gold."

"All gold? Or just your father's?"

"Just my father's," I confirm. "But it hasn't taken over my mind like it has his." I pray it never does.

"And we'll never let it," Aris reassures.

His eyes stay on mine as he leans forward. And then he presses his lips gently against mine. His other arm swoops behind me, pressing me harder against him.

I close my eyes and let myself melt against him. I want the heat from his arm around me to thaw the iciness that has kept me prisoner so long. The gold tugs at my mind, but I push it away. I don't want anything ruining this moment.

I focus on the trail of tingling skin his touch leaves behind as his fingers slide across my cheek. I let myself get lost in the warmth of his lips, in the way they draw me closer and closer until my arms wrap around him of their own accord, unwilling to let go.

When Aris finally pulls away, breathless, he lets his forehead rest against mine, like he's trying to give me the strength to face my curse.

I bite the sides of my cheek to keep a smile from sliding across my face. I can still taste him on my lips, a sweet honeyed mead.

I never dreamed I'd be kissed. I don't even know if I did it right. I don't even care.

Aris smiles down at me reassuringly. "Now that we know who we're up against and what they're really after, we can stop them. But first we have to get off this boat."

I nod, glad that we're in agreement. I feel like we could face anything together. And we just might have to if Royce gets his way.

I drop my voice as several other sailors walk by clearing debris and straightening water collection barrels. "It'll have to be while we're on the Island of Lost Souls."

"I'm sure we'll be able to find help on the island. It's our best chance," Aris says. "You and I will escape and find someone else who can help us go after the gold."

"And Hettie," I say. "We can't leave her behind."

"Of course," he says. "We'll find a reason for all of us to go to shore. But can Hettie keep the secret? Should we wait until we're on the island to tell her? I've heard from the crew she's been spending time with Rhat. I wouldn't want anything to slip out."

Hettie does tend to try to impress people with what she knows, but she won't let this slip. "She'll keep it quiet." If she doesn't, we're dead.

He nods. "All right." He puts one hand on my cheek, warming the skin. "Whatever happens, remember we're in this together. I'll do whatever it takes to get you and the gold home safely."

I nod. And I find I'm not scared, at least not as scared as I should be, especially with a place called the Island of Lost Souls looming somewhere ahead of us.

❀ ❀ ❀

I stay below deck the next few days, knowing we just have to make it to the Island of Lost Souls. Hettie, on the other hand, has focused on her scheme of figuring out Royce's plan by getting close to Rhat.

After I told her about the plan to escape on the island, she claimed we would be given away if she didn't keep up her charade with Rhat. She told me the two of them have been practicing sword fighting, climbing through the rigging, tying things in knots, and spending evenings in the crow's nest looking at the stars.

The only night I venture onto the deck is the night we near the coast of the Island of Lost Souls. The night we're going to escape.

The island comes into view just after midnight and looks barely twice the length of the entire castle grounds back home. Small, squat buildings dot the coast. No wonder most people don't know about it. The island would be hard to find amidst all this open water.

Phipps and Thipps sidle up to me, one on each side, as I stare out over the waves. Their presence is startling. I'm not used to people being willing to get so close, especially once they see me without my hood or veil.

"So," Phipps says, "my brother and I were thinking, that if the rumors are true and your father outlawed gold because all gold is attracted to you . . ."

Thipps jumps in. "Then we'd be happy to act as bodyguards when the gold comes flying at you right out of people's pockets."

"Not to mention we're good at spotting a full purse and could loosen the bottom a little," Phipps adds, "if you know what I mean."

They're talking so quickly I have to whip back and forth.

"Of course, we'd only want a nominal fee for our services," Thipps says.

"Nominal. Very nominal," Phipps assures me. "After all, we are taking the brunt of all that gold coming right at us."

They both stare at me expectantly, eyes bright and smiles wide.

This is certainly a rumor I haven't heard before. Gold flying out of pockets because it's attracted to my skin? It would almost be laughable if there was any truth to it. And while normally I hate people bringing up the rumors about my curse, the twins seem to have done it in such a way that it almost feels like something I should be excited about simply because they're so excited about it, like this is the biggest moment of their life and I'm lucky they're letting me in on it.

It hurts a little to let them down. "While I appreciate the offer," I say, "if gold were attracted to my skin, don't you think your gold tooth would've flown out of your mouth by now, Thipps?"

Phipps's smile falters and he sags forward on the railing.

Thipps's smile falters too for a second before he recovers. "Ahh, but it's not gold all the way through. It's mostly copper." He taps the tooth with his finger as if that proves the point.

I resist the urge to roll my eyes. At least they're not scared of my skin.

"Phipps, Thipps," Rhat calls, "help drop the anchor."

The men groan and push off the railing.

"Just think about our offer," Phipps says, drumming his hands against the wood.

Both men wait until I nod before scampering off, already arguing about which one had the idea first and should therefore get a bigger cut of the profits.

❦ ❦ ❦

We anchor the ship a distance from the coast.

"Should we wait until morning to go ashore, Captain?" Rhat asks.

"No, it's best to do it now while it's still dark. We don't want too many people knowing we were here. And," he adds, looking at me, "we don't want that gold getting any farther ahead."

"Aye, Captain," Rhat replies.

Sailors lower a longboat and various men climb down the ladder. Phipps and Thipps argue over who should sit on which side of the boat. From the deck, Hettie shyly waves at Rhat as he climbs down.

I look over at Aris and nod. We'd discussed how to approach this.

"I think I could give you a hand on shore," Aris says to Royce.

"I didn't expect anything less from you," Royce says. He motions for Aris to climb down.

I exhale. So far, so good.

Next, I present myself. I bolster myself so I don't wither under Royce's stare. "Hettie and I should come as well. We don't feel safe on your ship without you or Aris on board." I cast my eyes to where Brus stands not too far off.

Hettie moves to my side. She was a little huffy, claiming I may have misheard Rhat since she hadn't discovered any dark secrets from him, but she'd gone along with me when I said we had to get off the ship.

"No," Royce says simply before going back to staring over the railing at the men gathered in the boat below.

I gape. "What do you mean, no?"

His head whips toward me. "I realize princesses probably aren't told that word often," he says, "but it means you can't come."

"But—"

"If you feel unsafe onboard, you have no idea what's in store for you on that island. And if you think I'm taking a girl made of gold there, you've lost your mind."

"You have to—"

"I don't have to do anything," he says, brushing some of his shaggy blond hair away from his eyes. "And if you try to board the longboat, my men would be more than happy to detain you in the brig."

Behind Royce, Brus hoists up a rope used to let the longboat down. He keeps glancing over, obviously listening and eager to step forward should I not adhere to whatever Royce decrees. I ignore the small smile spreading across his face that reveals blackened teeth.

"Now, if you'll excuse me," Royce says. He tosses the rope he'd been winding to a nearby sailor and starts to descend the rope ladder leading down to the longboat.

I bite my lip. I need some way to get Hettie and me on that boat.

Thankfully, Aris comes to my rescue. "Royce," he calls, standing up in the boat and sending it rocking, "I would feel better having Princess Kora and her cousin come with us after what I heard happened several days ago with your sailors."

"And I would feel better not having a girl with golden skin with us on an island full of greedy, cutthroat pirates," Royce says in reply.

It's obvious he's trying to separate us. Wasn't that what he said? He'd deal with Aris at some point? Maybe even maroon him on an island. This island. Where Aris would be surrounded by cutthroats and thieves.

I wring my hands and then switch to pulling on the end of my braid. I pace back and forth. My heart thuds in time with each foot hitting the deck. The sound echoes hollowly through me.

Brus's eyes follow my path.

Frustrated, I close my eyes. Something tugs at my mind. Without meaning to, I reach out for the gold.

Suddenly, I know how I'm getting on that island.

CHAPTER 14

>>>>>>>>>>◉﹤﹤﹤﹤﹤﹤﹤﹤﹤

Wait," I call out breathlessly.

I race forward to where Royce is still climbing down the ladder. I drop to my knees and grab his wrist just as he is about to descend another step.

His head snaps up. He's far enough down that he's level with me for once. The intensity of his gaze pushes all thoughts from my mind.

"What?" He looks irritated, even more so than usual.

I rip my gloved hand away and absently rub it on my dress as I work to find my voice. "I have to come with you."

His fingers clench tighter around the ladder. "We've already been over that." He ducks his head to continue climbing down.

"You don't understand."

He pauses mid-step. "Then explain it. Fast."

"The gold," I whisper, "it's here."

That gets his attention. His voice drops. "All of it?"

I shake my head. "A piece of it. A coin. That's why I missed it. I didn't think they'd separate the treasure." Earlier, I'd only been looking for the aura of the tapestry, then tossing it away before I had to see Captain Skulls again. I'd been moving too quickly to notice if all the gold was there.

Royce eyes me, like he's wondering if I'm telling the truth. "They must have stopped here," he finally says. "Depending on how long they stopped, and whether we hurry, we might make up some ground."

"Then we need to hurry."

"Where's the coin now?"

I point in the direction I'd sensed it.

He sighs. "Where exactly?" His eyes are bright, but the lanterns of the ship cast an eerie glow over him.

"It doesn't work like that. I can't simply tell you where it is. It's more like . . . like I know when I'm getting closer, like I can see it in my mind." It'd be hard to explain to someone I wanted to explain it to, but it's even harder with Royce. I don't want to reveal anything more to him than necessary.

Royce hauls himself back onto the deck, nearly running into me at the top of the ladder. "Fine," he says. "It looks like you're coming to shore after all."

I nod, not sure if I should be frightened or excited.

"Come on, Hettie," I say, motioning to the ladder.

"There's no reason for her to come," Royce says, staring down at me. Challenging me? Does he suspect? He must.

I cast a glance toward the longboat. I can't catch Aris's eye.

"But . . ." I leave the word hanging. I have no excuse for why Hettie should come.

"Would you rather we leave the coin here?" Royce asks.

My eyes go to Hettie. Her eyes are wide as she stares at me, unsure what to do. She gives the barest shrug of her shoulders, questioning what comes next.

I can only stare back as precious seconds tick away.

Hettie's eyes narrow as she faces Royce. "You . . . you can't leave me here alone with all these men."

Royce crosses his arms. "I'm going to have a hard-enough

time making sure the princess comes back alive. I can't watch both of you, so if you value her life, I suggest you stay here."

"But . . ." Hettie stammers.

"You can bolt yourself in your room," he says.

"Anyone could break in."

Royce massages his forehead for a moment. "Fine." He takes a small golden key from his pocket. "This is the key to the brig. It's the only one. No one else is down there. You can lock yourself in a cell, and no one will be able to touch you."

Hettie's eyes jump from the key to me. Then she straightens and purses her lips. "That's not a fitting place for—"

Royce cuts her off. "You're not coming. So either go willingly, or I will have someone escort you because we're losing valuable time due to you."

Hettie stares at the outstretched key. She shoots me a look that says it all: *There goes our plan.*

Out of excuses, Hettie has no choice but to snatch the key, and I have no choice but to climb down the ladder.

I settle in next to Aris. Thipps is on my other side, and he grins and offers me a wink while Phipps mutters that he knew he should've sat there.

"I wouldn't mind gold skin myself," he says. "All I'd have to do is scratch a little, and I'd have enough to pay for drinks for a whole night."

As with many things the brothers say, I'm not sure if I should be amused or disgusted. I try to offer him a smile as I turn back to Aris and whisper, "A piece of the gold is on the island. That's why I was allowed to come."

He shakes his head. "We're as cursed as Midas," he mutters and runs his fingers through his hair.

His words tear through me faster than gold does, and I sit back as though I've been struck. I know it's a common phrase used by people down on their luck, but it is not one anyone has actually said around me before.

Aris looks up, and his eyes go wide when he sees my face. "I didn't mean that. I'm sorry." He leans over and quickly clasps my hands. "I know what your father has suffered. I've just spent too much time around superstitious sailors lately. And I've been going out of my mind worrying about you being on that island. It was bad enough when we had to travel there to escape, but now we also need to retrieve some of the gold—it won't be easy." His eyes search out mine. "Can you forgive me?"

I nod, and some of the tension drains from my shoulders. I should've realized how hard this is going to be. Whoever has it isn't simply going to hand it over. But Aris knows this island, and he knows how difficult it'll be to get the coin back, let alone find a boat to escape in. And I've been letting him shoulder that burden alone. I can't blame him for cracking under the pressure of it all.

Aris remains silent for a few moments before nodding and squeezing my hands in his. "Stay close to me. We'll make it through this together." He eyes Royce as the captain settles into the nearly empty front of the boat where the supplies will go.

Phipps and Thipps tell jokes in an attempt to lighten the tension in the longboat, at least until Royce quiets them. After that, only the slice of the oars into the water breaks the silence of the boat ride to shore. When we get there, Royce turns to me.

"Stay out of sight as much as possible."

I nod, knowing this is something I can do. I've excelled at staying out of sight for years.

We climb out of the longboat onto a long, rickety dock.

Several boards are missing, and it leans to the right. The dock has row upon row of empty offshoots meant for bigger ships that protrude far out into the water. Several other docks jut out parallel to us, but they all seem as empty and dilapidated. On some, entire sections have collapsed into the water, leaving jagged boards pointing out at all angles.

The only other boats I see are small longboats like ours pulled onto the shore farther down past the docks. I pray there are more docks somewhere containing the boat we need to get out of here.

Past the dock, stacked crates almost block the view of the meager town, but I can just barely make out slanted roofs and smoke from cooking fires rising into the air.

My eyes catch on a set of tall poles at the end of the dock. Headless bodies dangle from them. Their hands sway back and forth, as if motioning us not to go any farther.

In life, they must've been big, hulking men. But in death, the way their shoulders hunch forward over the ropes looped under their arms manages to make them look frightened even without faces to show their emotion. I wonder what could have led these men to such a fate.

The wind picks up, vaulting them once more into the silent dance of death. Tendrils of cold wind race down my back and feel like fingernails. I shiver.

Royce moves toward them and stops. "They look fresh," he says to Rhat.

"Aye, Captain," Rhat replies.

"He must have been here."

"It could just be another copycat, someone else trying to pick up his legacy. Despite the rumors, none of our sources have been able to confirm he's alive."

Phipps and Thipps move forward as I make my way around Royce and Rhat. "Remember our offer," Thipps starts to say before he sees the bodies. "Captain Skulls," he whispers. "Has to be his work."

"Can't be," Phipps replies. "He's dead."

"I heard he lives forever, that each skull he collects gives him another year of life."

"How many times do I have to tell you that's not true?" Phipps knocks his brother upside his head.

Thipps rubs the spot. "How do you know it isn't true? Sailors say he drinks the blood of his victims, sucks it right out of the head, and that the entire hull of his ship is filled with skulls. I've even heard that after battles, Skulls has his men bring in captives two at a time. They play a game of cutting the captives' throats very slowly, and whoever keeps theirs alive the longest wins an extra share of the loot." He switches from rubbing his head to rubbing his neck. "I don't want to die that way. I'd rather go down in battle itself than be taken prisoner by the likes of him."

Phipps rolls his eyes. "Worry about dying later. We've got work to do." He shoves his brother down the dock. His eyes return to the headless bodies more than once, though, and he visibly swallows.

Aris wraps his arms around me, angling me away from the gruesome sight. "Don't look," he says.

It's too late for that. I shudder at the memory of Captain Skulls standing over the head of that Lagonian soldier. "Do you think he's still here?" I say.

"Not if the rest of the gold isn't. He'll be with the gold. Or"—he nods toward the bodies—"he'll be busy adding those to his collection."

I take a deep breath, fearing the day I have to face the pirate captain.

"Whenever you're finished gawking," Aris calls over his shoulder to Royce, "the princess is ready."

Aris's words stir Royce back toward the group.

"All right," Royce says, gathering the other sailors close to him, although some still give me a wide berth. "Rhat, Aris, and I have our own business to attend to. Thipps, you stay and guard the longboat. Phipps, take the rest of the men and get all the supplies we can afford back to the ship as quickly as possible. We don't know what kind of situation we'll find ourselves in as we return to the ship, so load the supplies as quickly as you can."

Phipps nods and moves off in the opposite direction I sensed the coin. A group of sailors follows after him.

Once the men are gone, Royce pulls Rhat aside, but it's quiet enough for me to hear their words. "Go on ahead," he whispers. "Search the taverns. I want to know if he's here."

Rhat nods and heads off into the night.

Finally, Royce turns to me. "Which way is the coin?"

I glance back toward where Thipps is guarding the boat, but he isn't close enough to overhear. Plus, from his perch on the bow, he's already singing some song about life at sea.

I close my eyes and let the gold flash through to ensure it's still where I'd located it last. Then, I force my eyes open. I point in the direction I sensed it, and Aris moves forward, taking my arm.

But Royce stops us. "I want you to get us as close to the coin as you can," he says, "but don't enter any buildings without checking with me first."

I look toward Aris. He nods reassuringly.

I yank up the hood of the cloak I'd worn in preparation for making our escape, and we set off across the pathway leading up to the town. A row of whitewashed buildings stretches down the coast. At least they would've been white if it weren't for all the dirt and mud kicked up from what passes as a street. Light spills onto the maze of missing cobblestones. Tufts of grass and tangles of weeds have taken up residence in the gaps. Several thin cats slink through the shadows and disappear down dark alleyways situated between a few structures.

Raucous laughter from nearby buildings drowns out the hum of the ocean waves crashing against the shoreline. The night air tugs at my cloak, so I keep my head down. If there's anywhere I don't want to be exposed, it's here.

Several women showing more skin than could ever be considered decent stroll by. They call out to Aris and Royce. Royce ignores them, and Aris keeps his head down.

A group of men stumble from one of the doorways. A man's low voice floats out from the entryway as he sings:

> *"Away went my lass*
> *when I'd spent my last brass.*
> *What I wouldn't do for a barrel of gold.*
> *She said she'd never come back*
> *While I lived in a shack.*
> *What I wouldn't do for a barrel of gold.*
> *The gold, the gold,*
> *Grab it while you can.*
> *Or you'll end up like Midas, young man."*

Bile makes the slow climb up my throat over and over again

no matter how many times I swallow it down. I want to run in there and yell at them to stop. But as much as I will it, my feet won't move.

The door slams shut, cutting off the sound. It breaks the spell the words had over me.

"It's only a song," Aris says. "Don't let it affect you. Focus on the coin."

I nod.

It's hard to look away from the building. From the people who will never understand what my father went through. Or why.

The melody of the continuing song haunts me as we move down the street.

When we near the end of the pathway, I stop. Ahead, the wind races down toward cliff edges. On one side, dark rocks cut a jagged pathway into the sea.

I point to the second-to-last building on the street. Gray bricks lead up to a thin roof, and several windows let light out into the street. A sign reading The Cat's Cradle creaks above the door, and I notice two carved cats curled up inside the Cs.

"Are you sure this is the place?" Royce asks.

"It's inside," I confirm.

"In there?" Aris lets out a groan.

"What is this place?" I ask.

Aris relaxes his shoulders. "The owner, he's the one who made the island what it is. This tavern is where the most heartless pirates come to drink. It's not safe for you in there."

"Where exactly is the coin?" Royce interrupts.

Even in the darkness of the street, I can feel his eyes on me, boring through to my soul. When I look up into them, all

I see is the reflection of my own gold skin glowing faintly in the night.

"I told you, it doesn't work like that. It could be in a pocket or a shoe or a pouch. I won't know until I get close enough." True, I could close my eyes and maybe picture the room as I'd done when I envisioned Captain Skulls, but even then, I couldn't really describe it well enough to Royce to know where to go.

"There has to be another way," Aris says. He steps in closer. Our group is attracting unwanted stares from passersby. Every second we spend arguing, we risk more exposure.

One form slips out of the closest tavern and across the street toward us. It's Rhat.

"Everything okay, Captain?" he asks. "I've only got the Cat's Cradle left to check."

"We've got to get Kora inside there," Royce says. It's the first time he says my name without making it sound like a curse. He runs his fingers through his hair and turns to look at the building again, out of which we can hear shouting. It's hard to tell if the occupants are angry or just having a good time.

If Rhat wonders about why we need to get inside, he doesn't show it, which must mean Royce told him about my ability to find the gold.

"Sounds like they've already had quite a bit to drink," I say, "which could leave them incapacitated."

"Or more reckless," Royce replies.

"We can't go in there and search everyone," Aris says. "We need a better plan." He eyes a group of men who are studying us before going into the Cat's Cradle.

I wring my hands. "What if we caused some sort of distraction?" I ask. "If we could draw people out here and distract them, they'd be easier to search." I wish Phipps and Thipps were here. Didn't they say something about being good at loosening the bottoms of purses?

"The only things pirates would come out of the pub for would be free rum or a fight between two crews, of which we have neither," Aris explains.

"That's it." Royce spins around. "We don't need to draw them out. We'll start a fight inside."

"Captain," Rhat says, "there are only four of us."

"It'll be a controlled fight," Royce says. He turns to Aris. "You against me. Everyone will be so busy watching us, they won't notice when Kora and Rhat sneak in during the confusion." He turns to me. "Kora, once you locate the man who has the coin, signal Rhat, and he'll take every coin the scoundrel has on him."

"No," Aris says, his face hard. I don't think he's declining because he doesn't want a fight—he doesn't want me going into that tavern with only Rhat to protect me.

"We'll keep the fight as far from the door as possible." Royce continues as though he plans imaginary fights every day.

"Any number of things could go wrong," Aris says. He looks at me as he says it.

"What happened to wanting this trip to be like when we were kids?" Royce cuts in. "Don't you remember the time we started that brawl in the square so our fathers wouldn't find out it was us who let all the chickens out of their crates before they could be judged as part of the festival?"

"We were eight," Aris says. "That was entirely different."

"We needed a distraction, and it worked."

"You didn't even want Kora on the island, and now you want to take her into the Cat's Cradle while we initiate a fight?" Aris says.

"You know pirate rules," Royce replies. "You don't have any crew members in there who will back you. Neither do I. So no one else will step in. We throw a few punches, knock over some tables, toss a few drinks at each other to keep their attention. We only have to worry about being thrown out before Kora and Rhat can find the coin."

"And you think this will work?" Aris asks.

"Do you have a better plan?" When Aris doesn't answer, Royce continues. "You go ahead. Find a spot away from the door. I'll follow in a few minutes."

Aris opens his mouth to object, then closes it. He turns to me instead, pulling me a few steps from Royce and Rhat.

"If they try to take you away, scream." The weight of his words rests around me. "Be careful."

"You too," I say, careful not to let my gaze shift to Royce. "I don't think he means to fight fair."

"I know," he whispers. "But if I can fight off four men with nothing but a conch shell, I can take him." That bright smile of his finally returns.

He leans forward and kisses me, the kind of kiss that makes me wish he didn't have to go anywhere. He presses his hand against my back, pulling me closer, and I let myself lean into him.

When he finally pulls away, I can barely breathe. A blush rises in my cheeks when I realize I can still feel where his lips met mine.

"I'll see you soon," he says. I catch the warning in the words. Then he strides into the tavern with his shoulders thrown back.

And I'm left alone with Royce and Rhat.

CHAPTER 15

As soon as Aris disappears into The Cat's Cradle, I turn back to the others. I'm half expecting them to whisk me away and leave Aris to fend for himself in that den of debauchery. But Royce must want that coin first.

He waits a minute after Aris has entered before he turns to Rhat. "At the first sound of a scuffle, get in and then get out." With that, he's gone, disappearing into the building.

I shake my head.

Rhat looks like he wants to say something, but he stays silent, instead turning his attention to the tavern.

After a few moments, shouts erupt inside.

"I guess that's our cue," Rhat says.

He tucks me under his arm and steers me toward the pub.

We barely make it inside before we're hit with shards of a broken chair being smashed over a nearby man's head. Rhat tries to shield me, and we fall back against the now-closed door.

A bar runs along the left side of the room, while tables and chairs—which are currently being used as both weapons and shields—are situated in the rest of the room. The tavern smells of cheap ale, and the air feels sticky. Everyone has some sort of weapon in their hand and is in the middle of attacking someone else.

The din in the room is unimaginable. Glass bottles break into shards, which are then crunched under stomping feet. Men cry out as they fall to the floor and become covered in the broken glass.

A man with two side-by-side scars in the shape of Xs on his forehead spins Rhat around, but his eyes shift to me.

I realize too late that I shouldn't have looked up at him. His bulging eyes open and close several times to process what he's seeing beneath my hood. Before he can react further, Rhat punches him, sending the man reeling back into the fray.

"Where's the—" Rhat starts to say before another set of hands grab him from behind, sending me off balance as well.

I fall backward, landing on an overturned table. I roll to the side to avoid being crushed by a set of tall black boots, then scramble away, taking shelter under one of the last standing tables. Pain radiates through my palms. A quick look confirms the worst.

Broken glass has torn my gloves to shreds, and small lines of crimson blood stain the fabric. I pick several bits of glass out of my skin, wincing with each one.

I peek out from under the table looking for anyone familiar. At this point, I'd almost even be happy to see Royce.

It's like staring into a sea of chaos. Heads duck and reemerge several paces over. Teeth get knocked out and fly through the air. Grunts and groans turn into a form of communication after listening to them long enough. One man stumbles forward, blood trickling out of his mouth and staining his beard. He smiles at me, displaying a gap where his front teeth should be. Then he collapses.

I look up to avoid looking at him.

Along the rafters, several cats perch, their tails hanging down like chandeliers.

I don't have time to watch them long. When I dare glance down, a break in the chaos reveals a door opposite the one I'd come in. Something tugs inside me. I know that's where the gold is.

I look at my gloves. Only the fingers are intact. I'll have to be very, very careful not to touch the gold with my bare skin. But this might be my only chance to get the gold without Royce or Rhat there to take it away from me.

I scan once more for Aris. When I don't see him—or anyone I recognize—I make a decision I hope I don't regret and charge toward the door.

I rush through the crowd without incident and shove the door shut behind me. The silence is deafening compared to the room outside.

This part of the building looks to be both the storeroom of the tavern and the owner's living quarters judging from the pallet laid on the ground with blankets thrown over it. Tall barrels and several crates are stacked under the two small windows at the back of the room. A candle sits on each windowsill, casting flickering light. The bare gray walls close the room in like a miniature fortress.

My eyes adjust to the light while I search for the aura of the missing coin. I spot it coming from some additional blankets strewn about the floor.

I reach for the blankets, but stop. There's an orange cat curled up in them. The aura is coming from beneath the cat, shining through the floorboards.

The cat whisks its tail back and forth, watching me more intently than Royce does.

I go to reach for it. The cat gets to its feet and hisses before striking a paw in my direction.

I stumble a few feet back.

"Come on, kitty," I say, holding my hand out to it.

It hisses again.

I hiss back in frustration. I've never had much luck with animals back in the palace either, as if even they can sense the curse inside me. My father's old hunting dogs would howl uncontrollably whenever I got too close. The cats in the stables would hiss and arch their backs at me. Even the horses would thrash if I tried to rub their noses. One poor pageboy was thrown from his mount just because I'd ventured too close one day.

The cat before me continues to whisk its tail back and forth, seemingly counting off the seconds until someone bursts into the room and corners me. Outside the door, men shout, and there's a loud crashing noise.

I reach for the blanket the cat's standing on.

The cat's eyes glint. It leans forward, ready to spring. Its claws dig into the blanket, and I don't want them digging into me.

I untie my cloak and whip it around in front of me. The cat leaps. I manage to catch it in my cloak, bundling the thick fabric around the animal. It squirms and scratches, trying to break free from the wool, but eventually quiets. In fact, after a few seconds, the cat curls up inside the cloak, and I swear I can hear the cursed thing purring. I place the bundle in the corner, praying the cat doesn't leap out before I can find the coin.

Rushing back, I kick the blankets out of the way. I try lifting several floorboards until I find one that gives way, and in the darkened hole is a metal box. I pull it up and set it on the floor. The gleam from the coin inside seeps out.

I take a deep breath and flip open the lid. Coins from every nation sit atop several frayed papers. In the middle of the pile is the stolen coin.

It gleams brighter than any currency in the box, inviting me to touch it, to pick it up, but the memory of turning the guard to gold rushes to the forefront of my mind. Hands on either side of the box, I shut my eyes and steady myself.

Standing near the golden table in the tower was one thing. This is entirely another. I'm about to pick up a piece of gold wearing thin gloves. Torn gloves. I haven't touched gold since that fateful day in the tower, and now that the moment is here, I can't help but be terrified.

Your father needs you, I remind myself. *You can do this.*

I reach for the coin before I lose what's left of my courage. But before I grab it, the door behind me bursts open.

A small man, no taller than me, rushes in. His spectacles rest uneasily on his pointed nose, and an orange glow reflects off the top of his balding head

For a moment, I think the glow is a reflection of either my skin or the coin, but neither could cast light that far.

That's when I see the source. Behind the man, flames spread across the building and up the rafters long since deserted by the cats. Spilled drinks have caught the tendrils of fire and turned the floor into a maze of flames. I see the brawlers hurrying outside through the smoke that casts the entire room in a dark haze. The cat I threw into the corner makes its own mad dash out the door between the man's feet.

"He said you might come for the coin," the man says. He steps in my direction.

I don't need to bother asking who the man is referring to.

"I was hoping he was right," he adds. "I've heard your veins run gold."

He produces a small knife, and I take a few steps back. I shut the lid of the box and hold it up defensively.

Another man appears, towering over the little man and blocking the entire doorway with his body.

I clutch the box to my chest. My heart pounds louder the closer the coin gets to it. "The coin belongs to me," I say. I try to keep my breathing even. From the glimpse I'd gotten of the other room, everyone else has fled. I'm on my own.

"That coin was given to me for services rendered," the little man replies. He eases further into the room. The bigger man follows.

"Don't come any closer." I hold the box like I'm ready to swing it.

"Get me that box back," the shorter man says to the larger, "and then subdue her."

The larger man takes a few tentative steps forward.

I'm out of options; the box is the only weapon I have. Without looking, I fling open the lid, reach down, and wrap my fingers around the gold coin.

CHAPTER 16

The cold of the metal seeps through my gloves and chills me to the bone. But I haven't absorbed it. Not yet. It's curled up in my fingers, away from the slits in my glove.

The large man spreads his arms wide and lunges for me. I fling the metal box at him. It hits him square in the chest and bounces to the ground, breaking open and scattering its contents across the floor with a clang. The spilled coins reflect the light from the fire in the next room as more smoke pours in.

I'll never get out that way.

Something in the front of the building explodes, sending shards of wood and glass through the air. My attackers instinctively duck, and I use the distraction to dash backward toward the windows. I toss the candle on the sill over my shoulder before shoving the window open. Cool air rushes across my skin, reviving me.

I launch through the window, barely registering any pain as I roll to the ground. Then I'm on my feet, running. I hold the coin far out in front of me, afraid to let it too close.

There's a heavy thump behind me, which is followed by even heavier footfalls.

I find myself in some sort of alleyway behind the tavern. Dirt tracks run along the backs of the buildings and are hedged in by a brick wall on the other side.

Coughing, I stumble down the alleyway looking for a way out. But the buildings are connected to one another; no gaps lead back to the main road. And with my skin glowing ever so slightly in the darkness, there's no place I can hide.

Rapid breathing echoes down the alley behind me. His steps fall more quickly than mine.

Up ahead, a small light streaks between two buildings. I beg my legs to carry me toward it and find it's another alley. I turn down the path and see the main road ahead. As I whip around the corner, I can tell my pursuer is only a few steps behind. His arms dart out toward me.

I push harder until I burst into the street. People are everywhere, and I crash into a man before I can stop myself. I barely register his eyebrows shooting up when he sees me before I'm pushing myself off him, weaving farther into the crowd.

People with buckets are running around, shouting to others to join the fight against the fire. When I risk a look back, the large man from the tavern is still there. Still chasing me.

I use my lesser height to my advantage. I duck under arms, trying to stay out of view as I navigate in what I hope is the right direction.

I finally break through most of the crowd and realize I'm not far from the dock. I charge forward, and the crates and barrels stacked on the pier rise before me. The area is deserted. I run along it looking for the dock we'd tied our boat to, but it's so dark I can't make out much of anything.

"Thipps," I whisper. Wasn't he supposed to be guarding the boat? I know I shouldn't be going back toward Royce's men, but it's the only place I can think of to look for Aris.

Footsteps sound on the other side of the crates. Through the slats, the large man appears. And if I can see him, then he can see me. I duck behind a wall of barrels as the man moves onto the dock. The boards creak as he paces slowly along the stacks. Through the small gaps between barrels, I watch as he scans the crates, each step bringing him closer to my hiding place.

I realize I'm clutching the coin over my heart just as a shadow passes over me.

I hold my breath.

The board right in front of my barrels squeaks. My heart stops.

Before I can rethink my plan, I surge forward, sending the empty barrels flying into my pursuer. He stumbles off the dock and into the water.

I don't wait to see if he surfaces. I take off down the closest dock, hoping I'll find our boat at the end. But I only make it a few steps before a set of cold hands grabs me. The coin slips toward the slits in my gloves as I try in vain to wrench free.

"Captain knew you'd come for the gold."

I turn to find the man with the two Xs carved on his fore-head, the one I'd run into at the beginning of the fight. Judging by the look of him, he didn't fare too well. Dried blood crusts beneath his split lip, and his nose points farther to the left than it did earlier.

"He'll reward me nicely for bringing him your skull." He tightens his grip. "He's eager to know if it's as gold as the rest of you." His teeth glint yellow when he grins.

In the darkness, I think I can make out our tiny boat tied on the next dock over. I try to pull free again, to make it back over there, but the man's expecting my attempt. He pulls me closer and produces a knife. The blade is short and rusted, and several kinks in the metal indicate how well used it is. He holds it close to my face.

"It won't hurt much." His foul breath washes over me. "Captain's trained us to cut heads off just how he likes them." He totters slightly backward.

He's drunk, and I see a chance.

I fake pulling backward, and then when he's not anticipating it, I crash back into him. He tumbles to the side and careens over, dragging me along with him. He lets go of me midair in an attempt to break his own fall.

Instinctively, I put my hands down. I crash into the ground next to him with a cry. Pain shoots across my knuckles. The coin clatters across the dock until it skids to a stop on the edge.

I crawl toward it, but the man grabs my leg and pulls me back. I try to kick him away. He only pulls harder until I'm flat on my stomach.

"Let her go," a voice calls.

Thipps rushes forward from where he must've been guarding the boat. He's got one of the oars. He swings it, connecting with the man's middle.

The man collapses with a grunt.

I grab the coin as Thipps drops the oar and scrambles toward me.

He helps me to my feet, not even hesitating to reach out to me despite my skin. "Are you all right?" His face shows genuine concern.

I open my mouth to thank him.

But surprise flashes across Thipps's face, and a small gasp escapes his lips. He collapses forward, knocking into me. I barely catch him as we fall into a heap.

Behind him, the man with the two Xs looms, his knife now dripping blood.

"No." I focus on Thipps. I cling to him, forcing him to look at me. "No, Thipps."

He clutches my shoulder. "Tell Phipps . . ." He coughs up blood. "Tell him . . ." His eyes lose focus on my face, and his hand slips from my shoulder. He goes still. Blood pools on the dock around his back. It drips through the boards and into the ocean.

"No," I say again.

I search his face, watch his chest for any sign of movement, for any sign he's still alive. A weight settles heavily in my stomach.

"No." I clutch at his shirt.

"Thipps," I plead.

But his eyes stare blankly ahead.

I shake my head as uneven breaths rip from my chest.

This can't be happening.

Another man has died because of me. For me.

My eyes fall on the pirate standing before me. He points his knife at me. "The Captain'll be even happier when I bring back two skulls."

The man kicks Thipps's body to the side. It rolls toward the edge of the dock, opening the pathway between us. Then, he lunges toward me.

I duck out of the way of the knife speeding toward me. He swings again. I clench the coin tighter in my palm to keep it safe.

That's when I feel it.

The whole world goes cold. The smoky air in my lungs is replaced by metallic breath. A wave of gold sweeps through me. My vision fades and then snaps back.

Breathe, I command myself. If I breathe I know I haven't turned into a golden statue. My heart speeds up, which means it's still beating. When the gold hits my heart, I inhale sharply, praying my pulse doesn't stop entirely. But when the gold slides through the chambers, there's something different about the sensation. There's no feeling of worms wriggling beneath my skin. My skin doesn't even itch.

I feel powerful.

Everything around me has slowed down. The knife crashes toward me, but the gold shooting through my body is faster. I catch the pirate's wrists, and as soon as my skin touches his through the cuts in my gloves, gold rushes over his entire body, hardening him in place.

The man's face is frozen in a sneer. His covered eyes reflect the moonlight, taking on a milky appearance. I could almost imagine I'm looking into his soul if I were sure he still had one.

I hug my arms to my chest to try and replace some of the warmth the gold seems to have stolen from me. But it isn't helping. I feel colder than ever before, like I'll never be warm again.

I can't even wrap my mind around what I've done. Did I have another choice? Does it matter if I did? I can't change what I did now. But that doesn't stop the bile creeping up my throat.

I look away, and I spot Thipps's limp form lying motionless on the dock.

I crawl toward him and roll him onto his back. "Please," I whisper. But it's no use—he's gone. Tears prick at the corners of my eyes and slide down my cheeks.

I know I should move. I should look for Aris, but absorbing the gold has left me cold and exhausted.

I bury my head in my hands.

A voice cuts through the night.

"Did you do this?" Royce stands there staring at the statue of my attacker. Rhat gapes from behind him.

I don't answer. I clench my jaw and stare at him.

Rhat notices Thipps and rushes forward.

"Thipps." Rhat grabs Thipps's shoulders, and Thipps's head sags lifelessly backward. Rhat gently lowers the body back down, and his eyes turn to Royce, confirming the worst.

I scramble away from them until I'm on the end of the dock. Royce steps closer. "What happened?"

"He died saving me." I nearly choke on the words.

Royce pauses a few feet in front of me. He's on one side of the golden statue and Rhat is on the other, blocking my escape.

I take a step back, assessing if I can somehow make a swim for it, but I tumble on a loose board. Royce moves like he means to help, but I hold out my arm to stop him.

"Stay back," I shout. I wish Aris was here. But he's not, and I'm alone. And now Royce must have guessed what I can do, has had every horrible suspicion about me confirmed because of that gleaming statue. I know he'll lock me up now, keep me prisoner, his to turn things to gold until it kills me. That's the type of thing Uncle Pheus has worried about since I was seven.

"Are you all right?" Royce asks cautiously. "He didn't hurt you, did he?"

"Don't touch me. I'll turn you to gold if you come any closer." I shove my hand out farther in what I hope is a menacing fashion. I don't think I could actually bear absorbing gold again to fulfill that promise, but it's the only thing I have to keep him at bay.

"Kora, you're safe with me." He holds up his arms in surrender.

"Safe?" I laugh. It's a manic sound, but I can't help it. "I won't let you take me. I'll never turn anything to gold for you, and I'll never hand over my father's gold to you."

Royce sighs and runs his hand through his hair. "We can talk about that back on the ship. But we need to go before someone else finds us."

"I'd rather take my chances on this island."

His eyes don't leave mine. "I can help you, Kora." He holds his hand out to me.

I shake my head.

"I know you're scared," he says. "None of this is your fault." He motions to Thipps's body. "He died a hero, the way he would've wanted it. Don't let his sacrifice go to waste. We've got to get out of here." He stretches his hand out closer to me.

"There you are." A breathless Aris runs up, and I nearly cry with joy, even when I see he has a busted lip and his eyes are crazed. He pushes past Royce and pulls me into a hug. "Are you all right? I've been searching everywhere for you. I heard the tavern keeper shouting he'd give a chest of jewels to the man who brought him the golden girl. I thought I'd lost you."

I don't even care that Royce and Rhat now know my secret. Aris's arms around me have stopped me from going over the edge. Now that he's here, I feel like I can breathe without gold weighing down my chest.

"What happened?" Aris asks, pulling away to stare down at me. "Did you get the coin?"

"He followed me from the tavern"—I nod toward the statue—"and he was going to kill me. During the struggle, I . . . I turned him to gold." My voice is hoarse.

"It's all right," Aris soothes.

But it's not all right. I'm not all right.

"I killed him." I gag on the words. Even if I turn him back, he could kill himself just like the guard did. No, he will kill himself just like the guard did. Because I sent him to an unimaginable place.

"You're not a murderer. You're a survivor." Aris pulls back and looks at me. "You're a survivor," he repeats.

"Everything would've been fine if you hadn't ruined the plan," Royce says before I can reply.

Aris drops his arms and spins around. "I can't help that they jumped me as soon as I set foot inside. Not all of us can pass for pirates. They probably saw my clothes and knew I was a nobleman. I told you it was a bad plan."

Royce steps forward, matching Aris's posture. "Or maybe they—"

"Others are coming," Rhat interrupts. "We need to go." He moves forward and gently hoists Thipps's body over his shoulder.

But I can't go back yet. "I can't leave without the gold."

Royce shoots Aris one more warning look before turning to look at the statue. "I'm not sure all of us together could carry him, and I'm not leaving Thipps behind."

Boards creak farther down the dock as men run over the planks searching down the offshoots for where we might be hiding.

I take another breath. "I can change him back." Not that it'll do the man any good.

I don't look at them as I say the words. Instead, I approach the man slowly, holding the now copper coin between my gloved fingers.

Before one of them can stop me, I press my exposed palm against the back of the man's neck. He sputters to life, ramming his knife forward into empty air. Confusion rocks his face as his eyes dart over us.

"How'd you do that, you cursed witch?" he says, looking up. His eyes go wide when he sees us gathered around him, and his knife clatters to the dock.

Aris moves forward quickly with his sword drawn.

"Wait," Royce says. "Don't hurt him."

Aris smashes the hilt of his sword into the man's temple, sending him crashing into a heap next to his knife.

I drop the coin into my palm, and the gold passes through me back into the coin. I shiver.

"Do you want me to hold on to that?" Aris asks, nodding to the coin.

I release a sigh. It's like he knows what I need before I even do. I nod and drop the coin into his hand.

Royce shoves past us with a grunt. He kneels over the man, turning him onto his back. "Didn't you see the two Xs on his forehead?"

Aris inspects the hilt for blood before shoving it back into its sheath. "It's a common branding for double-crossers."

Royce sends him a look of disgust. "You don't recognize him?"

"I'm not in the practice of keeping company with pirates," Aris replies.

"They've got the fire out," Rhat warns. "Men are coming this way."

"He was on Captain Skulls's crew," Royce says. He has a faraway look in his eyes. "I'm sure of it."

"It's a common mark, Royce," Aris says. I can tell he doesn't want Royce to figure out that we already know Captain Skulls took the gold. "It probably just looks familiar. Let's get back to the ship."

"No," Royce says. "That's why I remember it. I couldn't imagine Skulls would sink low enough to hire mutineers on his own crew."

"If he was on Skulls's crew, that's all the more reason we should get out of here," Aris says.

Voices filter down the dock, and I can make out shapes moving our direction.

"We need to go, Royce," Aris says.

"We should have questioned him." Royce turns on Aris.

Footfalls pound toward us.

"He would've attacked Kora if I hadn't knocked him out," Aris says. "Her safety is more important."

"There's the golden girl," a voice calls out.

The words snap Royce out of whatever reverie he's stuck in. He pounds his fists on the dock before leaping to his feet.

"Run," Royce shouts. "Make for the longboat."

It's clear I picked the wrong dock. Royce crashes into Aris as we're forced to backtrack and make our way to the next one over. I fight to keep my balance on the uneven boards as we skim over them, nearly stumbling over a barnacle-crusted anchor resting on the dock. My running has become as jagged as my breathing. I push my thoughts away and focus on moving forward.

We make it to the beginning of the wrong dock I'd run down and rush past more lines of crates and piles of rope and ripped sails. The spot where our boat is tied comes into view.

Before we reach it, three men with swords step in front of us from behind the crates. We skid to a stop. I chance a glimpse behind us, but the men chasing us have caught up. The four of them slow their approach. The line of crates traps us on one side and the sea on the other.

We have nowhere left to run.

CHAPTER 17

ᚹᚹᚹᚹᚹᚹᚹᚹᚹ◉ᚹᚹᚹᚹᚹᚹᚹᚹᚹ

 ive us the girl," one man says. He stands taller than all the others and wears a bandana atop his hair. Muscles bulge beneath his shirt. His other companions inch forward.

Aris moves me beside him so that the barrels are at my back and he, Rhat, and Royce form a sort of triangle cage around me. Rhat slowly rests Thipps's body on the dock and draws his sword.

"It doesn't have to be like this," Royce says, but he too draws his sword and points it at the tall man.

"You're outnumbered," a skinny man with a long goatee says.

"For now," Royce replies.

Then, all at once, everything erupts around me. Men charge from both sides. Swords clang. The skinny man with the goatee spots me through the melee and runs toward me. I grab the sword from Thipps's belt. It's a wide blade almost as long as my arm. It's too heavy for me, and I'm not the only one who knows it.

The man smirks at me, crinkling up his goatee.

"Guess you can't turn people to gold just by looking at them, can you?" he says. He licks his lips.

I lunge for him, but he sidesteps my blade easily.

I curse my skin for scaring away the fencing teacher I should've had.

He swings his sword at me, and it passes dangerously close to my face as I dive out of the way. I drop my sword and try to roll upright, but my elbow crashes into the dock and radiates pain. I roll straight toward the line of crates and come to a stop mere inches from one of the sharp, upturned edges of a rusted anchor.

My attacker saunters over and leans down above me. He smiles, displaying a row of yellow teeth. But before he can speak, something smashes into his head, knocking him aside. Behind him, the small man from the pub drops the wooden fragment he's holding. "This one's mine," he says, stepping forward.

He pulls out a knife and motions for me to stand. The blade is thin, barely visible in the moonlight.

I swallow.

"Move," he says, indicating the direction we'd come from.

I slowly rise to my feet. As I do, I take measured breaths and scan the dock looking for help. But Aris and the others are still fighting other opponents. My sword is too far away for me to reach, and the anchor at my feet is way too heavy for me to lift.

The man is barely an arm's length away. How quickly would he react if I took off? Because the last thing I want to do is go anywhere with him.

"Now," he says. He jabs the knife closer to my stomach.

I'm still trying to think of a plan when Aris appears behind the man. My eyes must alert the tavern owner to his presence because he whips around, but he doesn't get a word out before Aris runs him through.

"She won't be going anywhere with you," Aris says and rips out his sword.

The man grabs his stomach. He curls in on himself and staggers a few feet away. He stumbles to his knees before collapsing into the water with a splash.

I exhale, and then Aris is there, with his arms around me. I want to crumple against him, but we're not safe here. So I don't fight it when he pulls away.

"We've got the coin," he says. "Let's get out of here." He tugs me toward the edge of the fight.

I pull back. "What about Hettie?"

"There's no time. Keeping the gold safe is more important." He yanks me forward once more.

I dig in my feet. How am I supposed to choose between abandoning my father and abandoning Hettie? Before I can explain this, the man with the goatee rises and lunges for Aris from behind. Aris staggers as the pirate crashes into him, releasing my hand and dropping his sword as he knocks into the crates, which rattle but don't fall. Aris turns quickly and charges the man. He drives him backward toward the water. Toward where jagged poles from a collapsed boat slip jut upward like talons waiting to shut around their prey.

Before I can cry out, Aris and the man splash into the water.

My heart stops. I rush to the edge of the dock.

The body of the man with the goatee lies impaled on the nearest board.

I stumble back and cover my mouth.

Rhat appears at my side. "Where's Aris?"

I shake my head and stare into the dark water. The ripples have stopped their uneven dance, and still, he hasn't surfaced.

I hear more footsteps pounding toward us, but I'm frozen. My future is tied to Aris. The world won't start again unless he's in it. I don't feel the breeze. I don't smell the smoke from the fire. I only feel coldness seeping through my skin and heading straight for my bones, for my heart, as I watch the water.

Every glint of moonlight feels like a betrayal, sending jolts of hope through me that Aris might be surfacing. But that's all they ever are, bits of light that can't even penetrate the darkness of the sea, that can't bring Aris's light back into my life.

"We need to go," Royce says, coming up on my other side with blood dripping from the tip of his sword.

"We have to go in after Aris," I say, my voice rising with panic. I kneel on the dock and hunt for any signs of life.

"If he hasn't resurfaced by now," Royce says, "he's not going to." His voice is so cold, unfeeling. "You won't find anything in that dark water anyway."

I stare into the inky depths. Royce has to be wrong. There must be some way to find him.

A jolt of hope shoots through me. "The coin. Aris has the coin." I shut my eyes, and instantly, the tainted gold tugs at me, begs me to come closer.

There.

I swing my arm around, pointing to where the light of the coin burns the brightest.

I open my eyes, and I'm pointing directly at Royce.

My heart stops.

He stares down at me, unblinking.

"You . . . you have the coin." It comes out as a statement, though I can't figure out how.

Royce slowly removes it from his pocket. It glints invitingly in the moonlight. "I thought it was safer that I keep it, so I took it from Aris when we collided on the last dock."

I shakily rise to my feet; there's nowhere to go. I stare down at the water as much to look for Aris as to see if it offers any escape, but I'm likely to end up like the man with the goatee.

Voices call down the dock, and I'm vaguely aware that they're shouting at me. About me. About the reward the tavern owner offered for my capture.

"We have to get back to the ship," Royce says, tucking the coin back into his coat pocket.

The dock shudders under the weight of additional bodies as more men race toward us.

I can't breathe. I can't move. My mind is churning faster than the tide. So is my stomach.

Rhat once again heaves Thipps over his shoulder.

"We have to go," Royce urges.

"No." I attempt a steadying breath. "We can't leave Aris. They'll tear him apart when they find him." And they will find him. I won't let myself think about the alternative. "We can't leave him here."

"That's what he gets for becoming involved with pirates." He reaches for my arm.

"Don't you have a heart?" I yank away. "He used to be your friend. Doesn't that mean anything to you?"

"I wouldn't have wasted time standing here if it didn't," he shoots back. "But it's too late for him. We can still make it to the boat, but we've got to go. Now."

"I'm not leaving without him." I glance to where the men are searching the dock we'd just left.

"Captain . . ." Rhat says in warning.

The boards under my feet rattle as the mob gets closer. The light from their lanterns is starting to reach us.

"We're out of time." Royce grabs my arm and pulls me down the dock. We rush past the fallen bodies of the men who'd attacked us. Some are groaning in pain. Others are still.

"Please," I beg Royce, "I'll turn anything you want to gold. Please go back for him." Tears stream down my face. "Please—he could still be alive." Even as I say the words, I stop struggling and let Royce lead me away. If I go back, I'll be taken prisoner. I'll be abandoning Hettie and my father. And Aris would want me to get away, even if it's with Royce. At least Royce wants me alive.

I can only imagine what the men will do to Aris if they find him. They'll torture him. They'll probably even kill him. All because he knows me.

My body goes numb at the thought.

We stumble into the longboat as Phipps and the others frantically toss supplies in.

I don't feel the edge of the boat dig into my side. I doubt I'd even feel it if I absorbed gold.

Royce shoves off just as the men catch up with us and leaves them standing on the dock. I block out their shouts. I stare at the water instead, looking for any sign Aris is still alive.

CHAPTER 18

꘍꘍꘍꘍꘍꘍꘍꘍꘍◉꘍꘍꘍꘍꘍꘍꘍꘍꘍

Royce takes his seat in the boat opposite me.

"Did you get everything we needed?" he asks Phipps as though he hasn't just left a man behind to die.

"Aye, Captain," Phipps says. He pats the massive amount of sail filling up the majority of the longboat. If he finds it odd Aris isn't with us, he doesn't mention it.

None of them do.

"Where's Thipps?" Phipps asks.

There's frantic movement in the boat followed by a gasp when his eyes land on his brother's body, laid out on another new sail folded in the front of the boat. I look away.

"He saved the princess," Royce says quietly.

"No," Phipps whispers. He falls to his knees next to his brother's form. "Thipps. Come on, Thipps." He pulls on the collar of his shirt, yanking him up. Thipps's head rolls backward.

"He's gone," Royce says in a gentle tone I've never heard from him before.

"No. No." Phipps scans the crew like this is some joke. His breathing grows more haggard with each face he seeks out. He shakes his brother. "Wake up."

"I'm sorry, Phipps," Royce says.

Phipps smooths back his brother's hair. "He can't be gone.

I never got to tell him he really was better at playing the accordion." His voice grows sharper, louder, with each declaration. "He doesn't know that I cheated whenever we arm wrestled. He didn't . . ." He breaks down into sobs, clinging to his brother's shirt. "I never told him he was my better half."

"He knew," Royce says. "He knew you loved him."

Phipps's knuckles have gone white where he grasps his brother's shirt. "No." His sobs cover the boat and leak out over the water. They rip through my ears and threaten to tear the rest of me apart, to break loose all the cries I'm holding in for Aris and for Thipps.

I clamp my hands over my ears, but that does little to dampen the sound. Each pain-filled cry lodges in my soul all the way back to the ship.

The island has become nothing more than a spot of light in the distance by the time a ladder clatters down the side of the ship. Men begin climbing and hoisting up the new supplies. Phipps wails and snaps at the sailors who try to take Thipps's body from him. He yells until they allow him to carry it himself. He struggles under the weight but slowly makes it up the ladder. Eventually, only Rhat, Royce, and I are left. I sit there with my arms crossed.

Rhat climbs up, and Royce rises to hold the ladder steady for him. Once Rhat reaches the top, Royce gestures for me.

I'm half tempted to knock him overboard and row the boat back myself to look for Aris. But who knows what I'd find at this point. And I'd still be leaving Hettie behind.

I stand and move toward the ladder. I pause at its base. "People have always called me a monster because of my skin," I say, "but you've proved you're a real monster." I jab a finger at him to illustrate my point. "I'm going to spend every moment of the rest of my life making your life as cursed as mine." I can practically see the coin glowing through his jacket pocket. Could I get to it before he is able to stop me? If I succeeded, I'd turn him to gold right here.

"It had to be done," Royce says.

I sneer. "You were only waiting for the right opportunity. I heard you and Rhat talking after we left Lagonia. You wanted a perfect way to be rid of Aris, and what better way than to leave him behind?"

He rubs his forehead, refusing to even look at me. "You don't know what you're talking about."

"I know you wanted to wait and see what I could do, what I was worth alive, but I'll never turn anything to gold for you."

"Is that what Aris wanted?" The small boat rocks back and forth as he leans forward. "I'm not him. I know gold won't make me happy. It might buy me a new ship, but no amount can buy me a loyal crew or bring back the men I lost to Captain Skulls. So you can keep your cursed gold. I never wanted it." He sits down hard, sending the boat reeling.

I plunk down to keep from falling overboard. "What do you mean you don't want the gold?"

"I only accepted your proposal because it meant I could shadow Aris. I thought if he had you, he'd lead me straight to Captain Skulls. I could finally get my revenge and my place in the armada back. I could finally prove Aris was the one who sunk my ship under Skulls's orders, that he was the one who lost the treaty."

He stares up at the stars. "I almost had it tonight too. That man with the two Xs on his head—I know he was part of Skulls's crew. He could've vouched that Skulls and Aris met up several weeks before we were set to carry the treaty." He shakes his head and stares at his lap.

I feel like I must still have gold in my ears. "Aris didn't sink your ship."

"Is that what he told you?" He finally musters the energy to meet my gaze.

I don't believe him. Yet there is so much pain behind his words, so much anger.

"How do you think he knew about this island?" Royce throws his arm back toward the fading lights twinkling over the water. "I hadn't even heard of it until a few weeks ago, when he claimed he had traced the woman who blew up my ship to here, knowing I'd bring him if there was any chance that woman was still around. Now, since I never found the woman on the island, I fear he met with Captain Skulls, probably to finalize his plans for robbing you before we sailed to your kingdom.

"So your cursing me won't do any good," he continues. "It seems I'm already as cursed as my father was. Looks like we have that in common." He leans against the edge of the boat as it jostles a few feet away from the ship.

"You're lying," I say. Royce has given me no reason to trust him in the past week, whereas Aris has always been kind, attentive, and honest. I can't doubt him. Not now. "And you certainly don't know anything about being cursed."

Royce laughs, but there's no humor in it. "Not all remnants are physical, Kora. I'd gladly show you my journal full of every detail, every pain, every nightmare caused by watching my own father be buried alive under a never-ending pile of gold." His features have taken on a pained sharpness. "But I'm pretty sure Aris burned it or threw it overboard just to spite me."

"That happened to Aris's father." I cross my arms over my chest. "You think he was too ashamed to tell me about it? He wasn't. And I hope Triton or Poseidon or whoever rules the seas sinks your ship a thousand times over for ever claiming it was you."

At this, Royce looks surprised. "That man has no shame." He shakes his head. "What else did he tell you? Did he tell you why he spends so much time at sea? Was it because his mother can't bear to look her own son in the eyes because every time she does, she only sees her husband?" His voice rises. "Did he tell you about the time he found his mother throwing everything of value from the house in the middle of the night because she thought it would bring him back?" He's practically shouting, and there's a wild look in his eyes. "Did he describe what it was like having to explain to her every morning that her husband was dead because she refused to believe it?"

My eyes go wide, and my mouth hangs open. But I don't know what to say.

"If he wanted my past so badly," Royce rages, "he should've been the one to explain to my mother that all the servants left because they wouldn't be paid in cursed gold. He should've been the one who had to drag his father's coffin by himself because no one else would touch it for fear of catching the curse." He raids his pockets, coming up with the coin he's always rubbing. "He should be the one carrying around a coin from a cursed treasure to remind himself that every decision he makes carries great weight. So he can know how one moment of weakness can ruin so many lives." He pitches the coin into the bottom of the boat. It clinks away under the benches.

Royce's lips form a tight line. "I'd gladly have given Aris those memories if he'd take the pain with them."

I'm speechless. I think about the journal tucked under my pillow. Whose words have I been reading? Those of the ever affectionate and vibrant Aris or those of the broken man in front of me?

"I wanted to warn you about him, but I didn't think you'd believe me," Royce says softly.

"You're the one who was talking about killing me and seeing what my powers are," I retort, though my heart isn't in it. In fact, my heart may be breaking.

The anger is gone from his voice, replaced by exhaustion. "What you overheard was Rhat and me trying to reason out what Aris wanted with you. If he was only after the gold, we thought he would've killed you already, so we figured he was after whatever powers you have. That's why I asked you on deck that one day what your curse entailed, but I can see why you didn't share that information with me now—I was trying to puzzle out what he wanted you for. And we knew then we needed to get him off the ship, but we couldn't figure out if you were working with him. But when you volunteered to go to the Island of Lost Souls, I figured you really did want to save your father, especially since Aris was so against going—probably because he knew he'd be recognized this time."

"But you were talking about ransoming me."

"Not you." Royce shakes his head. "Aris. That suggestion was Rhat's attempt at humor—he knew I didn't want Aris to die, yet at the same time we couldn't exactly let him go until we had proof."

"But you said he was broke . . ." I let the words whither before I can imply the same applies to the monarchy.

"His family's been broke for years. Why else do you think he took up with Skulls in the first place? He's a Wystlinos." He puffs out his chest in a mock imitation of Aris. "He's always thought he was too good for physical labor. He's always taken the easiest route. That's included a lot of drinking and gambling instead of working, which is probably why he was jumped before I got inside The Cat's Cradle. He likely owed them all money.

"And it's no wonder he fell in with Skulls's crew given all the time he spent at the taverns. I'm sure he was promised a substantial cut of everything Skulls plundered while the armada was away defending the country during the Orfland Wars. That's why he sold out his country and his friends to keep the war going by arranging for Skulls to steal the treaty, to keep the armada from returning to protect the coastal cities. If I'm right and Captain Skulls is still alive, then Aris doubtless owes him for botching up the treaty job by letting a second copy get through. I just need the proof, proof I might've had if Aris hadn't knocked out the man who attacked you."

I go over his words, looking for the flaws in his explanation. "Aris's family isn't broke. His family throws more lavish parties than the palace does."

"Did you attend any of them?" he asks. When I don't reply, he continues. "Once the money ran out, Aris simply told lavish, made-up tales about what happened at his supposed parties and told everyone the guest list was very exclusive—so exclusive, in fact, that no one was actually invited but you. Sure, once or twice when he won money playing Seascapes or through some other means, he'd actually throw one to keep up the pretense. But you got invites to parties that never existed to make it look like he still had money. He knew you were never going to come. It was all a sham. Everything about him was a sham."

"No," I breathe. I'm not sure what I'm denying anymore. "You're the one who wants my father's gold. You promised it to your men."

He shakes his head, sending his hair cascading forward. "I only did that to save you. If I hadn't promised them payment, they would've mutinied. Most of the sailors don't even know about my father's curse—they're men Aris hired when Captain Skulls destroyed my last ship. I've been trying to save up to hire a new crew, but with repairs and other setbacks, I haven't amassed much. I never actually would've given them the gold." When he looks at me, his eyes are pleading. Honest. My stomach flips over with every jolt of the boat.

Could Royce be telling the truth?

My mind flashes to every moment I've spent with Aris, from when he wasn't scared to offer me his arm to when he kissed me a few hours ago before going into The Cat's Cradle.

But there are other moments. Ones I pushed aside. Like when he'd snapped at me to stay out of his argument with Royce. Or when he'd said we were as cursed as my father. If his own father had been cursed, would he really say that about mine? And on the island, he'd suggested making our escape without Hettie. He said the gold was more important. He'd even lied to Royce from the beginning about why we needed his ship. Were those moments of weakness—of trying to protect me—or were they slips of his true character?

Could he really be that conniving? As conniving and strategic as he was during Seascapes, a game he could play without giving away any hint of his true strategies?

I don't want to believe I was so easily duped. He cared. Didn't he? He told me stories about Jipper. He danced with me. He was going to show me the world.

Or expose me to it.

The thought hits me, sucking the air from my lungs.

But he's the one who held me when I had my first vision of Captain Skulls.

And the one who told me not to tell Royce.

I bite the inside of my lip.

Aris is the one who wanted to go back to Lagonia at every setback—after discovering Hettie aboard and after the storm. Was he trying to protect me or slow me down?

Did he cut the sails loose and slash holes in them?

If he really is the one working with Captain Skulls, what Royce said holds true: Aris hadn't wanted to go to the Island of Lost Souls because he knew he'd be recognized.

When Royce insisted, he'd then told me we'd find help on that island. Yet, he'd been there before—hadn't he admitted it himself when he told me Royce was the one working with Skulls? Aris would've known there was nothing but pirates and thieves there.

My insides freeze at the thought.

He'd tricked me into telling him the secret of my power under the guise of protecting me from his uncle, the one looking for money to raise an army against my father. The same one he easily could be working with.

And after listening to Royce's account, it's also not that far-fetched to believe that the supposed disdain between Aris and his uncle was part of one more performance, one more lie Aris fed me.

My head shouts the answer, but my heart doesn't want to hear it. There has to be something I'm missing. Some flaw in Royce's explanation.

I can't find it.

The boat taps against the ship, startling me.

Royce scours the bottom of the boat for his coin, tucking it away in his pocket. He turns to look down at me.

"I'm not sure if you believe me or not," Royce says, interrupting my thoughts. "Aris has had years of practice lying to people. It's taken me years to sort out the lies he's fed me. So you can either believe me, and I'll continue helping you get your father's gold back as I promised I would, or I'll let you have this longboat. I won't keep you against your will. You can row back to the island to be with Aris if he's still alive. But you won't find anyone else to help you there."

Water gently laps against the boat while he waits for my decision. I stare up the ladder. Hettie is up there waiting and probably wondering why I haven't climbed up yet.

"Hettie is free to go too," he adds as if he's reading my thoughts, "if that's what's stalling your decision. I'll send her down if you want, but you need to decide now. The men on the dock will have undoubtedly sent a few boats after us."

I swing around to stare into the darkness leading back toward the island as though I'll be able to see other boats slicing through the water. But everything has gone calm.

I don't even know if Aris is still alive. I'm not sure I want him to be. Because the more I think about it, there's no way the words I read could belong to him. There's no way he could hide so much pain behind such a jovial smile. I wanted to believe it was possible because he gave me hope. But pain like that weighs down a soul. If it doesn't poison you, it makes you stoic and hard.

Like Royce.

I look away from the island. Away from Aris.

I stare at my tattered gloves. I feel just as ripped to pieces as they are. How had I been so easily fooled, so easily torn apart?

I stare out over the black waves and blink back tears.

I force myself to stand because, if I don't keep moving somehow, I'll cry enough tears to drown that whole cursed island and everyone on it. But even then, it wouldn't be enough to wash away what Aris did to me.

The boat rocks under the sudden movement.

Royce doesn't hesitate to reach out a hand to steady me. Even after he knows I can turn men to gold.

"I believe you," I say to Royce when our eyes meet. The words sound feeble in my mouth, but they're the best I can muster under the circumstances.

He doesn't take his hand away until I'm safely in front of the ladder. "Trust me, I know what you're feeling. Eventually, the hatred does go away." He looks back toward the docks we left. "Sometimes you almost pity him."

I try to absorb his words as I slowly climb up the ladder, but I can't. My hands shake on the rungs. I just want to collapse into bed and sleep for days. I don't want to think ever again. I don't want to feel anything for the rest of my life. Because as it turns out, the rumors are wrong— my heart isn't made of gold. It's very soft and very alive. And now it's shattered.

Hettie grabs me almost the instant I'm up the ladder. I let her drag me into a long hug. "They told me you were back, and then I saw them bring up that body, and I thought they lied to get me out of that horrible little cell . . ." She glances around us. "Where's Duke Wystlinos?"

"He's not coming," I mumble as sailors raise the anchor and secure the longboat.

I pull away from her and head for the stairs to our room. Men move all around me getting the ship ready to sail. I feel like I'm moving at a crawl compared to them.

I've only made it a few steps when Hettie asks again, "What do you mean he's not coming?" She looks over the side of the ship as though he would be down there even though the longboat is no longer in the water.

I hang my head, too tired to explain. The only thing that keeps me from bursting into tears all over again is the last shred of anger I have toward Aris. And that's quickly being overtaken by exhaustion.

"What happened?" Hettie prods. "I didn't spend an entire evening locked in a cell so you could leave me out of this too."

Royce saves me from having to answer by coming to my side and blocking my view of Hettie.

"I know you're tired," he says, "and I promise I'll let you sleep. But I need you to check on the gold one more time. In case anything else has been separated."

I can tell Royce is trying to be gentle, considerate. I can read it in the concerned wrinkles of his forehead that he hates asking me.

"There's something you should know," I say. "Captain Skulls took the gold."

His eyes go dark when I explain my earlier vision, but he takes it in stride. "I figured as much. He's been leaving corpses up and down the coast. But if it's too hard for you to face that again . . ."

I shake my head. My father still needs me.

I close my eyes and concentrate. I locate the coin first because of its proximity. I only intend to reach out a little, to find the aura of the others, but my sluggish mind doesn't react as quickly as it should. As soon as I sense the aura, my mind races toward it before I can push it away.

It's not just my mind. I jolt forward and open my eyes. I'm not standing on the deck with Royce in front of me.

I'm standing in the same ship cabin I'd seen in my earlier vision.

Sitting in a chair directly across from me, guarding a table piled with my father's gold, is Captain Skulls.

He leans forward and picks up his sword from its resting place across his knees. "I thought you'd come back," he says.

Then he stabs his blade into my stomach.

CHAPTER 19

〉〉〉〉〉〉〉〉◎〈〈〈〈〈〈〈〈〈

Captain Skulls plunges the sword deeper. He hovers so close I can smell alcohol on his breath. He smiles at my discomfort, revealing a mouth entirely filled with gold teeth.

I try to cry out, but no sound passes my lips.

"Nobody steals from me," he says, giving the blade a twist. His skin is stretched so thin across his face that barely any wrinkles appear when he smiles.

I stare down at the blade sticking out of my stomach. A silver skull forms the base of the hilt, the blade jutting out like a tongue. Although I can't feel the pain yet, I know in a moment I'll drop to my knees and bleed out on the dusty cabin floor. My fingers will fumble uselessly trying to close the wound. No one will even know where I've gone.

I'm not even sure where I've gone, where I'm going to die. My connection with the gold is changing too rapidly for me to understand.

Captain Skulls pulls the sword out and steps back. I look away, unable to watch my own blood drip from the tip of his blade, waiting for the moment my body gives out.

Nothing happens.

I grab my stomach. My fingers explore where a mark should've been. There's nothing. Not even a tear in my dress.

When I look up at Captain Skulls, his face burns with anger.

I'm as confused as he is, but somehow, I'm no more than an apparition here, a phantom version of myself, like the aura the cursed gold gives off. My real body must be back on the *Swanflight*, and all I want to do is get back there before I end up trapped in this nightmare.

Captain Skulls takes a swipe at my neck, one that would've knocked my head clear off if I'd been there in the flesh. The blade passes harmlessly through me.

He swings his sword once again toward me.

I can't stop myself from ducking out of the way even though I doubt his blade will have any effect this time.

"How is this possible?" he mutters. He stares at me with renewed interest.

I stumble backward. Something rattles above me on a shelf as Captain Skulls stomps closer, and my eyes dart about the room. Skulls line shelves meant for books. Some skulls have even been turned into candleholders and have hot red wax dripping out of eye sockets and down decaying teeth. There have to be dozens of them—dozens of men and women he's killed and skinned. I cover my mouth with my hand, horrified.

My reaction elicits a grin from him. "Beautiful, aren't they?"

"You're insane," I stammer.

"I'm a collector," he corrects.

"Give me my father's gold," I say. My voice is far from steady. My hands shake as I clutch at my skirt. "I'll find it no matter where you take it anyway."

"I know." His face hardens. "I was warned about that little skill of yours."

By Aris. I'm sure of it.

He leans in closer, his hot breath floating across me, and his gleaming teeth fill my vision. "But since it seems I can't kill you for trying to steal *my* gold, what I'm interested in are your other skills."

I go rigid.

"If the rumors are true," he says, "we could be allies in all things gold." His golden teeth pass so close to my skin. I have no idea what absorbing gold would do to me in this state. I don't want to test the limits of my abilities. Not here.

"Never." I duck away and stumble to the far side of the room. "I've already gotten the piece from the Island of Lost Souls, and now I'm coming for the rest of *my father's* gold."

"Did you now?" Disappointment stains his voice as he moves toward the pile of my father's treasure. He runs his fingers absently over the various pieces. "I left someone on the island to collect your skull if they couldn't take you alive." His eyes flick back to mine. "Tell me, is it made of gold?"

I straighten my shoulders as best I can. "You'll never find out."

He picks up one of the coins, weighing it in his hand. "No, I suppose I won't." His eyes meet mine. The reflection of my skin in his eyes is the only light I've ever seen them hold. "For you see, your . . . ability to locate the gold forced me to part with another piece to ensure the treasure could never be reunited to uphold my end of the bargain, which quite upsets me since I really had planned on keeping it all."

My throat goes dry as I count the golden objects piled on the table. One of the chalices is missing. "What have you done with it?"

I swallow. I can't even imagine where someone this twisted and demented could've hidden the gold. But I can imagine who he made a bargain with and who told him to hide it out of my reach: Archduke Ralton. He's the only one who would know enough and want my father to continue to fade away. Him and Aris.

"You know, that chalice cost me another skull." He drops the coin back into the pile. "My helmsman broke one of my precious prizes during that last storm and so knew he needed to volunteer to be the one to deliver the chalice. Sadly, he never made it back." His eyes flick back up to me. "But why risk going after the gold and making that your fate? Since you so kindly came to me and since you might still have some powers I can use, I'd rather not let your skull and your abilities fall into the hands of those cursed women when it's standing right in front of me."

I don't know what he's talking about, and I don't have time to figure it out because gold clinks together as he digs out the knife my father turned.

"My sword may not be able to touch you, but maybe something made of gold can pin you here until we figure out just what you can do."

I stagger away. Skulls clatter on shelves as he stumbles after me.

My father's gold winks invitingly as I scramble for a plan. There's one door, and that will only lead me farther into his ship. I don't know how I got here, so I'm not sure how I can get back.

Wait. My father's gold.

Just as Captain Skulls rears up behind me, I clamp my eyes shut. I shove away the aura of my father's gold sitting so close by as it tries to overwhelm my mind.

There.

But no, there are two blinking auras beckoning me. I don't

have time to search them out, to figure out which one's the coin. I pick the closest one and focus all my energy on it.

I leap forward. But I don't find myself safe on the *Swanflight*.

I splash into rough water. It's so dark I can't see anything except the white tips of the waves that threaten to pour over me.

I whip around in the water and kick frantically.

Then I see it. The glow I know no one else sees. The golden chalice rests about fifteen feet below the surface.

Something swims in front of the cup, sending distorting ripples forward. My heart skips a beat.

"Who dares to enter the lair of the Temptresses?" a female voice coos.

My skin grows cold.

He couldn't. He wouldn't.

Not the Temptresses of Triton.

From what I've read about them, they're considered only slightly less mythical than Jipper. They used to be human women whom Triton, son of Poseidon, fell in love with. But once his interest in them waned, he refused to return them to land, instead turning them into creatures of the sea. Part human and part aquatic. They supposedly guard a watery treasure trove, which, along with their enchanted voices, they use to lure greedy sailors to their deaths.

Something brushes past me in the water.

Somewhere, a woman laughs.

Before I can think, I cast out my mind once more and grab on to the golden aura of the coin.

I struggle to open my eyes. I'm lying on the deck, and Royce's face is pressed against mine, propelling oxygen into my lungs. He pulls away, his face a mix of torment and hope. I must've been away from my body too long. Darkness seeps in at the corners of my vision.

Breathe, I tell myself.

I cough, then gulp in air like I've never had any before.

My eyes slide over Hettie and Rhat. They land on Royce. He fades in and out of focus.

"Kora." He shouts my name, searching my face for some sort of recognition.

I try to hold on, but the fog is setting back in. "Temptresses, Triton, gold," I whisper before my eyelids droop closed.

CHAPTER 20

))))))))))◉((((((((((

I wake to find only a small candle lighting the room around me as I lie in bed, a bed I have to myself. Hettie is nowhere to be seen, and I wonder what time of day it is.

My head aches along with most of my body. I reach to massage my back but my hand brushes against Royce's journal. I slide it out and run my hands over the cracked leather and down the spine. I focus on the sections that have been ripped out. Whereas before, I guessed that signaled something Aris wanted to keep private, I can now only assume those pages included material that would have given away the journal's true owner.

I turn to the final pages.

❀ ❀ ❀

Maybe I'll never find another person who understands what it's like to have the curse always inside you. Someone who understands why I freeze when I hear coins clinking together.

Maybe no one ever will.

But I've stopped burying the pain. That only made the nightmares worse. No, the only way to move forward is to face it each time it rears its head. I can't put off wearing gold on my coat. I can't flee every time someone pulls out a pouch of coins in a marketplace or fear the stars turning into coins the way they do in my dreams.

So each night, I'll stand under those stars until that's all that they are. I'll keep coins in my pockets until the jingling no longer summons the darkness in my mind.

Because I am not my father's curse. I've been at sea long enough to know that now. It doesn't keep the nightmares from coming back. But it keeps the hopelessness from surfacing.

I couldn't save him, but I can still save myself.

❦ ❦ ❦

How do I reconcile the Royce I know with the man I found in those pages? The man who is so similar to me. The one I know understands. Because I see now that all those moments when he seemed cold or distant, it wasn't him plotting against me. It was him holding himself together, wondering if I was an enemy or an ally.

How could I have let Aris blind me? How could I have believed him that easily? But I know the answers. I was so desperate for attention, I didn't even think to question him. He seemed like everything I dreamed of. He offered me everything I wanted. He represented everything I wanted to be. Because he wasn't afraid to touch my skin, I'd let him waltz into my heart too, with his tales of adventure. No, his lies.

Aris deceived me, pretended to care about me. Worst of all, he used Royce's past to get close to me. Every moment, every word was rehearsed to enter into my good graces. He probably didn't believe in Jipper. He never wanted to take me sailing. It was all about the gold, about my power.

And I let him kiss me. Worse, I wanted him to. He must've been desperate indeed if he was that committed to his masquerade.

I blink back tears. I don't want to cry over him; he doesn't deserve it. But I can't stop the tears from coming. They slide down my cheeks and fall into the sheets wrapped around me.

I ball my hands into fists. If only I'd seen through him, the gold would still be safe back at the palace, Thipps would still be alive, and I wouldn't feel like my heart would be better off if it was still made of gold.

A gentle knock sounds at the door.

I wipe at my tears with my tattered gloves and shove the journal back under my pillow just as Hettie steps inside the cabin.

"Oh good, you're awake," she says. "You had us all worried." She looks like she didn't sleep well. Dark circles line her eyes, and her hair sticks out in all directions. "Are you okay? Rhat and Royce filled me in on most of what happened with Duke Wystlinos."

"I was so stupid to trust him," I say with a sigh. I lean back against the wall.

"Oh, Kora, he fooled us all." Hettie moves forward and pulls me into a hug. "He even fooled my father."

As I cling to her, something breaks loose inside me. Maybe the golden coating around my heart. But I can't hold back the tears any longer. Sobs shake my chest. Hettie holds me tighter, and I let her. I don't know how long I cling to her, but by the time I'm done sobbing I feel empty. Not in a depleted way, but the slightest bit lighter.

I find her hand and squeeze it. I sniffle until I've found my voice. "I've missed you, Hettie."

She's quiet for a moment.

"I know," she finally says.

I snort. Her response is so typically Hettie.

"What happened to us?" she asks.

"You stopped coming to visit after the incident." My voice is hoarse after crying for so long.

She sits up and her face becomes serious. "I wanted to come. My father said I shouldn't visit you, that it wasn't safe. I didn't care. I got a bucket of river water to try dunking you in again because I didn't want to see you suffering. I tried to sneak into your room so many times that my father locked me in mine. When I learned to pick the lock, he posted guards outside my room for months." Her hair tumbles over her shoulders as she looks down at her lap. "During all that time, you never came to visit *me*. I thought you didn't care anymore."

"Of course I cared." I sit up to match her. "I was convinced you thought I was too terrifying to play with." I lower my gaze. "I guess I believed that was true too, that if even my father couldn't bear to look at me, how could anyone else?"

Every time my father shuddered at my arrival, every time his eyes sought out the gold instead of me, it was like he was turning me to gold all over again, freezing me out of his life.

Hettie gapes. "The only reason your father can't stand looking at you is because he can't bear the shame he thinks he'll find there. He leaves you alone because he thinks you hate him."

"But I don't." Maybe I did when I'd first been turned back, when I blamed him for everything. That was before I realized how trapped he is by what remains of the curse. Now, I pity him.

"He is convinced you do," Hettie says. "You're both too stubborn to talk about it, so you go on making stupid assumptions."

I open my mouth to refute her claims, but then I close it.

"Are you sure?" I ask, half hope and half fear.

"It's not like I've had years to study you both or anything," she retorts. "Although, you're probably better off than me and my father. I think the only reason he remembers I'm alive is because so much of the cook's budget goes toward making toasted almond tarts for me."

"He loves you," I say. "He simply has a tough exterior. He also has a multitude of responsibilities, more than he ever planned for."

She shakes her head. "He's never once said he loves me."

"He will," I say. "I bet when we get back, he'll be so happy that he'll say it a thousand times."

"That's *if* I go back," Hettie says. "I might stay on board." Her eyes drift to the deck above us, reminding me of the way my father always looks toward the tower, of how I once glanced toward the deck.

"You really like him, don't you?" I ask. A slight pang races through me, but I shove it down. I don't want to think about *him* ever again. My only consolation is that my heart hurts worse for having trusted him than it does from his absence.

"I really do." She flops onto her back and pulls a pillow over her face. She raises it up just enough for me to hear, "And I think he really likes me too."

"What happened to all those counts and dukes you were going to marry?" I tease.

"I don't care about them," her muffled words sound through the pillow. "They're all so stuffy, so like my father. Rhat doesn't hold me back. He doesn't tell me I can't do things. He makes me eat weird food concoctions, and I pretend to hate it. But I don't. He's been teaching me to fight, and he doesn't care that it's not ladylike. He probably wouldn't care if I ordered a thousand almond tarts and ate them all in one sitting. He makes me want to be a better person." She pauses. "Don't comment on that."

I laugh. And I'm so glad she had the foresight to stow aboard. Just as her father has always been the support my father needed, maybe she's the support I need.

She rolls over and props herself on one elbow. "You know who else is surprisingly nice when you get to know him?"

I raise my eyebrows as I blot away the remaining pathways the tears left on my cheeks.

"Royce," she answers. "He's actually pretty decent when he's not sitting there brooding. He even taught me a few moves this afternoon. He's lightened up a lot now that Duke Wystlinos is gone."

I manage not to wince at her reference to Aris. A sort of numbness is settling over me, ebbing away the pain as it takes hold. My head hurts too much to think about Royce right now, but not replying only encourages Hettie.

"And I happen to know," she continues, getting that gleam in her eye she always gets when she's about to do something she knows her father wouldn't approve of, "that he isn't promised to anyone. Well, he was, but once the girl's family found out his father was cursed, they called things off."

I groan. I can already tell where this is going. And my head definitely hurts too much for that. "Hettie, I haven't even processed everything with . . . well, you know."

And I definitely don't want to make the same mistake I made with Aris. I don't want to develop feelings for Royce just because we share a past.

"Don't spend another moment thinking about him," she instructs me. "If you'd seen Royce up there sword fighting shirtless"—she mock fans herself—"you wouldn't even remember Duke Wystlinos's name."

"Hettie!"

"What?" She throws her hands up innocently. "I just think you should give him a chance."

Before I can reply, she tosses the pillow aside and rolls off the bed. "Speaking of Royce, I was supposed to let him know if you were alive or not. And, if you promise to think about what I said"—she smiles broadly—"I'll even bring you some food."

I roll my eyes as she disappears through the door. I don't think she'll ever learn to be subtle. But she's Hettie. And she reminds me of home. And right now, that's what I need more than anything.

CHAPTER 21

After eating several barley rolls drizzled with honey and a mountain of figs, I figure I can't put off telling Royce about the missing gold chalice any longer. I wrap his journal in one of my cloaks as I make my way to the deck.

But as I pass the door leading down to the crew's quarters, muffled cries echo out.

I pause. Phipps. It has to be.

Would he even want to see me? Would I only make his pain worse? I figure I have to try. I owe that to Thipps.

I creak down the stairs into the room. Two layers of wooden beds are built into one wall while the rest of the room is a maze of light-colored hammocks tied to posts.

Someone sniffles. "I'll be up in just a moment, Captain," Phipps says. "Just needed to get . . . to get my lucky dagger."

Phipps is already sitting up on his bed and wiping his eyes when I step into view. I barely even notice his gold earring.

"Oh, Princess, I thought you were the captain." He quickly stands and ducks his head, busying himself by pulling up the sheet. His eyes are bloodshot, and his hair is more unkempt than usual. All hints of his usual cheerfulness are gone.

"Phipps, I'm so sorry about your brother."

His hands still. He closes his eyes, and it takes him a moment to open them again.

"He saved my life," I say, "and I'll never forget that."

"Thank you." Phipps straightens. "But don't go blaming yourself. Thipps probably thought he'd get to lord it over me for all eternity if he saved a princess." He scoffs. "You know what he'd say if he were here?"

I shake my head.

"He'd ask if you'd considered our offer." He forces a smile, but there's no jovialness like there'd been a day ago.

I smile in return. "And I would tell him he's already more than earned his share."

"He'd be happy at that." His gaze drifts upward. "He'd be happy all right." He quickly wipes at his eyes. "I should be getting back up before Captain comes looking for me."

I nod and let him lead the way to the deck.

Night air greets me.

Royce is exactly where I expect to find him after reading his journal entry about watching the stars at night. He's leaning over one of the railings.

A cool breeze washes over the deck. It ruffles his hair and the pages of the book he's reading, although I'm not sure how he can stand to read in the weak light of the lanterns. He must hear me approach because he turns toward me. He flips the back of his book closed over his finger, marking his place.

"How are you feeling?" he asks. His hair is just as messy as when I last saw it, but when his eyes fall on me, the usual hardness is gone. Or maybe it was never there at all.

"Better." I clear my throat. "But when I . . . collapsed, I saw a vision. I think Captain Skulls hid a piece of gold with the Temptresses of Triton."

Royce nods. "I was hoping you wouldn't say that, but that's what we deduced from your last words to us. We're headed to the general area where the Temptresses are rumored to be, but a more exact heading would help." His eyes are soft. "If you're up for it."

I close my eyes and let my mind reach out. There's a flash of gold and then I'm surrounded by cold water. The cup's a few feet below me. Enough light emanates from it for me to see gold coins scattered around each side.

A shadowy creature launches toward me. I scream and jerk backward, breaking my connection with the gold.

Royce's arm steadies me as I stumble back to myself.

"Are you all right?" he asks. He keeps his hand on my arm until I nod.

Slowly, I explain what I saw.

He shakes his head. "Rhat thought the treasure might be under-water. He's volunteered to go with you and Hettie to retrieve it."

"Hettie?" I question.

"Since the Temptresses's voices are rumored to be enchanted, luring men to their deaths, we think a woman could ignore their spell. Hettie didn't want you going by yourself, so she said she'd go as well."

I'm surprised by Hettie's willingness to help, then remind myself I've been thinking of her the wrong way too—she's the same cousin I remember from childhood, not the distant one I'd imagined these past ten years.

As I think through Royce's plan, I run my fingers through my hair. I desperately need a chance to wash it and get out the bits of ash left over from the fire on the island. But that'll have to wait.

"Didn't *Captain Corelli's Account of the Sea* talk about the Temptresses and how to defeat them?" I ask. When I wasn't reading about Jipper, I'd pull *Captain Corelli's Account of the Sea* into bed with me. I'd run my fingers down the thick pages and imagine a world outside my palace prison. But I can't remember what Captain Corelli said she thought could be used against the Temptresses. I remember thinking it was odd, that I couldn't believe it would work. That's probably why I don't remember the tactic.

"I've never read it," Royce says.

I nod. I forgot that most people haven't. Very few copies exist because Captain Corelli was the first female captain to sail the seas. No one would take her explorations seriously, so the only copies were the ones she handwrote herself. Captain Corelli was Sunisan, like my mother, and my mother had brought her copy with her when she'd come to marry my father.

"I wish I could remember what it said," I say. "Hopefully I'll remember by the time we face them."

Royce clears his throat. "I won't be going. Rhat will."

"You're not coming?" Everything I know about Royce points to him never wanting to sit out a fight.

He drops his head, causing his hair to eclipse his eyes. "Rhat and I agreed that only one man should go. Neither of us wanted to leave you and Hettie with the likes of Brus in case we don't make it back. Rhat argued that because of his skill as a pearl diver and because . . ." He clears his throat.

"It's because of the gold, isn't it?" I ask. I unwrap his journal. "Aris gave this to me. He said it was his, that it would help me understand him better. But I guess it helped me understand you."

He slides the journal from my hands.

"You read it?" He doesn't look up from where he's running his finger down the remnants of one of the torn-out pages.

"Yes."

His hand falters.

"I suppose in a strange way, I'm glad," he says. "My crew, the ones who know, they try to help in their own ways, although they think ignoring the curse is the best way to deal with it. I, however, can't pretend it didn't happen, that my father didn't matter. He was a great man, but all people remember is his death. They don't remember how he'd stop to help a traveler whose cart lost a wheel or how he let all our tenants stay in the manor house when fire ravaged through their farms."

"That's what I'm afraid of with my father," I admit. "People only see him as Midas, the king with the Golden Touch."

When Royce looks at me, his eyes are intense. "That doesn't have to be us. It took me a long time to learn it, but we're not destined to repeat their mistakes."

"I hope so." I hold his gaze.

He smiles softly. "We're not."

The way I find myself staring at his smile reminds me too much of how I used to look at Aris. I look away quickly.

Royce must sense my change in mood because he says, "I'm sorry about what happened with Aris, that I didn't warn you sooner."

"It's not your fault," I say.

"I know how it feels," he replies. He stares out at the murky waves stretching into the distance, his face unreadable in the dark. "Her name was Isadora," he says quietly. "We were betrothed before my father was cursed. She came to me the very night my father died and tossed the ring at my feet. She wouldn't even get close enough to me to place it in my hand. We never spoke again."

"I'm sorry," I stammer.

"Don't be," he says. "I never could've been happy with someone like that. What if my father had been cursed after we were married? What would she have done then?" He shakes his head, his hair scattering over his forehead. "I guess my point is that it's better you found out who Aris really was before . . . Well, before anything worse could happen."

"I just wish I'd been smart enough to see through his charade," I say with a sigh.

He touches my arm lightly. "Don't apologize for wanting to believe the best of people," he says. "From what I heard from Hettie, it wasn't even your idea to bring him to the palace. None of this is your fault."

I nod. "My uncle thought a match between us would appease Archduke Ralton, Aris's uncle, who's gathering troops to rebel against my father." I run my gloved hands along the railing. The tattered bits catch on the wood.

"I'm surprised your uncle didn't know better. He's the one who questioned both Aris and me after the Orfland treaty disaster. I was sure if anyone could get the truth out of Aris, it was your uncle. He detained me for three days straight, giving me barely any food and waking me up at all hours of the night for questioning. But Aris, he let go after one day. My former friend is a better liar than even I give him credit for."

"I can't even imagine what my uncle will say when he finds out," I reply. "Between that and Hettie running away, I'm not sure I want to be nearby when that happens."

"I'm pretty sure your cousin can handle that one." He laughs.

"You should've seen her up here fighting earlier. I feel sorry for anyone who makes her angry." His eyes are curious when the moonlight hits them. "Can you fight like that?"

I shake my head. "Hettie and I used to sneak into the training grounds and watch the guards practice. Hettie always said she was going to be a guard someday because all they had to do was stand around. She'd make me mock fight with sticks in the garden, but I don't think that counts as training. And even that stopped after . . ." I gesture to my skin.

"I get it," Royce says. "And I'm sure Hettie could teach you a thing or two now. But if she's too busy, I could teach you to fight. Just a few moves, though, in case something goes wrong when we meet Captain Skulls. Unless . . ." He nods toward my hands. "Unless you plan to defend yourself with your power."

"I don't want to use it again. I didn't want to use it last time," I say. Images of the man with the two Xs on his forehead pop into my mind. "I know what it's like to be trapped inside that shell. I'm not sure anyone deserves that."

"Not even Aris?"

"Maybe him," I concede. "I just hate the way the gold clings to . . . to my soul when I absorb it."

"When you absorb it?"

"That's how it works," I say. "I have to touch something gold first. When I do, I then absorb it whether I want to or not. Then the next thing I touch turns to gold."

"So you can't turn anything you want to gold?"

I shake my head. "And I wouldn't want to. Even if I could control what I change."

"See"—he shakes the journal in my direction—"I was right.

Neither of us is destined to repeat our father's mistakes." He tucks his journal under the book he'd been reading.

The spine of that book is so tattered that I can't read the words, but the lanterns swing toward us and glint off the cover. I'd know that cover anywhere.

"*The Magical Mysteries of Jipper and Other Islands*," I whisper before I can stop myself.

That book had been my link to the outside world. It described islands in such vivid detail that I could imagine I was there. It's half the reason I wanted to sail the world.

"'To those who cry that Jipper be nothing more than musings of drunk men and even drunker philosophers, I ask you, when did you last grasp the wind? When did you last hold the tide in your hands? I ask you, why can the sun rise and sink each day and not an island?'" he quotes the opening lines.

"'For though the tides rise and fall, men say an island cannot. What fools men are,'" I continue. "I can't believe you've read it before."

We grin at each other in the dark.

"Do you really think Jipper exists?" I ask, remembering the last time I asked such a question.

He nods. "Every source I've found says that when the sun sets, the island disappears. I've always been more interested in what happens if you're stuck on the island when the sun sets."

"Some people think you die," I say.

He actually laughs, and it's a nice sound. "Maybe you die. Maybe you go wherever the island appears next. Who knows? Maybe after we take on the Temptresses, I'll be feeling a little better about my luck and will sail there next to find out."

"I've always wanted to see it," I say. I rest my elbows on the railing and stare out at the waves.

"Then let's go." Royce matches my posture. Our elbows are nearly touching.

"Just like that?" I ask.

"After we get your father's gold back, of course." He turns slightly toward me, his face inches from mine.

The crash of endless waves echoes across the ocean as we stare at each other.

After a few heartbeats, Royce clears his throat and drops his gaze.

He pushes off the railing. "You seem to know it well, but just in case you want to read it again." He hands me his copy of *The Magical Mysteries of Jipper and Other Islands*.

I can't help but run my fingers over the cover. "Thank you," I whisper.

He gazes down at me.

We're standing so close.

Too close. It is too much like when Aris last kissed me. The rawness of the memory makes my breath catch in my throat.

"I should go check on Hettie," I tell him, stepping away. "Good night," I say over my shoulder as I head across the deck with the book.

"Good night," Royce calls softly after me.

I catch one last glimpse of him staring up at the stars before I descend into the hallway.

I lean against the wall inside the door for a moment, letting the cool night breeze wash over me. *Royce isn't Aris*, I tell myself. But in my mind, they're so closely linked, especially since Aris pretended to be Royce in so many ways. It's so hard to sort out what's real and what's fiction. But it's even harder to like the qualities in Royce that I know are real because I once thought they belonged to Aris.

Because I once loved them in someone else.

CHAPTER 22

༛༛༛༛༛༛༛༛༛༛❀༺༺༺༺༺༺༺༺༺༺

The next few days bleed together, though I can sense the cup growing closer and closer as we cut through the waves. The men must feel it in their own way too because I often spot them staring off into the distance. Sometimes they shiver. Sometimes they whisper to Triton, asking him for protection.

When I see their fear, I can't help but wonder if we're facing the Temptresses for nothing. What if the curse has already stolen my father from me? I contemplate sending a messenger pigeon to Uncle Pheus, but I don't know if his response will arrive in time.

Then I remember I don't need pigeons.

After a moment of concentration, I arrive in my ghostly state in the tower room. The golden table twinkles invitingly, but I turn toward the door, soon realizing no one has bothered to clean up the shards of wood on the floor. I hop over the mess and dash down the stairs into the hallway. I know I have to hurry while in this form to avoid ending up like I did after staying too long on Captain Skulls's ship.

There's a shriek to my left. I glance over my shoulder and see a maid has thrown the tray she was carrying into the air and has her skirts hiked around her knees, running in the other direction.

Half the staff already thinks of me as a ghost. What does it matter if the other half do?

I put the maid out of my mind and hurry toward my father's room. His door is ajar, and I slip inside. A shaft of light from the hallway illuminates his sleeping form.

As I move closer, I watch my father's chest rise and fall. His face is ashen, and despite the stubble staining his cheeks, they appear hollow.

He fidgets in his sleep and calls out my name. Then, with a start, he opens his eyes. Bright blue, but with flecks of gold. Have those metallic tones always been there?

When his eyes find mine, he says my name again and smiles, causing my heart to leap into my throat.

His eyes hold warmth. For me.

"I knew you'd come back to me." His hand shakes as it drifts toward me. In that moment, I'm not a young woman, not a princess, but a child scared of the dark. And my father has finally come to chase the monsters away.

It's not long before his eyes slide backward, and his hand falls back to his side.

But his reaction is what I needed. I know that he's still in there. Somewhere. And I can still save him.

As I begin to reach out to the coin on the ship, a hinge squeak startles me. I turn and find my uncle in the doorway. His eyes go wide and he calls out to me, but I'm already pulling away. There's too much to explain to Uncle Pheus right now, and I don't want to have to answer for Hettie. Soon, we'll all be able to return home and set things right.

I just need my father to hold on until I can bring *all* the gold back.

That's the thought coursing through me when the ship stops on the fourth night after leaving the Island of Lost Souls.

Nothing creaks, nothing rocks, nothing breathes. Well, except Hettie, who's snoring softly beside me.

I nudge her arm far more gently than any nudges she's given me the past few nights. "We've stopped."

"I wish *you'd* stop." She rolls over to where she thinks I can't reach and pulls a pillow over her head.

"Hettie, wake up. We're there."

"Oh, fine," she says, "I'm awake." She sits up and looks out the window. She seems distracted, and I know her thoughts must be on Rhat.

She doesn't even complain as she pulls on the clothing Rhat found for her on board—loose trousers and a white shirt with the typical Kalakhosian trim design running down the sleeves and outlining the small area where silver cords crisscross over her collarbones.

She secures her pants with rope and has the shirt tucked far inside.

She's managed to look like a put-together castaway. I can only imagine what I'm going to look like.

I pull on my own set of pants. The trousers are rough and about four sizes too big.

"Oh, here," Hettie says, stalking over. She lashes a rope through the belt loops of the trousers and secures them with a complicated knot. She smiles to herself, pleased with her own handiwork.

"Rhat taught it to me," she says when she sees I'm scrutinizing her.

The pants have an awkward gathering in the front, but at

least they won't be falling down. I pull on the shirt and tuck it in. It pools down to my knees. I roll up the long sleeves. As a final adjustment, I pull the silver cords tight, exposing less of my skin. I already feel exposed enough without a dress on, without layers of fabric between me and the world.

I pull on my sturdiest pair of gloves because I know what I'll be encountering. Gold and lots of it.

But I've survived my other encounters. I can do this. I have to.

The silence is even heavier above deck. A bright moon casts a long trail across the still water. Few crew members are out, and those who are look warily at cliffs in the distance.

I just make out a channel running between two of those cliffs. From this distance, it looks like it's paved with gold.

Waves crash between the high bluffs as they race to escape out the other end. The water in the passageway moves faster than anything else around it, as if even it's frightened by what its depths conceal. This won't be anything like swimming at the seashore I'd visited as a child.

Shallow golden pools line the edges of the channel, each one glowing unnaturally. The Temptresses' treasures eerily glint, their glow ebbing right beneath the surface. No wonder men come to try their luck against the sirens. A fortune awaits any man who can overpower them.

I scrunch up my brow when I realize I haven't seen one of the Temptresses. All the golden pools seem unguarded. No fierce warrior women with spears made of stones and coral wait to pounce on us the moment we near the rocks.

I take a deep breath and look away. Royce anxiously moves toward me.

"Is the longboat ready?" I ask. I know he had hoped we'd

arrive while the sun was still out, but we both knew we couldn't wait. My father needs every moment he can get.

"The men are preparing it now."

Rhat and Hettie appear, walking closely together, their shoulders touching. They keep glancing at each other, but neither says anything.

"Kora," Royce says, "get the boat as close to the cup as you can. Rhat will go down after it. He should be the only one going in that water."

We all nod.

"We've taken certain precautions," Royce continues as Rhat shoves bits of cloth into his ears. "Hopefully this will help guard against their voices." He hands Hettie and me matching bits of cloth. "In case you're not immune."

I shove the cloths in my rope waistband as Phipps and a few others lower the longboat down the side of the ship.

Royce lowers his voice and stares out toward the rocks. "Should anything go wrong . . ." He pauses. That pause holds us all; no one wants to finish the thought. I take a deep breath. "Then come back to the ship," he finishes. "We'll regroup from here."

We go silent. Each of us know who's most likely not to return. I try to avoid looking at Rhat. I want to tell him that he doesn't have to come. But since the cup is underwater, I can't deny we'll need him.

As we move toward the ladder leading down to the longboat, the other sailors form a line. Each one nods to Rhat, taking off their hats to the comrade they fear they'll never see again, the comrade they wouldn't trade places with for all the gold in the Temptresses' lair.

Rhat ties a rope around his waist, knotting it securely.

"The other end's attached to the longboat," he explains, "so you can pull me up if you need to."

Rhat pauses before Royce. They clasp each other on the shoulder.

"Be safe, my friend," Royce says. The two share a long look that speaks to their friendship. Then, Rhat climbs down to the boat and helps Hettie do the same.

I move to follow, but Royce lightly touches my shoulder.

He pulls out a thin knife and presses the hilt into my hands.

"Rhat will be tied to the boat." He won't meet my gaze. "If he's not going to make it up, cut the rope."

I stare blankly at the knife then down to the boat where Rhat and Hettie sit next to each other.

"The Temptresses are supposed to be incredibly strong," he continues, "stronger than ten men. If they get a hold of him, they'll pull the boat down as well. None of you will make it back." He clenches his jaw and looks away. "Rhat's aware of what I'm asking you to do. He knew the risks when he volunteered." Royce clears his throat. "I'm giving this to you because I don't think Hettie could do it."

I can't process what he's asking of me. The knife weighs down my hand despite its small size, and I look up to Royce and shake my head. I try to give him the knife back, but he refuses to take it.

"Rhat made me promise Hettie would make it back to the ship alive," he says. "And I promised you I'd help get your father's gold back." He looks down at the knife. "I hope you don't have to use it, but it might be the only way I get a chance at keeping those promises." His eyes are pleading. I know it must be just as hard for him to ask this of me as it will be to actually carry it out.

I swallow and nod, not at all certain I will be able to use the blade.

"Thank you," Royce says. His eyes hold me a moment. "Be safe." He looks like he wants to say more, but doesn't.

Slowly, I tuck the knife into my makeshift belt, and Royce helps me onto the ladder. The moment his hands are free, I can already see him reaching for the coin he keeps in his pocket. I wouldn't be surprised if he's rubbed a hole clear through by the time we get back.

Hettie holds up a lantern to light my way as I descend. In addition to her lantern, four torches are lashed to the edges of the boat so we can see as much as possible.

I take my place at the other oar. Hettie sits sandwiched between Rhat and me, where her fingers clench and unclench the handle of the lantern. Royce was right about one thing: Hettie could never cut that rope.

We drift away and begin rowing.

The current picks up quickly, steering us toward the opening between the cliffs. The rocks speed toward us faster than they should, as though the water wants this over as quickly as we do. The closer we get, the faster it flows. Water sloshes into the boat, and I nervously glance back at the *Swanflight*. What if we don't even make it to the Temptresses at all?

"Slow, slow," Rhat shouts. He reaches over to stop me from rowing, but my oar is no longer in the water. Still, the boat hurtles ever closer to the rocks.

"We're going too fast," Hettie says. She grips Rhat's arm, digging her fingernails in.

"Stick your paddle in and pull against the water," Rhat tells me.

I do what he says, but it makes no difference. Jagged out-croppings of rocks look like teeth waiting to chew us up, and gold and silver treasures hidden under the water flash by. Some magic is drawing us closer, and soon the rocks rear up in front of us. The hull of the longboat twists as the waves catch hold of it, and we careen straight toward one of the cliffs. I slam my oar down in the water, forcing the water to pull against it. It has no effect. And the cliff looms ahead.

Hettie screams.

I shut my eyes, awaiting impact.

CHAPTER 23

ᎶᎶᎶᎶᎶᎶᎶᎶᎶᎶ◉ᎦᎦᎦᎦᎦᎦᎦᎦᎦᎦ

Instead of the crash I'm expecting to hear, everything goes quiet.

Slowly, I open my eyes. The sea has gone still. Not a single ripple disturbs the water. Hettie gradually releases the grip she has on Rhat's arm.

Something doesn't feel right.

Shadows ripple around the golden treasures, but nothing else moves. I don't see a single fish. Even they seem smart enough to stay away from here.

The boat stopped inches from one of the rock cliffs, and submerged at the cliff's base I notice shallow ledges dotted with deeper pools, all lit by no source I can find. Each ledge and pool holds a feast of treasures. Strands of engorged pearls, bejeweled crowns, silver plates, and golden statues line the rocks. It's the coins that draw my attention. Deeper in the water, between the ledges on either side, the coins create a solid layer that runs off farther into the dark water, like a golden stream.

Royce definitely wouldn't have liked this place. I certainly don't. I pretend my gloves feel slick from sea spray and not from my sweating palms.

I wouldn't even have to get my elbows wet to reach some

of the treasures closer to the boat. What happens if I touch the gold underwater?

I don't want to think about it. I can't afford to—I'm already terrified as it is.

Next to me, Hettie's hand hovers over the water, right above a tiara covered in sapphires, ready to slip in and grab the point waiting right below the water line. I slap her hand away. "Don't touch anything."

Hettie winces and rubs her hand. "You didn't have to hit me. I wasn't going to take it."

Aside from our voices, the world around us remains unnervingly silent. I seek out the cup as quickly as I can and find it's only a few feet ahead of me. Thankfully, light from one of the pools spills over so that I can just see it. It's lying amongst a few golden platters and other items tossed atop the pathway of golden coins. It sparkles brighter than anything else around it, which is hard to do in a sea that literally looks like molten gold.

The water there is maybe twenty feet deep. I'd have trouble reaching it, but I'm sure Rhat won't.

"Rhat," I turn to point out the cup's location. But Rhat isn't listening. He's staring into the water on his side of the boat.

"Rhat," I say louder, thinking he can't hear because of the cloth in his ears.

He doesn't look up. Instead, he leans closer to the water.

"What do you see?" Hettie asks, afraid to look.

Something splashes behind the boat, and I spin around. One of the torches sizzles out as water spatters over it.

I turn back to warn the others. I'm too late; Rhat keels over the side of the boat. I slam against the opposite side as the boat rocks in adjustment to the weight shift.

"No," Hettie screams. She frantically pulls at the rope attached to Rhat's waist with her free hand, but it doesn't do much good with her other hand still holding on to the lantern. The boat dips and takes on a few inches of water as the rope pulls taut and lurches the boat farther into the water.

Rhat floats several yards in front of the boat. Around him, three shimmering figures with human shapes twist and twirl. Their skin looks like running water. They have long, flowing hair that tangles like two rivers meeting. They are clear yet solid.

The Temptresses have arrived.

They're oddly beautiful, like moving ice sculptures, flowing through the water as though they've choreographed every movement together. Their arms arch forward and back, and then, like birds diving into the sea, they dive at Rhat.

They seize him and pull him farther down, causing the boat to dip forward again.

I grab on to the rope behind Hettie. She strains in front of me, the frayed cord rubbing her hand until it starts to bleed. I lean forward to get a better grip, and the hilt of the dagger in my belt loop presses against my ribs. I ignore it. Rhat was once a pearl diver. He can probably hold his breath longer than almost anyone. We still have time.

Soon, my gloves slip on the rope. They're silk and not meant to grasp anything rougher than a teacup. It isn't long before the threads break. The rope chews into my scarred palms, and I bite back a cry.

The scent of metallic blood mixes with the saltiness of the sea.

Rhat kicks at his captors, and for a moment, he breaks free. He bobs to the surface, his eyes wide. Hettie leans forward, dropping the rope. She tosses the lantern, and it lands on one of the dry ledges of the cliff face. With frantic eyes, she stretches her arm out to Rhat. But then the Temptresses reappear, pinning Rhat's arms to his sides. They pull, and Rhat sinks like a stone toward the piles of gold.

The boat goes with him, water pouring over the edges. Hettie screams and leaps up, causing the boat to rock and sink even more.

The other torch at the back of the boat goes out, and water continues to stream in. If I want any chance of getting Hettie and myself back to the *Swanflight*, I've got to cut the rope. Now.

The golden water illuminates the scene below us, and I stare at Rhat. His kicking and squirming have slowed. The Temptresses surround him, and they're not going anywhere. They're content to slowly drown him.

I grab the knife from my belt. I pull the rope taut with one hand and press the knife against it. I pause. The moment I cut the rope, I sentence Rhat to death.

Somewhere behind me, Hettie is screaming the same word over and over again: no.

I can't tell if she's screaming at the Temptresses or at what I and my knife are poised to do.

I take a deep breath and make my decision. I pull the knife away from the rope and tuck it back into my belt.

"Hettie," I say, "do you see that cup down there?" I point to the one gleaming brighter than anything else.

She stares into the dark water. "I think so."

"After I jump in and distract the Temptresses, swim down and get it."

"No."

"Hettie, there's no time for arguing," I say.

"You get the cup. I'm going to go down there and show those Temptresses that they messed with the wrong woman this time." There's a gleam in her eye I've never seen before. And I think maybe the Temptresses *have* messed with the wrong woman.

I nod.

Hettie splashes over the side into the water.

I jump over the other side. Cold water swallows me, but I fight back to the surface, choking as I emerge.

In an instant, one of the Temptresses arrives. She doesn't touch me. Instead she circles, spinning in endless loops around me, watching, waiting.

When she's behind me, all I can feel is the swoosh of water pressing against my body. I throw my arms out, turning around, trying to keep her in sight.

Maybe she won't attack me. I decide to risk it and put my swimming skills to the test. I take a deep breath and dive toward the cup.

Something yanks me back by my hair, causing me to expel all my air. I'm pulled to the surface.

"Foolish woman," the Temptress hisses. "You and the other female leave now and we won't hurt you." Her words flow like water out of her mouth. "Stay, and you'll receive his fate."

"Please, he's my friend," I say.

The Temptress laughs. "Males can never be trusted." Using her inhuman strength, she tosses me back into the boat, where I land in a heap. The water sloshing around the bottom absorbs most of the impact. Thankfully, the front end of the boat sits above the waterline, no longer taking on liquid.

"We don't want to hurt you," the Temptress says. "Especially since you look to be as cursed as we are." She rises out of the water so her elbows rest on the edge of the boat. A graceful hand absently twirls a strand of waterfall hair. I imagine she must've been quite pretty when she was a human, given her high cheekbones and full lips.

With a flick of her fingers, she sends water toward the last two torches. They sputter out.

I swallow. All the salt water I've inhaled has dried out my throat.

"No doubt a man made you that way." The Temptress's voice winds around me, like a gentle tide pulling a seashell back into its grasp. "I can sense your pain. It's the same pain my sisters and I share. We can help you channel it. You could become one of us and get back at the men who hurt you, the ones who used you."

The rest of the world falls away as her words conjure up images of Aris in my mind. Of all the moments he wanted to leave Hettie behind and make a run for it. Of every time he touched me, pretending to care for me when it was all a lie.

"Don't let men ruin your life any longer," the Temptress coos.

I start to nod, but the action shakes loose the hold her words have on me. I fumble for the rags Royce gave me to put in my ears, but the hand of the Temptress darts out, stopping me.

"Revenge is sweet," she continues.

I stare up into her face. It's so lovely. So kind.

"Don't let them lie to you anymore. Don't let them trick you anymore. Don't let them hurt you anymore."

Her words hold such truth. It's like I'm as transparent to her as she is to me.

She smiles softly. "I want what's best for you. And that's to get away from those who want to use you."

I try to speak.

The Temptress shushes me. "Think of all the men who've hurt you. All the ones you couldn't trust."

My father's face when I turned to gold flashes before me. Uncle Pheus jumping when I turned the library rug to gold. Overhearing Rhat and Royce. Aris. They've all hurt me. They've scarred me.

I glance to where Rhat lies motionless on the bottom of the sea floor guarded by one Temptress. Deep shadows play across his face. I don't need him. He'll just hurt me if I save him.

Hettie's standing on a shelf whacking a Temptress with a silver platter. She's screaming something I can't comprehend. I open my mouth, but was it to tell her to stop or to keep going? Before I can make up my mind, the Temptress draws my attention once more.

"They need to pay for their sins." Her voice is harsher now. "They need to learn that they can't hurt us just because we're women. We need to show them how strong we are."

That's what I want. I want my father, my uncle, my people to know I can rule.

She holds out a transparent, watery hand. "Join us."

I extend my hand forward.

I meet her gaze. Her eyes are as bright as the reflection of the gold pool I can see through her body. To anyone else, it might seem like a halo, a golden aura, a warm, beckoning light. The only light amidst all this darkness.

Not to me.

My hand freezes.

If I'd been anyone else other than the cursed daughter of King Midas, I might've taken her outstretched hand. I might've given in to the promises she offered. But I've seen enough golden auras to know to stay away from them. They don't hold the promises and riches you think they will.

And she's wrong about the men in my life too. They're already seeing how strong I am because I'm the one outside the palace saving my father—saving my kingdom. I'm the one out here facing the Temptresses, and now it's up to me to save Rhat too.

I rip my hand away, and the hold she has over me shatters.

Her smile drops. Her face takes on darker undertones, the deep blues and blacks reserved for the depths of the oceans.

I stumble away from her. "No," I say. I shake away the remaining effects her words had on me.

Was I really willing to let Rhat die that easily? To give up on my father?

I stand up, looking down at the Temptress. She has no power over me now. I pull the knife from my belt.

Her eyes narrow. She grabs the edge of the boat. "If you'll not join us, then you've sided with mankind. And we've sworn to kill mankind." She begins rocking the boat.

I waver, trying to keep my balance.

The Temptress lets out a screech, using all her strength to drive one side of the boat down into the water.

Before I can find anything to cling to, I vault over her head into the water, losing my grip on the knife.

A loud crack sounds behind me.

Bubbles float all around my body, clouding my vision. Through them, I can make out the boat broken in two, sinking fast to the bottom.

I kick back to the surface. The water has become choppy

again, as tumultuous as when we first arrived. The current pushes me. I can't see the Temptress anywhere.

"Kora," Hettie calls. She reaches out to me, but a watery claw grabs her ankle, pulling her into the water too.

The Temptress who grabbed her wraps her arms around Hettie. My cousin struggles against her captor, bubbles escaping from her lips.

I dive toward Hettie, but I only get halfway before another Temptress appears next to me. She wraps her icy hand around my leg and drags me through the water. I kick with my other leg hoping to connect with some part of her, but she's too nimble.

She shoves me toward the bottom.

Above me, the surface has become a liquid reflection of the gold along the bottom. The gold I'm about to crash into.

I glimpse both Hettie and Rhat pinned to the bottom, and for her part, Hettie is still struggling. The Temptress switches her grip to pin me next to them, but my kick connects with her chest as she moves to wrap her arms around me.

I make a break for the surface and grab on to the ledge as a wave flings me forward. I flop onto my back, and there's a moment of pain. Then I feel it. Right there on my neck. I've touched something gold.

Every fatigued muscle springs back to life, energized by the gold, each fiber fortified by metal strands that wrap themselves around every available surface. The whole world is my canvas. I can reach out and paint anything gold.

The Temptress speeds toward me with a look of renewed rage on her face and her hands extended like claws. I don't have time to move before she leaps. Her nails dig into my shoulders.

I scream.

The gold pulses around inside me, but she doesn't turn.

Water. She's made of water, which is too pure to be affected.

A wave crashes over us, breaking the siren's hold and dragging her back into the water. Before she can catch me, I leap to my feet, running across the ledge. The Temptress keeps pace in the water below me, reaching out to try to grab my foot. I jump over her scrabbling hand.

I need a weapon. I grab a silver candlestick, and the gold that had been pounding around inside me drains into it. I swing it at her when she leaps up again, but my aim is flawed. She catches it, trying to pull me into the water.

I let it go.

I quicken my pace over the shelf. Platters and gilded treasures pass beneath my feet. It's hard to figure out what's gold and what's not. I avoid it all.

Up ahead, the lantern rests on the shelf. The fire winks invitingly.

Fire.

That had been what Captain Corelli had said she thought could defeat the Temptresses. I'd forgotten about it because it seemed so farfetched. They were made of water. Why would fire affect them?

But I pray Captain Corelli was right because she's my only hope now.

I dive toward the lantern just as the Temptress leaps out of the water. She pulls herself up the shelf so her upper body is visible. I swing the handle just as her face appears next to me.

The lantern crashes into her. Glass shards from the broken panes reflect light as they soar around us.

A stream of oil bottled at the bottom explodes over the

Temptress. It covers her watery body, running down it, mixing with it. It catches the flame and becomes a ball of fire.

She screams, clawing at her face. Her body sizzles everywhere the flame touches. Bubbles rise to the surface and release thick white mist. She's boiling from the inside out.

Then, all at once, water explodes in all directions. It fizzes where it lands in the cool ocean.

I shield my face with my arm and stumble back against the cliff wall. Scalding water bites through the sleeves of my shirt and leaves small burns on my arms.

Loud screeches pierce the air, and the two remaining Temptresses speed toward me. I raise the lantern, which still has just enough oil to keep burning, threateningly toward them. They glare up at me through the water and I stare back.

They must not like what they see in my eyes, or within the lantern, because they turn and flee, leaving a trail of bubbles in their wake.

As soon as they're out of sight, the water calms.

A flurry of movement on the ledge across from me catches my attention. Rhat and Hettie climb up the piles of treasure, the latter coughing up water as she ascends. I let out a sigh. Hettie looks like a freshly washed cat. The water has tamed her hair, taking away several inches of volume.

Despite her appearance, she doesn't seem to have lost any energy. "We did it," she laughs. She holds up the cup that makes everything else look cheap due to its inner glow.

Rhat smiles, pulling Hettie into a hug. How is he even alive?

"I thought you were dead," I call over to him. "You were under the water for so long."

"An old pearl diver's trick," Rhat says, as if that explains everything. "Stay calm and don't move—it helps you conserve air." Rhat unties the rope that secured him to the sunken boat and tosses it into the water.

The splash is echoed by another one. For a moment, I think the Temptresses have come back, but the sound's coming from the mouth of the cliffs. Royce's oars splash into the water as he rows another longboat toward us.

"I saw the boat go down and heard you screaming," he says as he glides toward us. "I couldn't sit the fight out after that. Are the Temptresses gone?"

"Aye," Rhat says. "Kora took care of them."

"I knew you could do it," Royce says, taking my hand and helping me into the boat.

"Let's just get out of here before they come back," I say. My shoulders ache where the Temptress dug into them.

"What about all this gold?" Hettie protests as Royce rows over to them. She's already draped several strands of pearls around her neck and is holding up some gold earrings.

I'm about to respond, but Royce beats me to it.

"No time," Royce says. "Kora's right. We don't want to be here when they get back."

Royce really isn't like Aris. He doesn't care about the gold. A wealth of treasure sits unguarded at his feet, and he's not interested. Not even to fix his ship.

Rhat pulls out a burlap sack from the back of his trousers. "But, Captain," he says, "I brought this just in case. I thought at the very least we could grab a few things to tide the men over since we won't actually be giving them Kora's gold." He looks at Royce expectantly.

Royce rolls his eyes. "You have until we row over to you."

Rhat whoops and hollers. He starts shoving everything he can into his bag.

Hettie grabs an emerald-laced silver tiara and a strand of sapphires as they wait for us to row the short distance to them. I doubt she has any plans to share with the crew.

By the time we reach them, Rhat's bag is full and both he and Hettie have heaps of gold clutched to their chests. They toss it into the boat, far from me, and climb in.

"You know," Hettie says as Royce and Rhat fight the current back to the *Swanflight*, "those Temptresses really weren't as bad as everyone said." She holds up a gold ring with a square ruby set atop the band. "And I rather like their sense of style."

Whether it's due to pure exhaustion or a small bit of happiness that no matter what changes, Hettie will always be Hettie, I can't help but laugh as we head back to the ship.

CHAPTER 24

When we get back to the boat, every muscle in my body aches. Climbing the ladder is pure torture, though my shoulders have stopped bleeding. When I risk a glance under my shirt, I see five small holes on each shoulder—marks I know will scar.

The crew crowds around the deck, pushing to see how Rhat fared. The moment his head appears at the top of the ladder, the other sailors let out a rising cry. The gold he's carrying gets an even bigger welcome. Rhat stands with his arms above his head, basking in his hero's welcome.

The men all rush to congratulate him. He starts digging around in his bag, tossing out coins and small items to the men. Brus catches a golden vase. When he turns around, there's a genuine smile on his face. I wouldn't say it makes him look any more pleasant, but at least he doesn't look poised to slit my throat for once.

After everyone's received a piece or two, Rhat holds up a hand, quieting the men. He pushes through them, making his way to me. He gives Hettie a smile as he passes her, and her cheeks go bright crimson.

"I may be the first man to survive an encounter with the Temptresses of Triton," he says, angling to face the sailors, "but

I wouldn't be here if Princess Kora and Lady Hettie hadn't saved me. This gold is a gift from them." He grabs one of my hands and one of Hettie's and holds them in the air. "Let's hear it for the true heroes!"

The men let out a good holler in our honor.

Brus doesn't join in, but he doesn't protest either. Instead, I find him looking at me. I'm not sure what he sees, but our eyes meet for a moment before he meanders off to compare his treasure with the rest of the crew's. And I realize that might be as close as he gets to an apology.

Amidst the hoopla, Rhat leans and whispers into my ear, "Thank you."

"Thank Captain Corelli," I say. "Her theory was right."

Rhat laughs and gives my hand a squeeze before dropping it and pulling Hettie into a makeshift dance as they join the others celebrating.

Hettie slaps a silver tiara laced with emeralds on my hair as she goes by, and motions for me to join them, but I shake my head.

I stroll to the railing and look out to sea. Already the golden pools have reverted to darkness, and the cliffs are fading into the distance. When I look down at my hands, I see my skin sparkling slightly in the moonlight. I pull off my gloves, wincing a little at the fresh wounds from the rope. At least the salt water has cleaned them nicely.

Cool wind rushes between my fingers. I wiggle them, letting them play in the breeze.

Has it really been ten years since I've felt this sensation? Or any real sensation? I stare down at my deflated gloves resting on the railing. I pick them up and weigh them in my palm. They're so delicate. So easily torn apart. I used to believe the same of myself.

Without thinking about it, I heave my gloves into the ocean. They tumble into the waves and are quickly swallowed.

Those certainly aren't my only pair of gloves. I have at least another six sets, but at the moment, I don't care.

I lean against the railing, running my fingers across the wood. It's weathered and rough and in need of repair. Yet it feels wonderful. It feels alive. I run my hands along it, feeling each crack, smoothing down each splinter. I trace a finger down a nearby rope, pressing against each coarse strand.

I realize I don't even remember what a human hand feels like in my own. And then I realize I want to find out.

I'm not going to let my gloves hold me back, and I shouldn't let the ghost of Aris hold me back either.

I search for Royce among the crowd. I spot him leaning back against the mast with his arms folded across his chest, an amused look on his face. When he sees me watching, he pushes off and comes over. "No gloves?" He raises his brows, but doesn't look afraid.

"Not for now," I say, already picturing carrying the gold off Captain Skulls's ship.

"Gloves and Temptresses in one day." He smiles. "I'm impressed."

Royce leans on the railing next to me so that our arms are touching. I can feel the heat radiating off his body.

I shiver.

"You're freezing," he says. "You should head downstairs and change out of those wet clothes."

I shake my head. "Not yet. I want to see the sunrise. It's always been my favorite time of day." And today it means more than ever. Today, I survived more gold than I've ever seen.

He looks down at me. "Why's that?"

"It means the nightmares are over."

He nods knowingly. Then he seems to remember something and digs in his pocket. "Here." He holds out what I think is a strand of pearls.

As I pick it up, the pearls unwind, and the center bauble comes into view. It's a thin seashell no longer than my pinkie. Lines of pink and yellow stripe out from the center. The back is cast in silver, no doubt to make it stronger.

"The shell is called a sunrise tellin," he supplies. "I thought someone who loves the sea as much as you do should have one."

I run my finger across the shell's glossy surface. It's the smoothest thing I've ever felt.

"It's the only item I did grab from the Temptresses' lair when Rhat and Hettie were climbing in because it reminded me of you, like a sunrise on the outside and strong on the inside." He shuffles his feet, strangely nervous.

My eyes go to his. There's no way he could know how much this means to me, how it makes me think of my mother and all the seashells I collected after she died.

"I like it very much," I manage.

He holds his hand out for the necklace. The pearls clink together as I pool it in his palms.

His fingers brush against my neck as he gently collects my hair and swoops it to the side. He loops the necklace around me before securing it.

For the first time, metal touching my skin doesn't feel slimy. The silver doesn't feel like it's going to melt right off and absorb into me.

"Thank you," I say.

He smiles, and we fall silent as the sun rises quietly into the sky, trailing pinks and purples behind it. A morning breeze accompanies the dawn, and I shiver again. I tuck my fingers under my arms to keep them warm.

"If you insist on staying out here, the least I can do is help you stay warm," Royce says. He pulls off his jacket—a simple gray one with no gold, I note with relief—and drapes it over my shoulders.

It smells like the ocean, wild and yet familiar. I pull it close as we both turn to watch the sunrise.

"Thank you," he says after a while. "For saving Rhat. You could've cut the rope and gotten out of there, but you didn't. It took real bravery to make that decision."

"I wouldn't have been able to live with myself if I took him from Hettie." I glance over to where the two of them are still dancing, though now they just sway in one another's arms. "I've never seen her so happy."

"At any rate," Royce continues, "I know Rhat and the crew won't soon forget it. They value loyalty above all else. They'll do their best to get your gold back."

His words remind me we've only recovered two pieces, and there are nine more to go. My eyes close on instinct to seek out the gold, and even before I open them again, I know I won't find Royce standing in front of me. The scent of spilled wine overpowers my nostrils.

I'm in Captain Skulls's cabin once more.

He stands by the window drinking out of a golden chalice, the mate to the one now on the *Swanflight*.

Seeing his pale lips on one of the cups my parents used to toast their wedding makes fury rise through my body. He sips deeply and turns toward me, only looking mildly surprised to see me standing on his ship.

The empty eyes of all the skulls around the room bore into me.

"You're alive." A grin spreads across his face. "I was so afraid I'd have to find a way to best the Temptresses myself in order to retrieve your skull. That would have been terribly inconvenient."

"I defeated the Temptresses," I say, straightening. "Now I'm coming for you."

Several of the skulls' jaws click and clack as the ship moves, almost like they're talking. I shudder at the sound.

"You won't get the gold without a fight." The captain puts the chalice down on a small table next to him. "You've never been in a real battle, Princess. You've never seen the lifeless eyes or heard the moans that escape the lips of your friends when they're lying there with swords through their chests." He takes several steps closer. I hold my ground. He can't hurt me in this form. I think. "If you agree to surrender, I'll let all your friends go free. I'll even give back your father's gold. All you have to do is promise to work with me."

I look away, noticing the floor of his cabin is stained with blood. Almost every plank of wood has been dyed the rusted color. It's darker under the table. But it's no dye that turned those boards. If I bring the men to face him, how many of them would end up in here, either as a game of sport for his men or as part of his collection?

My stomach recoils.

I imagine Hettie in the hands of his crew. I can't let that happen.

I also can't trust Captain Skulls.

"No deal," I say. "You won't hold up your end of the bargain no matter what I agree to."

He frowns, making his already narrow face look even longer. "I was afraid you'd be this way." He steeples his fingers under his chin. "After my men kill the crew you travel with, you'll be much more amenable. If you're not, I'll drop every single piece of your father's gold into the deepest part of the ocean I can find. Then you'll never get it back."

"You wouldn't," I stammer.

He laughs. He moves toward the table, picking up the golden necklace. He pushes open one of the windows and dangles it out. "Why wouldn't I, when I know you can make me more?"

"I can't turn things to gold," I say. My heart leaps into my throat. I fight to stay calm, to not give him reason to suspect I'm lying, as panic at seeing the necklace swinging above the waves sets in.

He lets the necklace slip farther through his fingers. "That's not what I've heard." He swings the chain back and forth. "Now, run along back to the *Swanflight* and tell Royce he can find me where we met last time near Port Tamur, the time he thought he killed me. I am growing tired of this game of cat and mouse. I'm ready to see what you can do." He picks up the golden chalice once more and takes a swig.

I know Royce won't like the meeting point. But neither of us seem to have any say in the matter, especially since I can't risk not meeting Captain Skulls, lest he dump the rest of the gold in the ocean.

"We'll be there," I say.

"Good," Captain Skulls replies, pulling the necklace back

inside and tossing it on the table. "I'll see you there in about seven days. I've got to make a little stop first."

His golden teeth gleam as he grins.

Immediately, I let the cabin fade as I focus on the cup and coin.

I wake to find myself collapsed in Royce's arms once more.

His blue eyes are focused on mine. It's almost blinding how bright they are compared to Captain Skulls's. The ocean breeze drags strands of his hair across his forehead.

"Are you going to make a habit of this?" Royce asks, a smile playing about his lips.

"I've got a message from Captain Skulls."

He sobers instantly and helps me to my feet.

"He wants to meet."

"Where?"

"Where you almost killed him last time off the coast of Port Tamur."

If the news disturbs him, he doesn't let it show. He simply nods, accepting it.

"What else did he say? Did he give any clues about what he's planning? He's always planning something."

"He wanted me to surrender. He said he'd let everyone else go." Even though I know I can't trust him, the offer is tempting. I'd give anything to keep Hettie and Royce and Rhat and my father safe.

"He'll double-cross you faster than you can blink."

"I know," I say, sighing. "I didn't agree to his terms."

He places his arm on my shoulder. "I knew you wouldn't. Now we just have to find a way we can all get out of this alive when he outguns us nearly two to one."

"He won't use his cannons," I say, "not while I'm on board. He won't risk it. He wants me alive." Then another thought kills my newfound joy. "But we can't use ours either. We can't risk sinking his ship while the gold's on it."

"We'll think of something," Royce tells me.

I hope he's right.

CHAPTER 25

>>>>>>>>>>◉<<<<<<<<<<

The sea stretches out wide around us. The world has melted into one blue sphere, darker below, lighter above, and melding in the middle. Every other color seems brighter in comparison.

The only thing that stretches on longer are the days.

Everyone seems to feel it.

Thankfully, Royce and Hettie haven't given me much time to stay idle. A week isn't much time to learn fencing basics, but I'm trying.

At least it keeps me from worrying about my father. I visit him nearly every night, spending as much time as I dare by his side before returning to my body. I pretend that my presence gives him strength, just like sitting by his gold once did. I can't physically touch him in my visions, but I place my hand over his all the same. I tell him about our voyage and how we're getting closer to the gold each day, and I end each visit by planting a shadowy kiss on his forehead before fading back to the ship, to where my own body is bruised from training.

"You've got to keep your shoulders back like this." Royce adjusts my posture once more, turning my shoulders gently toward where he'd been standing a moment ago. Thankfully, the claw marks from the Temptresses have all but healed.

"Again," he says, taking up a position across from me.

We're using broken pieces of blunted wood from the ship as makeshift swords since Royce thought real blades would be too dangerous. I tighten my grip on the polished piece I'm using as I plan my next attack.

Hettie and Rhat watch from the railing, resting after their own bout, which Hettie won.

I leap forward, driving my wooden fragment toward Royce's. He steps back, absorbing my blow with his and tripping me at the same time.

Somehow, he still manages to catch me around my waist before I slip backward.

"See," he says, still holding me in his arms, "I can show you how to block a move a thousand times, but pirates aren't going to fight fair. You've got to think more about your surroundings, about what you're not defending."

He sets me on my feet. "Again."

He's by far the most aggressive teacher I've ever had. He doesn't stop pushing me even when sweat streaks down my face like molten gold. I wipe it away and raise my weapon.

I charge forward as I did last time, and I can see the disappointment in Royce's face as I repeat the same move he just criticized. It changes to surprise the instant I drop to my knees and swing at his calves, a move I've copied from watching Hettie.

"Ouch," he cries, hopping on one foot until the pain eases.

That elicits a chuckle from Rhat and a cheer from Hettie.

"Weren't expecting that, were you?" I grin.

Royce shoots Hettie a look and rubs his calf. "Better."

I get back into position. This time, Royce doesn't hold back. Our weapons meet in the air with a loud smack.

While we're vying for control, I wink at him. It's another trick

I've learned from my cousin—she has no qualms about using her femininity to distract Rhat when they fight.

The move has the same effect on Royce. He pulls back just a little, and while he's distracted, I grab the smaller piece of wood tucked into the back of my shirt that's meant to represent a dagger. I ram it into his ribs.

He doubles over, dropping his mock sword. It rolls across the deck, where it's stopped by Rhat's foot.

"Okay," Royce wheezes, straightening. "I think that's enough for now."

"Maybe for you," Rhat calls. "I want a rematch, and this time, no winking." He puts his hands on his hips and stares at Hettie.

She holds her hand up innocently. "No winking. I've got it." Then she moves forward and smiles deviously at Rhat. "You didn't say anything about kissing though."

Rhat smiles and sweeps her into his arms, pressing his lips against hers.

While he's distracted, Hettie slips her own makeshift dagger from her belt and rams it into his side.

"Ouf." Rhat stumbles away.

"Rule number two," Hettie quips. "Never take your eyes off your opponent."

"My eyes were most certainly on you," Rhat says.

"They were closed."

"Oh, were they?" Rhat replies. "Better check again to be sure." He shoves his face toward her.

"No, stop," Hettie cries through bouts of laughter. Once Rhat actually succeeds in kissing her, Hettie shoves him away. She tries to hide the smile on her face but doesn't succeed. "You'll pay for that," she says.

"I hope so," Rhat says as Hettie leaps at him with her makeshift sword.

They begin moving back and forth across the deck, exchanging blows.

Royce rolls his eyes at the scene. "Can you believe those two?"

I laugh. "I never would've pictured them together, but they do seem to work."

"Not the hair, not the hair," Hettie shrieks as Rhat pulls her backward for another kiss.

I shake my head at them, then I flex my bare fingers after holding the wood for so long. Cuts still crisscross my palm from the glass in The Cat's Cradle and from pulling the rope back at the Temptress's lair.

They don't look like the hands of a princess anymore.

Royce notices and takes the weapon from me. "We're not pushing you too hard, are we?"

I shake my head. "I want to be ready to face Captain Skulls."

"As do I," he replies. He lets his weight rest on the railing.

"How'd you beat him the first time?" I ask.

"The last time we met," Royce says, sweeping hair away from his face, "he fired one small shot directed at my hull. We would've slowly sank, but he made one small miscalculation—he was expecting me to have a larger ship like I did before. The *Swanflight* sits much lower in the water than his. He aimed too high and missed the hull entirely.

"But," he continues, "I've been thinking this time, we could turn the tables on him and shoot first."

"What about my father's gold?"

"If we fire one well-placed cannonball, we could effectively sink his ship without sinking it immediately. It would give us plenty of time to get the gold and get back to the ship. He wouldn't be able to follow us then because he'd be taking on too much water." Royce becomes more animated as he explains, "If we get the first shot in, he'll also be even less likely to open fire because he'll know his ship will never make it back to port. He'll have to try and take the *Swanflight*. All his men will be forced over to our ship, leaving his ship abandoned. We'll sneak aboard and get the gold and then move the gold back to our ship and finish off Skulls and his crew."

"You're sure the ship won't sink before we can get to the gold?"

"I've seen my fair share of sinking boats," he says. "We'll have time."

It's so risky, but it also seems like the only way because Captain Skulls could so easily do the same thing to us—shoot out the hull and force us to scramble over to his ship to survive.

"I just wish we had more men," he continues. He shakes his head, causing more loose strands to cover his face. "Last time, I had nearly double what I have now, not to mention Aris. Whatever his flaws, he's a master swordsman. He must've taken down at least five of Skulls's crew. Although, maybe that was all an act."

Royce leans against the railing and lets out a sigh. "I tried so hard to help him. I told him there was good money in sailing. I got him a commission on my ship, but he didn't want a life of hard work. I just never thought he'd see turning to Skulls as the answer to his family's money problems."

He shakes his head slowly. "If I'd known what he was planning, I never would have brought him to the palace. I was so blinded by the drive to clear my name that I had to know what he was up to." He looks into my eyes. "I'm sorry."

I can feel the emotion behind his gaze. "I needed to get out of the palace. I've learned more about myself out here in a few weeks then I did in the past ten years." But I'm not the only one who should be getting their life back. "When we return," I add, "I'll have my father clear your name and reinstate you in the Royal Armada. I'll make sure everyone knows you had nothing to do with stealing the treaty."

Royce is silent for a moment. "Thank you," he finally says, his voice soft. "That would mean the world to me." The afternoon sun lights up his face, highlighting his strong jawline.

"You deserve it," I say, "for helping me save my father."

He presses his lips together. "I hope you won't hold what I said about him when we first met against me."

I shrug. "No one knows the truth of what he's gone through. If there are people who believe the worst, I can't blame them for that. Our country has suffered for a long time, and most people think it's because of him. Some of it is. But I'm hoping to change that."

"If you even accomplish half of what you have out here once you return to Lagonia," Royce says, "you're going to make a great ruler someday."

"You really think people will want me as their queen?" I gesture to my skin, not bothering to point out the obvious. Although, when I'm with Royce, I forget I have golden skin because he's never been afraid to touch me.

"Once they get to know you, they'll love you." There's a pause, where Royce looks like he's said too much, and my heartbeat picks up speed. Then he pushes away from the railing. "First, we have to make sure you make it back to the palace." He hands me back my makeshift sword. "How about another go?"

My muscles groan in protest, but I take the piece of wood, spurred on by the thought that maybe I really could rule someday. "All right."

I need all the practice I can get. I can sense the gold getting closer, and when we reach Captain Skulls, I'm going to put up quite a fight.

CHAPTER 26

〉〉〉〉〉〉〉〉〉〉◉〈〈〈〈〈〈〈〈〈〈

The scent of gold is in the air when I wake several days later. The breeze carries it over the waves and dances it around my head. I look out the cabin window expecting to see a sail on the horizon, but it's not there … yet. Darkness still wraps the sky. But I know the cursed items are approaching.

I dress mindfully, aware of each action. My shoulders protest, as do half my other muscles from my continued training. I opt for the pants and shirt I wore when I faced the Temptresses, knowing that in a fight, a dress will slow me down.

The last item I pull out are my gloves, knowing I'll have to be prepared today. I feel like I'm putting on armor. I guess in some ways, I am.

I try to eat a few bites from the breakfast tray outside our door. But my stomach feels like Hettie's must have her first day aboard.

When I give up, Hettie finally wakes. "Why didn't you tell me there was food?" she asks, yawning and stretching. She hops out of bed and picks off my plate before retrieving hers.

I let her take the rest without comment.

I pull Hettie into a hug while she's got half a piece of bread hanging out of her mouth. "You be careful," I say.

She gulps down the bread. "Don't worry. I'll show those pirates a thing or two about sword fighting."

"I don't doubt it."

I leave her to finish eating while I head up the stairs. I nearly run directly into Royce on his way down. Behind him on deck, everything that's not tied down is in motion. Men hauling cannonballs run by. Barrels are rolled out of the way to make room for the inevitable fighting that's going to spill over to our ship.

Royce has donned his jacket again. The one with the golden threads and buttons.

It doesn't bother me so much now.

He moves to the far side of the step I am on so we are side by side and offers me as much of a smile as he can muster. "It's close, isn't it?" he says.

I nod.

He lets out a sigh. His hand finds mine.

I smile up at him, and his lips relax into a real smile.

"Kora . . ." He turns to face me. "These last few days . . . they've been . . ." he starts. His thumb finds the skin of my wrist above my glove. It moves back and forth, sending a pleasant tingle up my arm. "I mean, just in case something happens, I wanted you to know . . ." His eyes don't leave mine.

He cups my cheek. "Be safe out there today."

I nod, not taking my eyes from his. Up close, dark blue streaks run through each iris, almost like waves. I don't ever want to look away. I want to memorize them, suddenly afraid of what might happen in the next few hours.

Royce must sense it too because he pulls me closer, careful not to let the gold of his jacket graze my skin. His other hand gradually slides around my back, anchoring me to him. Then his lips are on mine. They taste like the sea breeze, salty and light.

It's a kiss that says everything he couldn't. It's intense at first but slowly turns softer, gentler, more pleading, as though he realizes how little time we have. I don't even feel the morning cold anymore.

For the first time, the gold doesn't tug at me. My thoughts are only of him. Of the warmth of his skin on mine. Of his hand cradling my back. Of his body pressing against mine.

When the only thing I can hear is my heart pulsing through me and I feel like my lungs might explode, I finally pull away. Royce rests his forehead against mine while we both catch our breath.

"Captain." Rhat clears his throat, and I pivot my head slightly to see he's stopped on the stairs and waits for us to both turn toward him.

Royce pulls away reluctantly.

"His ship's within sight," Rhat says.

"All right," Royce replies. He focuses back on me. "I guess it's time."

"I guess so." I stand there one more moment before following them both up the stairs and toward the rigging.

I stare up the ropes toward the crow's nest. Royce figured it would be the hardest place for Captain Skulls's crew to reach.

"Up you go," Rhat says. He lifts me so I'm clinging to the ropes. Behind me is a straight drop to the ocean.

I turn my attention back to the rigging as Rhat moves behind me to make sure I don't let go and end up tumbling overboard. He attempts to hold the netting steady, but the ropes still shake beneath me. Slowly, I pull myself up. The rigging narrows the closer I get to the crow's nest. It starts to toss and twist under my weight and desperate grabs for handholds.

"Almost there," Royce calls from the deck below.

I look down.

That's a mistake. I close my eyes.

I toss away the golden aura before it can beg me to come closer.

When I open my eyes again, a ship is barreling toward us. I didn't notice it earlier because its dark sails blend in with the morning shadows. The sails snap forward, the skull and crossbones painted on them unmistakable.

Instead of a mermaid gracing the front of the ship, there's a carved skeleton with its arms stretched out to either side. Each palm holds a skull.

I force myself the rest of the way up the rigging and drop headfirst into the crow's nest. My hand goes to the sunrise tellin necklace hanging around my neck. I rub my fingers across it as I sit in the bucket-shaped landing area catching my breath.

I didn't realize how taxing such a short climb would be. Phipps always makes it look so easy. He's been spending more and more time up here since his brother died, watching and waiting just as anxiously for Captain Skulls's ship to come into view. I can read it in the hollowness of his eyes and the set of his jaw—he wants revenge.

I find a sword and small dagger lying on the floor of the crow's nest that Rhat placed up there earlier for me. I'm not supposed to need them, but I belt the sword around my waist and shove my dagger through the loop in my pants.

There's also a small rope in case I'm forced to cut the rigging to prevent Skulls's men from climbing up to me and need a way to climb down later. One end is tied to the point of the mast sticking up through the middle of the crow's nest.

From my position, I hear the taunts of the sailors as the ships near one another.

I lower myself below the crow's nest's rim.

"Send over the princess," Captain Skulls shouts, "and I'll spare you all."

"Never," Royce shouts. "This ends today, Skulls."

Royce told me to stay out of sight, but I can't help peeking over the rim.

The ship is lined up parallel with ours, offering its side primed with cannons, though none have fired yet. As we suspected, Captain Skulls must not want to open fire because it risks killing me. I just pray our plan to fire at his ship works.

My stomach drops, though, when I see the sheer number of men lining the side brandishing weapons, ready to board as the ships drift closer. How can we ever fight that many? I glance at our own deck. It's looks practically deserted in comparison.

It takes me a moment to notice there's something different about Skulls's crew. I squint. All of them are wearing skull masks over their faces, giving them the appearance of the undead. And I'm almost certain they're made from real skulls.

"Take his ship!" Captain Skulls orders his men.

"No," I breathe. Our crew will be slaughtered.

His men let out a deafening cry. The first bits of sunlight glance off my skin as I cover my ears, and I turn to see the sun rising like a golden orb from its bed of clouds. I look down at Captain Skulls's ship again, a plan forming in my mind.

If there's one thing I've learned aboard the *Swanflight*, it's that sailors are the most superstitious people I've ever met.

I quickly undo my braid and run my fingers through my hair, loosening the strands. I yank up my sleeves, grab the rope tied to the mast, and leap onto the crow's nest ledge. The rope pulls taut, preventing me from plummeting to the deck below.

Sunrays hit my skin, sending light in every direction. I raise my arms and let the sun do its work.

The men preparing to make the leap across to our ship pause. Some shield their eyes, unable to see me against the sun. Some stand with both weapons and mouths slack.

I can't even imagine what I look like to them. I'd like to think I appear like the rising sun. Like I am the one who made it rise because I control all things golden.

"I've come for my gold," I shout. My voice shakes slightly. It's not easy keeping my balance on the thin ledge.

The sun is rising quickly. I'll soon lose my backdrop.

"If you throw down your weapons now and surrender, I'll spare your lives," I call.

There are murmurs among the crew.

"Resist and I'll turn each and every one of you to gold," I shout. I spread my arms wide to heighten the effect and hope I look menacing.

"A golden siren," someone cries.

"It's the ghost of Midas's daughter," another calls.

"We're all cursed," a third voice cries.

"I can feel it. I can feel the gold on me," a high-pitched voice squeals.

Then the screams all blend together.

Some men rip off their masks and jump overboard, including the one who said he felt the gold on him. Others throw their weapons into the sea.

Even after my own encounter with superstitious sailors, I never thought so many would be fooled.

We might actually stand a chance.

"It's a trick, you fools," Captain Skulls's voice rings out. "If another one of you throws down your sword, I'll run you through myself. Bring me that girl." There's a pause, and then he screams, "Now!"

Slowly, the men pull themselves together. Some throw glances at me as they send grappling hooks biting into the *Swanflight's* railing. The ships merge together with a jolt.

My thin slippers slide on the ledge, and I flounder to keep my balance.

"See," Captain Skulls shouts, "she's just a girl. That's merely the sun, not some golden halo."

My small slipup seems to rouse the men. They start hopping onto the *Swanflight*, and soon swords clash and voices rise into the air. I leap back into the crow's nest, disappointed that all I could offer my crew was a delay.

Below me, men are spread out on the deck. Most of the sailors form a ring around the mast where I am. Rhat and Royce are down by the base of the rigging to protect me. I know if someone gets past them, I'm in real trouble.

Captain Skulls points the tip of his sword in my direction and offers a little nod. He's coming for me. He's doesn't wear captain's blue like Royce does; he's in a black coat laced with crimson threads that almost look like drops of blood streaming down his body. He slowly works his way toward me.

I ignore him. There's someone else I want to find more.

I scan past Phipps and Brus fighting back to back. And then I see her.

Hettie's holding a man twice her size at bay. Her hair bobs around her as she ducks and dives around blows. She kicks the pirate in the stomach, sending him reeling back into the chaos. She doesn't waste any time following him.

I circle around the mast to keep an eye on her, but instead I see one of Skulls's crew slip through the crowd. He leaps onto the rigging and starts climbing. He doesn't even need to use his legs. He just pulls himself up by his arms, a dagger clamped between his teeth. His eyes are set so deep behind his mask that looking into the eyeholes is like looking into an abyss.

I refuse to let the mask have its intended effect on me and instead yank at my own dagger. I begin sawing through the ropes, but he's faster than I expect. I cut two of the three ropes holding up the rigging and still he continues unfazed. I'm sawing through the last rope when he grabs my arm. My dagger falls to the deck below.

He tries to pull me out of the crow's nest, his fingernails digging into my skin. I cry out. He yanks my sleeve, but the fabric rips. The man reels backward, giving me just enough time to recover. I slam my hand into his mask. There's a sickening crunch as the skull cracks. My attacker whirls backward before losing his handhold and plummeting into the water.

I stumble back against the far side of the crow's nest and stay there a moment, gathering myself.

I hear a strangled cry from below, one that stands out because of its high pitch. My stomach feels like it just fell into the water too. I whip around and search for Hettie's recognizable mass of auburn hair.

My relief at seeing that she hasn't been hurt is short lived because she's being pulled onto Captain Skulls's ship.

The absolute only thing worse is recognizing the person who captured her.

I blink several times, hoping I'm wrong.

But when he turns around, there's no mistaking his face, one I know so well.

Aris.

CHAPTER 27

"Let her go!" I scream.

He turns to look at me, and I lean so far against the ledge of the crow's nest I nearly fall out.

"I don't want to hurt her," Aris shouts back. "Surrender, and I'll let her go!"

I stare down at the deck. Both Rhat and Royce are fighting multiple opponents. They've spread out from their original positions and seem lucky to be holding their own. Skulls's men have scrambled over the ship, filling up every empty space. I don't spot anyone from our crew who isn't fighting at least two men at once.

Metal clashing against metal fills the air, and strangled cries reach me as some of the men go down. The deck's already beginning to look like the floor of Captain Skulls's cabin due to all the blood spreading across it.

I'm safe up here with the rigging virtually in tatters, but I can't reach anyone else who can help Hettie. Not that there's anyone free to help her.

I turn to check on Aris. He's pulling her farther across the deck.

I don't want to let her out of my sight.

That decides it.

I whip off my gloves and tuck them into my belt so they don't rip. I heave the rope over the side of the crow's nest and throw myself over, maneuvering until my feet become entwined. I may not have liked the rigging, but it was a lot better than the single rope. The wind thrashes it below me, causing me to sway.

I ease myself down since there's no one to catch me this time.

By the time I reach the bottom and hop onto the deck, everyone has shifted position. I hastily pull on my gloves as I scan the decks. I don't spot Rhat or Royce anywhere. I don't even see my dagger.

A man in a skull mask tries to grab me, and I plunge through the crowd to escape, bouncing off backs and glancing past swinging arms. Someone cries out behind me, but I can't bear to turn and look.

My slippers have a hard time getting any traction on the blood-soaked deck, and I slide into a big-bellied sailor who's missing an ear. He turns, ripping the knife he holds in each hand from where they'd been lodged in Brus's stomach. Brus silently drops to the deck.

The pirate's smile when he spots me is just visible past several missing teeth in his skull mask.

I pull my sword and point it at him to keep him at bay. My hands are already sweating inside my gloves. When he moves toward me, I panic and ram my sword at the man, the exact move Royce told me not to do.

He deflects it easily with his knife.

Just like I did with Royce, I make the same move again, and this time, I duck down, running my blade across the pirate's leg and leaving a deep gash.

He cries out, but doesn't fall.

He feints forward with his blades, and I'm so busy watching the knives that I don't see his foot swing around.

My legs go out from under me, and I land on my back with a thud. A throbbing pain ricochets through my head, but at least I've managed to hold on to my sword.

When I roll over, Brus's lifeless eyes look back at me.

Before I can react, the pirate grabs my leg and drags me away across the deck. All I can smell is blood. I'm not sure if it's my own or what's covering the deck.

Grabbing my sword in both hands, I heave my upper body forward and bring the blade crashing into the pirate's arm.

He screams and lets go. I scramble to my feet, pulling my blade free. There's a sickening *thunk* as the metal scrapes against bone.

His eyes go glassy, and he drops to his knees, cradling his wounded arm. His shirt is already drenched in blood by the time I surge past him.

I barely make it to where the grappling hooks, shaped like demon's claws, hold the ships together when the man with the two Xs on his forehead appears, ripping off his skull mask.

"Surprise," he says, his breath every bit as foul as the first time we met.

Memories of Thipps crashing onto the dock, of holding his lifeless body, flash before me. Without thinking, I launch myself at the man. A guttural roar rips through me.

He grabs my arms as he ducks away from my blade.

I try to kick him, but he moves easily out of the way, never breaking his grasp on my arms. My wrists burn as he twists them, trying to break my grip on my sword. He's stronger than me, driving me backward. My back rams into the railing not far from one of the grappling hooks.

My grip begins to weaken.

He leans in, his eyes wild and gleaming. He's enjoying this. "Bet you didn't think we'd meet again," he says.

"I could say the same thing," a voice calls behind the man.

Phipps comes charging forward. He yanks the pirate away from me and tosses him to the deck.

"I . . . I killed you," the man with the Xs stammers.

"Now it's my turn to do it to you," Phipps says. Before the pirate can get one of his knives free, Phipps rams his sword forward, straight into the man's stomach. "This is for my brother."

The man's eyes go wide before he slumps down against the deck.

Phipps rips his sword out. There are tears in his eyes. He blinks them back and yells, "For Thipps," as he runs back into the fray.

Another scream echoes his.

Hettie.

I climb onto the railing and make the short jump to Captain Skulls's ship, which is nearly empty since all the men were trying to get to me on the *Swanflight*.

Another set of feet pound down behind me. I look up into the grinning face of Captain Skulls.

"Why, if it isn't the golden girl in the flesh," he says. Every step he takes toward me lasts a lifetime, his feet thudding loudly against the deck.

I edge backward. I breathe in deep, haggard gasps.

"I loved your trick with the sun. I wish I'd thought of it. I might have you do a repeat performance for all the towns we raid. Lagonia will fear you more than they do your father."

I raise my sword. "Never."

He stops mere inches from it. "Maybe this will change your

tune." He motions and Aris moves into my line of vision. He clutches Hettie in front of him. Captain Skulls smirks at me. "I made a little stop at the Island of Lost Souls just for you."

"You're the ugliest, vilest, most black-hearted, foul creature I've ever met," Hettie spits at Aris as he yanks her forward. She's lost her sword and has resorted to clawing at his arms.

But Hettie's right. I can't believe I ever thought Aris was attractive. His eyes are too calculating, his features too sharp. His smile isn't kind; it's cruel.

"Hello, Kora," Aris says. "Did you miss me?"

"You disgust me," I spit back.

"The same could be said of you," he replies. "At least when you make me a very rich man, it will almost make all those times I had to touch you worth it."

I swallow down his insults before they can affect my concentration. "I'll never turn anything to gold for you." I point my sword at him while Hettie continues her attempt to struggle free.

"Make her cooperate," Captain Skulls snaps at Aris, nodding in my direction. "That's why you're here. You said you could control her."

Control me? Anger burns through my veins at the thought.

"Put the sword down, Kora," Aris says. "Now." He presses his blade against Hettie's skin. She stops struggling when a small trickle of blood appears. I gasp.

I want to think he won't do it, but he will.

"Surrender," Captain Skulls says.

I'm not taking any risks with Hettie's life. For now, I'll have to comply. "Fine," I say. I drop the sword at my feet.

"Kick it over here."

I do as he asks.

"Good. Now come over here nice and slow."

A single cannon fires.

Wood explodes. The ship lurches beneath me, pulling away from the *Swanflight*, which can hopefully only mean one thing: the cannonball found its mark.

Captain Skulls lets out a frustrated cry and clenches his jaw, making his cheeks look even shallower.

Now I just have to get the gold before the ship sinks. But before I can go after the gold, I need to get Hettie back on the *Swanflight*.

I rip off one of my gloves and toss it onto the deck. "I'm going to turn you both to gold."

Aris laughs. "We both know you haven't absorbed any. If you had, you'd be a raving mess like when I found you on the dock after turning my friend to gold."

"I've come a long way since then," I say.

Captain Skulls's eyes are even darker when they turn on me. "Not far enough," he intones, motioning for me to cross the rest of the deck and join him.

"Let her go first," I say. I need to get Hettie off the ship as quickly as possible.

"That's not how this works."

I shake my head. I need more time.

Before I can figure out what to do, someone blurs past me, tackling both Hettie and Aris to the deck.

It's Royce.

Hettie rolls toward the other side of the ship as the men grapple with each other, and I rush to her side to help her stand, propping her against the railing. She looks unharmed.

A few paces away from us, Royce lands a punch to Aris's

jaw. Aris stumbles backward, wiping a smear of blood from his lip. Then he charges Royce, driving him backward until Royce crashes into the railing next to us.

Aris laughs, picking up the sword he'd dropped when Royce first attacked, and takes up a position a few feet from Captain Skulls. They have us all cornered against the railing.

None of us have weapons. I spot Royce's sword across the deck where he must've lost it tackling Aris. Mine's not too far away. But neither are close enough to reach before Captain Skulls or Aris run us through.

"This has always been how it would end," Aris says to Royce.

"It's not over yet," Royce retorts.

Captain Skulls points his sword at us and smiles. "It *is* over. For two of you at least."

"Wait," I call, bringing his attention back to me. "I'll go with you, but let them go."

"The time for bargaining has expired," Captain Skulls replies dryly.

"Then I'll jump overboard right now." I press against the railing. "I'll never turn anything to gold for you, and all you'll be left with is what you've stolen from my father. Gold that curses whoever possesses it," I add for good measure, praying Captain Skulls is even a fraction as superstitious as his crew. But I don't even care about his answer because a plan is starting to form in my mind.

Captain Skulls studies me. "If you come without any fuss, I'll let her go free," Captain Skulls finally says with a nod to Hettie. "But Royce needs to learn his lesson."

"Fine," I say before anyone else can speak.

"As soon as you walk over here, she's free to go."

I start forward.

Royce lunges forward. "Kora, no." He grabs my arm as I hoped he would. "He's lying. He's going to kill us all anyway."

"You said I'd make a good leader." I take a deep breath, preparing myself before gently grabbing his wrist and prying it away with my bare hand. I inhale sharply and let out a metallic-scented breath. "This is me leading." My eyes plead with him to understand.

It's clear he doesn't; he stares at me in confusion. I pull away from him as quickly as I can and take slow, measured steps backward to make sure he doesn't follow me, doesn't reach out for me again.

"Don't do this, Kora," Hettie pleads.

"I have to. For all of us." I turn away from them. It's the hardest thing I've ever done.

"Take her below and chain her up until we take the *Swanflight*," Captain Skulls says.

"With pleasure," Aris says.

"No," Royce cries, as I move forward and Aris grabs my hand to pull me below.

The instant Aris's hand touches my bare skin, he turns to gold.

shiver as the last of the gold vanishes from my insides.

Someone lets out an audible gasp, and I turn back to face the others. Royce has his wrist raised, staring at his now brass cufflink. His eyes meet mine in amazement.

I quickly move toward my fallen sword. I swing around and aim the blade at Captain Skulls.

Royce leaps forward and picks up his, adding his strength to mine.

"Impressive," Captain Skulls says. "For once, I'm glad all the rumors are true. Although, I would've enjoyed killing him myself and collecting his skull after he'd repaid his debt to me."

"He's not dead," I say. "He's trapped. Just like you will be until you can be brought to court."

"Then your father can stay trapped in his curse too," Captain Skulls says. He turns and heads straight for the door that leads below deck.

My mind snaps to the gold. He's going to throw it overboard.

"The gold," I say to Royce just as the ship shifts beneath us.

Royce and I crash against the railing, nearly landing on top of Hettie. I drop my sword to avoid stabbing her, and it rolls down the deck.

There's a loud noise behind us. The statue that was Aris smashes through the railing and splashes into the sea.

It glimmers as the depths swallow it.

Shocked, I stare after him. I'd planned to set him free eventually, once he was handed over to the authorities. But now—now he'll be stuck in a golden prison forever. Unable to escape. The thought makes my stomach twist, not out of guilt, but out of fear of that fate. I'm not sure even Aris deserves that for eternity.

"Come on," Royce shouts, drawing my attention. He takes my hand and pulls me after Captain Skulls. "Hettie, find Rhat. Tell him to get the *Swanflight* clear."

Hettie nods and dashes off, picking up my sword as she goes.

"Stay behind me," Royce says as we move toward the stairs Captain Skulls took. "Which way's the gold?"

I'm about to say it's in Skulls's cabin, where I've seen it so many times before. But that's not where the aura is coming from. It's pulsing lower in the ship. Much lower. "I think it's in the hull. He's moved it toward the bottom of the ship."

I panic. What if it's already underwater?

I stumble, but Royce's grip keeps me upright. He pulls me through a hallway, and I expect each door we pass to be thrown open to reveal Captain Skulls. We climb down a set of stairs, weaving our way through the pirate ship. Royce is about to head down one more staircase when I stop him.

"There," I say, pointing to a closed door. "That's where the gold is."

Without waiting for him to acknowledge my words, I throw open the door. It leads into the brig, and the room is dark except for two lanterns hung at the front of the room. Cells run along both walls. Down here, the water has risen to our ankles.

Once we're inside, I catch glimpses of my father's gold inside one of the cells. It's shifted toward the back of the ship as it sinks and is buried under a pile of human skulls.

The ones tilted sideways look questioningly at me. Through me.

The ship moans and shifts. One skull rolls off the pile. It breaks in two with a sickening crunch.

Royce grabs the door to the cell and yanks several times. The metal clangs but doesn't budge. He resorts to kicking the bars. Nothing happens.

"Looking for this?" Captain Skulls emerges like a ghost from the darkness at the end of the hallway. He dangles a large key by a string.

"Hand it over," Royce says, raising his sword.

"The only way you're entering that cell," he says, looping the string over his neck, "is when you're part of my collection." He pulls out his sword, aiming it toward us.

Royce quickly moves forward in the crowded space. The walkway between the cells is barely large enough for one broad-shouldered man, but Captain Skulls meets his attack. Their swords clang against each other's and the bars as they work to find space to maneuver. They lock blades, and Royce brings his elbow up, smashing it across Captain Skulls's face.

Captain Skulls stumbles backward clutching his nose. Royce presses him farther back toward the shadows.

They're past the cell where the gold is locked, so I rush forward. I examine the hinges, then kick them, hit them, and pull on them. The bars don't move. I'm trying to pry them apart with my fingernails when I hear footsteps creep down the staircase outside the brig.

I panic. There's nowhere to run. Royce and Captain Skulls are at my back, and I don't have a weapon. But Royce's coat is still within reach. If only I could touch his buttons without distracting him. I'm turning toward him when a figure appears in the doorway.

I leap backward, but it's Hettie. She has my sword in one hand and a thin dagger in the other.

"I've been looking everywhere for you," she says. "We've got most of Skulls's crew beaten. There's still some fighting, but we're winning. Thanks to you turning Aris to gold, more men surrendered." She takes in the scene in the brig. "Where's your father's gold? This thing is about to sink."

I point to the locked cell. "Captain Skulls has the key."

Her mouth hangs open. "The gold's in there?"

I nod. I expect her to complain or run out screaming. But that was the old Hettie. The new Hettie shoots Royce a look, but I know the passageway is too narrow for her to even try helping him in a fight. She seems to decide the same.

"Move over." She shoves me out of the way and kneels in front of the lock, jamming her dagger into the keyhole and wiggling it back and forth.

"What are you doing?" I ask.

"Remember how my father"—she shoves the dagger farther in—"posted soldiers outside my room to keep me from visiting you after you got turned back? This is why."

Her words are breathless and distracted as she works. The blade scratches against the metal lock. "I'm used to doing it from the inside with a hairpin, but I should be able to get it."

Grunts and swords slicing against metal echo from the other end of the room.

"Hurry, Hettie," I plead.

"I know I make this look easy"—she scrunches her eyes together and stares into the lock—"but I've never seen a lock like this one before, and I can't tell if the dagger is too big to reach all the way to the back." She rams her shoulder forward.

Something clicks, and the door creaks open.

I ease into the cell, holding on to the bars. The floor slants straight toward the pile. And the only thing worse than sliding face-first into a pile of gold is sliding face-first into a pile of gold *and* human skulls.

"Let me do this," Hettie says. "I'd really like you not to turn the ship to gold while I'm on it." She breezes past me, letting the angle of the ship slide her right to the foot of the pile. She starts throwing skulls toward the edges of the cell.

She pulls the necklace and chalice out first and shoves those into her pockets; then she digs deeper into the pile.

"The pheasant," I point, "it's right there."

"I know," she says, still not picking it up. "What are the smaller objects? I want to get those in my pockets first since they'll take longer to find."

"Look for two coins. They'll be the hardest."

She starts mumbling about finding coins in a skull stack and about how she never thought her life would come to this.

I glance toward Royce. He's holding his own against Skulls, but neither has gained any ground.

I risk closing my eyes.

This close to the gold, it's easy to focus on just one object. I isolate a coin.

"Try that skull there," I point to one toward the bottom of the pile.

Hettie picks it up. A coin rattles out of the hollow cavity. She shoves it in her pocket while I'm busy locating the next one.

I guide her toward the bottom middle of the pile. She secures the coin with the other.

Next, she hauls up the platter, which she balances between her hip and one hand. She continues digging with the other. She pulls out the rose and the pheasant next, stacking them on the tray.

"What else is there? I'm not sure how much more I can carry." The platter slips against her hip under the weight of the pheasant.

I scan the items. "The tapestry," which I can spot the end of, "and a knife."

"I'm not sure I can carry the tapestry right now. Where's the knife?" Hettie asks. She irreverently kicks skulls in every direction.

I close my eyes. My mind doesn't go toward the pile. A small aura shines back in the shadows. Back where Captain Skulls is standing.

My eyes bolt open.

The ship jerks downward again, and Hettie nearly loses her grip on the platter. More water trickles through the doorway and along the floor. It pools against the skulls before continuing along the room.

"Get out of here," Royce calls.

"Skulls has my father's golden knife," I cry.

"I'll get it," he says without breaking stride. "Go."

"Kora, help me," Hettie says. She's struggling to make it up the incline while laden down with gold. I hold on to the bars and lean forward, grabbing her wrist. I steadily pull her forward.

"What about the tapestry?" she asks.

"I'll get it." I pull my sleeve down over my fingers and then slide into the pile of skulls, ignoring the cracks and snaps. I yank the tapestry out. It's heavy, but I manage to tuck it under my arm without touching it. I ease up the incline until I'm close enough to haul myself forward using the bars.

"Let's go," I say.

Hettie slowly moves forward.

I risk one more glance at Royce. Sweat runs down his neck. I hope I'm not imagining that Captain Skulls's blows are coming less and less often, but I don't have time to stop and be sure.

I give Royce one last look as I shove Hettie up the stairs.

CHAPTER 29

〉〉〉〉〉〉〉〉〉〉❀❬❬❬❬❬❬❬❬❬❬❬

Hettie nearly stumbles on the steps as we make our mad dash for the deck. I keep my hand on her back to steady her as we move up the stairs. We weave our way through the ship and back up to the open air.

If I thought crossing the cell was hard, the deck looks like a mountain in comparison.

My eyes follow the opposite path, toward the rising water. The one that will result in us sliding straight into the ocean and losing the gold if we fall.

Hettie and I pause in the doorway.

Rhat spots us. "Come on," he yells from the deck of the *Swanflight*. It looks like the fighting has stopped. Groups of men are being led to the brig while others lie unmoving on the deck. I turn away before I recognize anyone.

My eyes move back to Rhat as he pulls up a long plank of wood and lays it between the *Swanflight*'s railing and the outermost edge of the railing of the ship we're on.

He hops across it and slides to meet us in the doorway. "Where's Royce?"

"Still fighting Captain Skulls," I tell him.

"He can take care of himself," Rhat says. "Come on, I've got to get the ship clear. That plank won't stay there long."

He takes the platter and the items heaped upon it from Hettie. She grabs one of his arms, and I loop my free one through the other. With his added strength, we make it across the deck. We switch our grip to the railing. Rhat goes up first. He hands off the platter and reaches for me.

"Hettie first," I say.

He nods.

He helps her on to the plank and holds her hand as long as he can while she balances across. The plank shifts an inch while she's on it, and I suck in my breath. Hettie crouches low to keep her balance, and once the plank stops moving, she inches forward until she jumps onto the even deck of the *Swanflight*.

I hand Rhat the tapestry, and he shuffles it quickly across before coming back for me. He holds his hand out for me to grab.

I hesitate. Something's pulling at my mind. It's the knife. It's not moving any closer.

"Kora," he says, "we're out of time. The plank's about to fall. Come on."

"Go," I say. There are two things I'm not leaving on this ship.

"Kora." Rhat holds his hand back toward me.

"Get the ship clear," I shout.

Rhat jumps back to the *Swanflight*, dangling from the railing as the plank splashes into the water. He easily pulls himself up. "Make sure you get away from the ship before it goes under," he calls. "And watch out for the mast and sails. They won't hold long at that angle."

I race back through the ship. There's more than a foot of water to trudge through now. My pants cling to my legs, and a chill runs through my body.

I stumble into the brig to find Captain Skulls holding Royce underwater. A cut on Royce's scalp leaks blood, turning the water around him faintly pink.

"No," I scream. I scramble forward, my heart pounding as I fight to get to Royce.

Captain Skulls releases his grip and turns on me. His eyes are bloodshot, and there's a long gash on his cheek. Blood runs down his hollow face.

He slowly rises to his feet. Behind him, Royce's body bobs to the surface, face up. I think his eyes flutter for a moment, but I don't have time to make sure because Captain Skulls advances. He brings the golden knife around and slashes at me.

I leap back.

Captain Skulls keeps pressing his attack until we're nearly back to the stairs. He swings again, and I race upward, panic rising as I leave Royce behind.

I stumble onto the deck, Captain Skulls close behind me. His steps are unstable, and he has a deep cut across his side that I didn't notice before. His free hand is putting pressure against it.

"So it comes down to us," Captain Skulls says. He slowly shuffles forward, planting his feet carefully on the slanted deck as he moves up higher, cutting off my route back to the *Swanflight*. "I was saving this for you." He waves the knife around. "Once you made me a rich man, I was going to add your golden skull to my collection. It would've been my favorite."

I glare at him. "I'll turn you to gold just like I did Aris."

He laughs. "If you could, you would've already." He lumbers closer, knife at the ready.

I let him come. The sooner I get that gold, the sooner I can make it back to Royce. And there's only one way I can think of to get it.

Captain Skulls slices the blade toward me.

I duck far enough out of the way to avoid serious injury, though the knife edge bites into my arm.

I'm expecting coldness from absorbing the gold. What I'm not expecting is how much pain it brings with it. The blade cut deeper than I thought.

I stagger backward into the tallest mast before Captain Skulls can bring the now silver knife back up. I rest against the mast, careful not to let my skin touch it, and cover the wound with my hand. Blood seeps through my fingers. The gold courses through me so violently I can't tell if it has drowned out my heartbeat or if it's slowing on its own because of all the blood I've lost.

Captain Skulls's lips spread into a satisfied grin. He knows as well as I do that I have nowhere left to run. Not with him blocking the path to the *Swanflight*.

"Who knows," he says. "Maybe when you're dead, you'll still be able to turn things to gold." He raises the knife.

I'm too weak, too distracted by the gold to react in time. In those last few moments before the knife descends, I hear my father saying my name over and over again.

Except, when my eyes focus, it's not my father.

It's Royce.

He's diving toward me, trying to pull me away from the mast to save me, all while trying to keep us both from tumbling down the deck.

Over his shoulder, the blade crashes down. Except, it's no longer aimed at me.

I don't have time to think. Royce is about to die. I lean forward and kiss him just as the knife slams into his back.

CHAPTER 30

Royce's lips hold no warmth. They don't press back against mine. They harden at my touch.

The force of the knife driving into Royce's back knocks me away from him, but Royce doesn't move. His golden arms reach for me, and even the blood on his face has frozen. He sports the smallest look of surprise.

Captain Skulls cries out in frustration as the knife clatters to the deck and slides away toward a line of barrels, which must mean I turned Royce in time.

The first part of my plan has worked. I've saved Royce.

I lock eyes with Captain Skulls over Royce's shoulder. His lips are pulled back in a snarl, and he looks as if he's going to kill me with his bare hands.

He takes one step toward me.

The ship lurches violently, falling even more to one side.

Captain Skulls disappears down the deck. I don't know if he hits the railing and goes overboard or not because I'm too busy watching Royce's statue skid away. All I can picture is Royce joining Aris at the bottom of the sea.

I slide after him.

I grab his outstretched hand before he can tumble into the railing.

"Are you all right?" I ask the moment the gold drains back into my body. I search his face for any signs of insanity. Will he react like the guard? Will he jump into the ocean screaming about getting the gold off his body? I tighten my grip on his hand.

His eyes are wide, blinking against the sunlight. "Is that how most of your kisses go? No wonder you scared all your suitors away," he jokes.

Instantly, my shoulders relax. He's going to be fine.

I would smack his arm with my gloved hand and tell him that's not funny, but the ship seems to be tilting more and more by the moment. Our feet keep slipping before finding their traction, taking us closer and closer to the water. The mast above us groans. Rhat's words come back to me; I definitely don't want to be standing here when it falls. If the mast didn't kill us, getting trapped under the sails could.

Royce eyes the mast before jumping to me, to the cut on my arm. "What happened?"

"I had to absorb the gold somehow." It's still bleeding and hurts to move, but there is a bigger problem: I still have the gold inside me. I wince as the pounding pressure builds up again. It pulsates right behind my eyes, likes it's urging them to find another target already.

Royce must read my expression. "You need something else to turn to gold?"

I nod. We're still holding hands. I'm afraid if I let go and fall, he'll reach out to grab me, to save me, and then the gold will adhere to him again, dragging him to the bottom of the ocean.

Royce spots the knife where it landed not far from us.

"Hold on." He waits until I'm stable and slides down the deck toward the knife. Then, he crawls back toward me. He holds it out for me, and I wrap my fingers around the blade. The gold drains out of me, and as soon as it does, the ache in my arm flares up in its place.

I suck in a sharp breath.

But something else drowns out the sound. The masts creak as the ship continues to tilt toward the sea. Several of the ropes attached to the rigging snap off the main mast only a few feet from us. We duck to avoid the wooden splinters.

"We've got to get away from that mast." Royce takes the knife from me, tucking it into his belt. "Come on. We're going to have to jump off the ship." He scans the deck we're on, looking for the best option. "We need to get up there." Royce points to the helm on the next deck up, where the ship's railing hasn't yet been swallowed by the water.

I look to where he means. If we jump from there, we won't risk hitting the railing like we will here. And at least we'll be away from the main mast if it falls, although the shorter mast up there doesn't look any more stable.

"We can climb over the railing there," Royce continues, "and we'll be closer to the back of the ship and can hopefully swim free before that mizzenmast snaps. But we've got to hurry."

As I cradle my injured arm, Royce tucks me against him, helping me keep my balance as we struggle up the deck to the staircase leading up to the helm that isn't underwater yet. I'm only vaguely aware of the gold buttons gleaming down his jacket and the knife in his belt as we jostle forward.

Royce lets go as we both brace ourselves and fight up the tilted steps. He keeps glancing back to make sure I'm doing all right.

A salty breeze pushes me up the steps, while behind me, the main mast groans again.

"Hurry," Royce says. He reaches out for the hand that still has the glove on it.

I take his hand and dash up the final steps. We cling to the side of the ship.

"Stay close, and don't let go as we work our way toward the railing," Royce says.

So we don't slide full force into the other side of the ship, we latch onto the rungs running in front of the helm and inch toward the ship's wheel. As we get closer, I realize it's not a normal ship's wheel made of wooden pegs. No, this wheel has a skull at its center. Around it, long bones shoot out at even intervals to a wooden outer wheel, and where pegs used to turn the wheel should sit, human skulls have been put in their place.

My stomach recoils. I look away. Just as I do, a flurry of movement catches my eye.

Captain Skulls has snuck up the steps behind us. He stares at me with a snarl on his face.

Before I can warn Royce, there's a loud crack, followed by several thousand smaller cracks as the mizzenmast above us splinters in two. The broken portion collapses into the ocean, but beams and debris rain toward us.

"Look out," I cry as part of a lower sail still attached to a beam falls straight toward Royce. I shove him out of the way, sending him tumbling down the deck. The sail comes down between us like a shroud, and the beam crashes into the helm, sending bones, wood, and skulls spilling around my feet.

But that's not the worst part. I hadn't been thinking when I'd shoved Royce out of the way. I'd been so eager to get him to move that I'd reached out with my ungloved hand. And I must've touched one of his golden buttons because gold is pounding around inside me, begging to be set free.

But before I can search for something to transfer the gold to, a sound behind me catches my attention. I whip around to find Captain Skulls not far away. He slides down the deck toward me, grabbing a pointed piece of debris.

He advances quickly. I duck down as he swings the piece of wood toward me. I try to scramble away, but my feet are caught in the sail. I lose my balance and put my hands down to steady myself.

But I don't pay attention to where my hands land. Instantly, the gold drains out of me.

Panicked, I look down to see it's found its way into one of the cracked skulls from the broken wheel.

Captain Skulls's shadow falls over me.

My heart stops.

There's no time to think, to find a weapon. I slide my fingers into the skull's eyeholes. In one swift move as I straighten, I use the momentum of my body to carry my arms around as I smash the golden skull into Captain Skulls's temple.

It connects with a sickening crunch of bone on bone.

Captain Skulls's eyes roll up, and he crumples at my feet. His body collapses into the sail, pulling part of it down around him. Blood gushes out of the spot where the skull connected with his head before eventually slowing to a trickle. I stand there a few moments to make sure he doesn't rise, but his chest has stopped moving. I drop the golden skull at his feet, finally giving him what he always wanted.

And now it is time for me to get what I want.

I take a breath and scan the deck. Royce is fighting his way up the deck toward me. He's got the golden knife in one hand and the other pressed against his ribs.

I climb over the fallen sail and slide toward him. "Are you okay?"

He nods. "I just hit the railing hard. I'll be fine. What about Captain Skulls?"

He scans the deck, ready for an attack.

"He's dead," I say, looking back to where his feet are visible in the tangled sail.

"Then let's get off this boat." Royce tucks the knife away and takes my hand. "Can you swim with your injured arm?"

I nod. I don't think I have much choice.

We scoot down the deck until the railing bites into us. The water is so close. The part of the mast that broke off floats not too far out from the boat, surrounded by other debris.

Royce helps me climb up the railing before following. "Swim as hard as you can away from the ship," he says. He takes my hand and gives me one reassuring smile. Then we're vaulting forward into the water.

I lose his hand as soon as the water swallows us. Bubbles cloud around us. Salt water stings my arm, threatening to paralyze it. I fight my way to the surface, my arm burning with every movement. When I emerge, I can hear Royce splashing beside me.

I'm not sure if it's the waves or the pull of the boat sinking under, but I feel like I'm not making much headway. My arm throbs and more and more salt water seems to enter my bloodstream with every movement.

I'm not sure how many more strokes I can take.

Then, Royce is there. His hair is plastered over his face, and he whips it away. He pulls me farther from the sinking boat. "Just float on your back," he says. He waits for me to kick my feet up before doing the same.

I let the water cradle me. After a few moments, the sound of splashing oars rouses me, and I see the spare longboat from the *Swanflight*.

Rhat and Phipps lean over the edge as they near us.

"Careful of her arm," Royce warns as they pull me into the boat. He heaves himself up next to me as Rhat and Phipps turn the boat around.

We give the sinking pirate ship a wide berth on our way back to the *Swanflight*. The sails with the skulls painted on them have already sunk. I couldn't be happier that I'll never have to see them again, or their captain. No more dreading closing my eyes and ending up in his cabin. No more skulls watching my every move. No more fear of the gold being lost forever.

Soon, the ocean swallows what remains of Captain Skulls's ship, the waves calming. It looks like another beautiful, peaceful morning.

Weary but happy faces greet us aboard the *Swanflight*. Most have cuts and bruises, but even still, a cheer goes up as Royce steps aboard, the last one to return to the ship. Their captain is back, and they've won the day.

Hettie lets out a relieved sigh when she sees me. Ignoring the pain in my arm, I pull her into a hug, and it already feels like I have my family back. And when I get home, I'll hand the gold back to my father. Even though I'll have to be wearing gloves while I do it, my father will see that I'm not afraid. Maybe, just maybe, that'll be enough to show him that he can fight the hold it has over him.

Because sometimes all it takes is knowing you're not in it alone, that you have a crew who's got your back. I look around the ship. The men aren't cowering away from me. They're celebrating at my side.

I hoist my hand in the air and whoop and holler along with the rest of the crew because we're safe, we have the gold, and we're going home.

CHAPTER 31

The journey back to Lagonia stretches on. Ten days feel like a decade. I stick to my cabin, giving the men room to grieve their losses, to hold their funerals without the reminder of the reason they died gleaming in front of them.

It gives me time to visit my father.

I hoped he would grow stronger as the gold grew closer, but I don't notice much change in him. When I visit, I notice his lips have lost any color they held, and his skin is nearly transparent. I can't bear to stay long at his side, afraid his chest will cease moving entirely.

I always return to my body drained.

At least I'm sleeping through the night. I thought having the gold on board would be the cause of a lot of restless nights. But I barely even notice the aura anymore.

I do notice the looks Royce gives me, quick glances before looking away. We haven't really spoken much since the battle. Since I kissed him.

I convince myself it's for the best. After we make port, Royce will return to his life at sea, and I'll go back to life in the palace. That will be that. Why fight the inevitable?

But Hettie doesn't seem to share my feelings.

She bursts into the cabin one afternoon while I'm reading.

"There's going to be dancing tonight since we make port tomorrow," she says, swaying about the room and rummaging through my trunk for something she can fit into. "You're coming," she continues, straightening and holding one of my dresses across her body. "You need to get out of this cabin. You're starting to look pale . . . well, paler gold." She drops the dress and begins rummaging again. She reemerges with a red dress. She tosses it at me. "Put it on."

"I can't . . ."

She crosses her arms and stares at me. "Don't make me put it on you myself."

I run my hands over the silky fabric, the feeling reminding me of my nearly forgotten days as a princess. I force myself to meet her gaze. "We're not going to see them again. After tomorrow." There's no nice way of putting it.

Hettie acts as if I haven't spoken. She pulls a blue dress with a flared skirt over her head. "If you're not up there in ten minutes, I'm telling my father it was your idea to bring me on this trip." She smirks and flounces out of the room before I can reply.

That was our biggest threat when we were younger, one of us telling Uncle Pheus on the other. My father let us have the run of the palace. It was Uncle Pheus we had to watch out for.

I can't help but laugh.

Then I moan. My arm still hurts, but Royce wrapped it nicely after Hettie sewed it up. Who knew all those embroidery lessons about tiny stitches would actually be good for something someday?

I stare down at my arms, at the skin I always thought was ugly. But I'm not that same girl anymore. Royce helped me see past that.

And since I'm made of gold, I should start acting like it for once. I was made to shine. If I crawl back to the shadows now, I'll never make it out again.

Part of me doesn't care if Royce breaks my heart. I know I'll regret it if I don't see him tonight before I'm stuck inside the palace again.

I grab the dress and haul myself out of bed. After I've changed and pulled my hair loose from its braid, I stop in front of the mirror on the wall.

An unexpected face greets me. It's been so long since I've seen anything other than the distorted reflection I'd catch in the palace windows or in the fountains. I look older, more like my mother does in her portrait. I run my bare hand over my cheek, then fan my hair out across my shoulders. It shimmers as it catches the light filtering in through the window.

I smile at myself before I make my way up to the deck.

Music drifts through the air, though there's a distinct lack of accordion music. When I emerge into the twilight, Thipps's accordion has been placed on a barrel between the other musicians. Phipps stands next to it.

The men cheer when they see me arrive. I smile and wave, but then look away before I notice all the missing crew members.

Phipps is the first to approach. He's a little tipsy. "I've never danced with a princess before," he says. "I'm thinking I'm never going to get another chance. Will you dance with me?" He bows and offers me his hand.

His eyes are full of hope. When he smiles, I notice one of his front teeth is missing, and I'm pretty sure it was there before the battle the other day. But it's one of the nicest smiles I've ever seen.

I take his hand with a grand flourish, and he pulls me out onto the dance floor. His dancing style is more spinning in circles than anything formal. I find it's much more fun than anything my tutors ever tried to teach me.

"Thank you for saving me during the fight," I say.

"I *had* to." Phipps hiccups. "I couldn't let Thipps be the only one to do it, you know? Everyone would only remember his hero . . . heroics." He hiccups out that last word.

He spins me around, nearly losing his grip on my hand before pulling me back in.

"You should really feel sorry for me," Phipps says. "Thipps died a hero, and now I've got to spend every day trying to top that. I'm not certain he didn't stab himself just so he could look like the better brother."

I can't help but offer him a small smile as we twirl around the cramped area circled in by sailors.

Phipps only steps on my foot once, which throws us off balance, though he doesn't seem to notice. He just keeps spinning, but I'm not sure how much longer we'll stay upright.

Then a hand clamps each of us on the shoulder. "Careful there," Royce says. "We don't want to have to tell the king his daughter survived the Temptresses of Triton and Captain Skulls only to be done in by your dancing."

The crew laughs.

Phipps half laughs, half hiccups.

"Aye, Captain." He spins off on his own, bragging about how he got to dance with a princess and how Thipps couldn't say that.

I'm left staring at Royce.

"May I?" He offers me his hand as though we're standing in the palace ballroom.

I swallow. There's no way to back out now.

I take his hand, and he sweeps me into his arms, leading me into a dance that's a mixture of formal steps and free spinning. It's easy to catch on.

His touch is light but reassuring, and he's careful not to put too much pressure on my injured arm.

I look up into his face, into the eyes I'd always thought held cruelty and deceit but were really hiding pain. They're kinder now.

I'm hoping that means he's not mad. "I'm sorry I turned you to gold," I say softly. I stare squarely at his chest. "I know it's a terrifying place to be. It was the only way I could think to protect you from Captain Skulls's blade."

"It wasn't pleasant," he admits. "But I think that the real reason I hated it so much was because it meant I couldn't get to you. I couldn't stop Skulls from hurting you."

He gently sways against me, changing the direction we're heading.

I forget a step because I'm replaying his words again. He cares more about me than being turned to gold.

"Looks like you've been drinking whatever Phipps has been drinking," he jokes.

He twirls me out and then pulls me back in, catching me in his arms. "That was much better."

I laugh.

I almost wish I could freeze us in this moment. I don't want the sun to set. I don't want the morning to come. I don't want to say good-bye.

Because just like that, it's over when Royce says, "I've got your father's gold locked away in a large chest all ready for tomorrow."

"Thank you," I force myself to reply. "For everything."

Around us, the sky has become a mix of pinks and oranges. There are even hints of gold tucked away behind some of the clouds. He notices me watching the sunset and angles us so I can see it better. But I can't enjoy it. It only reminds me how little time I have left outside the palace, and I hate myself for thinking it. My father needs the gold back. I need to go back.

But I'm going to miss this. I'm going to miss him.

He smiles down at me. "You've given me my life back. I feel like you've given me the world."

It's funny. I could say the same thing about him.

We become lost in the tempo of the music. It's slower than when I danced with Phipps.

Royce draws me closer to his body, and I look up at him. He's smiling softly, almost wistfully. I wonder how much he misses court life and dancing. I wonder if he'd ever come back to it. Come back with me.

I lower my gaze to his chest because I can't ask that of him. Even if I could, the music stops before I can say the words.

We both hesitate a moment before dropping our arms.

"I'd ask for another dance, but I'm pretty sure my crew would mutiny if I kept you to myself all evening." He bows low, kissing my hand. A tingle runs up my arm.

I curtsy, but the movement is clumsy. I want to make some joke about how at least he didn't turn to gold that time when he kissed me. But by the time I straighten, he's already striding across the deck, and I'm being swallowed by a circle of men all eager to dance with a princess. Even one made of gold.

I pick a random arm reaching out to me as the music starts up again and Hettie and Rhat go twirling past.

As I spin away, I see Royce watching me from the edge of the circle. His eyes never leave me.

I try to keep his gaze, but I keep spinning around and around until he becomes a blur.

〉〉〉〉〉〉〉〉〉〉◎〈〈〈〈〈〈〈〈〈〈〈〈

CHAPTER 32

A light wind blows freely across the deck as morning dawns and Lagonia comes into sight. The city rises above the sea, and sunrays fall around it, shrouding the palace in light. It's unchanged from when I left, and yet everything feels different somehow.

The buildings stand tall, saluting me, their victorious princess. Except no one can ever know the real reason I left, if they know I left at all. That doesn't mean things can't be different, though. I know my father will see that when I give him the gold back.

I run my fingers across the necklace Royce gave me and take one last look around the deck of the *Swanflight* as we approach the entrance to the harbor. Hettie's perched atop a barrel eating a pickle next to Rhat, and Phipps waves to me from his spot in the replaced rigging. I wave in return. Royce cuts a striking figure at the helm as the wind ruffles his hair. He looks so much more relaxed now. I wish I felt that relaxed.

He comes over carrying a long chest as we turn toward the opening of the harbor, and I don't have to ask what's in it. It's got an inner glow that makes it look like he's locked up the sun. At least to me.

"Ready?"

Before I can answer, Hettie does. "I'm not going." She slides off the barrel and saunters over.

I sigh. I should've known she'd be nervous to see her father after running away.

"I'm sure your father missed you," I say. "He'll be so overjoyed to see you that he won't punish you."

Hettie shakes her head. "I don't want to see him. I've never been as happy as I was these past few weeks on the *Swanflight*. He'll take that away and never let me leave ever again."

"You can't hide on the ship forever," I counter.

"I don't know. I've gotten pretty good at hiding in barrels."

"Come on." I hold my hand out to her. "We're in this together. Besides, I bet there's bound to be a big feast tonight."

Hettie stares at my outstretched hand. I always could tempt her with food. She's about to take my hand, but before she does, cannon fire echoes across the harbor. A cannonball crashes into the water mere feet in front of the ship, sending up a plume of water.

Royce drops the chest and reaches out to steady me. Hettie falls to the deck. The ship descends into shouting and chaos.

"What was that?" Rhat calls as we sail into the harbor.

Inside the harbor, half the armada waits. The ship closest to us still has smoke floating away from one of its cannons.

"Why are they firing at us?" Hettie asks, climbing to her feet.

"Maybe they think we're pirates," I say. I run to the railing and wave my arms, hoping seeing a golden girl will stop them from firing instead of encouraging it.

"Stop," I scream at the nearest ship. "Stop, I'm Princess Kora." I know the men on the ship can hear me. They're close enough that I can almost make out their faces.

A second shot rings out, landing several feet away again. I grab the railing to stay on my feet.

"Get away from there," Royce pulls me back. "I don't think they believe we're pirates. I think they know exactly who we are."

"But . . ." I trail off. Why would Uncle Pheus have the armada fire on us?

He wouldn't. Which can only mean . . .

"Archduke Ralton," I breathe. Just when I thought I was done with every connection to Aris, his uncle has to ruin everything.

"Do you want us to fire back?" Royce asks.

Numbly, I stare down the gauntlet the armada has created leading up to the dock. There's no way our one ship can take out all of them. I can't imagine the lives that would be lost. On both sides.

I shake my head.

Royce keeps his hands on my shoulders as he shouts, "Rhat, run up the white flag of surrender."

"Do we have one of those, Captain?" Rhat asks.

"Make one," Royce replies.

My stomach feels like a cannonball blasted right through it. If Archduke Ralton has command of the armada, he must be in control of the palace. I don't know what this means for my father and Uncle Pheus. My father had been so weak when I'd last visited him. I can't stop the tears that slip down my cheeks.

Royce wraps his arms around me, and I bury my face against his chest. His heart beats, strong and pure. It's the most comforting sound in the world.

The sounds of men shouting, unneeded cannonballs being dropped, and feet stomping across the deck blur to the background.

I'm not sure how long we stay that way. It doesn't feel like very long before a man wearing the uniform of a Lagonian soldier rips us apart and shoves us toward a small boat. He makes Royce carry the gold since none of the soldiers want to touch it.

Hettie, Rhat, Royce, the gold, and I end up in one boat. Once we reach land, we're herded into a cart, where one of the soldiers forces a cloak on me, pulling the hood low.

I don't bother resisting.

No royal welcome awaits us at the palace. Only one of my father's stewards and a group of soldiers standing in two lines down the steps greet us. The steward ushers us quickly up the steps. Guards fall in around us.

I'm not sure where they've taken the rest of the crew.

"Please," I whisper to the steward, "is my father alive?"

He doesn't answer. He continues leading the way deeper into the palace.

"Please, I just want to know . . ."

The steward stops in front of a large set of doors. They don't lead to the main hall. They lead to the council room.

"You're to go in alone," the steward says.

"No." Royce steps forward.

So do several armed guards.

"It's all right." I put my hand out to stop him. I have only one bargaining chip, and his life is something I'm going to be bargaining for. I need him alive.

I slide the chest of gold from his grip. It's heavy, but I can manage until I can put it on the table inside.

With one final look around what's left of our crew, I enter the room.

The musty scent of an unused room overwhelms me. Dust

particles float around in the shafts of sunlight. Long tapestries cover the walls, and a thick red carpet muffles my steps as I venture farther inside. The fireplace nestled in the wall is unlit, and no speck of burnt ash indicates its usage. Large windows frame the door to the balcony at the far end of the room where my father used to give proclamations years ago. But the room and balcony have sat unused since The Touch came to my father.

I can't imagine why Ralton wants to meet me here unless he wants me to make some proclamation from the balcony about how weak my father is and how he's handing over the throne. Or how cursed I am.

The door clicks shut behind me.

When my eyes adjust to the light, to my surprise, it's not Ralton I see sitting at the far end of the long table that dominates the room.

It's my father.

He sits in an ornate wooden chair, hunched forward, his crown barely stable on his head. The beard he's grown in my absence looks even more unkempt than when I last saw it.

I drop the chest and rush forward.

"Father." The word tastes foreign in my mouth. I hesitate only a moment before kneeling and reaching out to touch his arm. His head lifts slightly, looking for the source, but it rolls back down. He looks as though he's aged decades.

I shake my head in disbelief. The gold is back. He's supposed to be fine. He's supposed to be better. I take solace in the fact that at least he was able to make it all the way here. Maybe he just needs more time close to the gold to regain his strength.

"Don't worry," I say. "I'll find a way to fix this." I rub his arm soothingly.

"You've done quite enough already," a voice behind me says.

I whip around to find Uncle Pheus. I didn't even hear him come in. For all I know, he could've been sitting in one of the chairs flanking the doors this whole time.

"Uncle Pheus," I say, relief flooding through me. "You're all right."

"Indeed," he says.

He doesn't appear injured, but his hair looks grayer than I remember.

"We need to find a way out of here," I say. "Captain Royce and his first mate are just outside. Together we might be able to overpower the guards before Archduke Ralton arrives."

He shakes his head. "I'm afraid we're not going anywhere."

"We have to try. I don't care about fighting for the throne. As long as we escape, that's all that matters."

Uncle Pheus sighs. It's the same sigh he used when he had to explain something to me as a child. "I had my doubts you'd make it back alive, but you're to be commended." He picks up the chest, carrying it to the end of the table opposite me. The chest lands with a thud. He pockets the key sticking out of the lock. Then, he moves down the opposite side of the table. Closer to me. "And to think, none of this would have been possible if you hadn't suffered part of your father's curse."

"I can handle the gold now," I say, rising from my father's side. "We can fight against Ralton."

"I had Archduke Ralton executed this morning for his role in your kidnapping."

I shake my head confused. "I wasn't kidnapped."

"As far as anyone else is concerned, you were, resulting in a battle here in our very own harbor." He points out the windows to where the armada is still visible. "Fortunately, the pirates were caught and are on their way to the dungeon now."

A scuffle sounds in the hallway outside the door. I hear Royce yell something about not going anywhere without me, but I can't make out the rest of what's said.

"No." I shake my head—he isn't making any sense.

"Unfortunately, my men were too late to save our dear princess. And your poor father died out of grief. Don't worry. I'll give you both a moving eulogy."

I stare at him in disbelief. "You . . . you ordered the armada to fire on the *Swanflight*?"

He shrugs his shoulders noncommittally. "It's time Lagonia had a real king."

My mind's reeling. "He's your brother. You've taken care of him all these years."

"After years of watching him waste away and ruin this country, I couldn't take it any longer," Uncle Pheus says. "Then when I heard that fool Ralton was trying to raise an army, I couldn't let him take it away from me. I had to secure the monarchy. I had it all planned out. The gold would fade away and so would my brother."

"I thought you cared about Lagonia, about my father," I say, shocked that he could have deceived me for so long.

"That Oracle got it wrong. It should've been me from the very beginning. I didn't even think Midas would make it out of those mountains with that stupid donkey. I was going to start a new life on my own, but they went and made him king."

I stare at my uncle as though I'm seeing him for the first time.

"He's a shadow. He's *my* shadow," he continues. "I've been the real king for years. It's time to make it official in name."

I race toward the door. Pheus makes no move to stop me. I pull on the handles. The door doesn't budge. My next thought is that I need a weapon, so I hurry over to the chest that holds the gold; but it's locked.

"You really don't have a fear of gold now, do you?" Pheus grabs the chest. He hefts it up and tosses it through the window. The chest skids across the broken glass out onto the balcony and crashes into the low stone railing already decayed from years of disuse. Shards of stone crumble down on top of the chest as it comes to a stop.

"No," I scream.

"I wouldn't let that out of my sight," Pheus says, pointing out the window toward the chest. "What do you think would happen if it fell off the balcony? All that broken and chipped gold. Maybe all that damage will be enough to send your father over the edge. Too bad it didn't happen the first time I had someone steal it."

I look at the pale form of my father unmoving in his chair. Another blow to the gold might be too much for him to withstand.

Anger swells up inside me, fueling my words. "I can't believe you let those thieves into the palace." I try to keep him talking while I come up with a plan of my own, but everything in the room is too big or too useless to use as a weapon.

He laughs. "It was almost too easy. When I interrogated Duke Wystlinos about the treaty and his involvement with Captain Skulls, he broke after less than a day. I knew not executing him would indebt him to me. Of course, after I learned about your connection to the gold, I ordered him to kill you at sea, but he must've gotten it in his head to see what you could do. Same as that greedy pirate. I instructed him to leave all the gold with the Temptresses of Triton in exchange for my armada leaving him alone for a time. But I'd already assumed he would end up being greedy. I just figured as long as the gold was gone, that was good enough. All I wasn't counting on was you.

"You were too weak to pose a threat to my rule, but your ability to sense the gold ruined my original plan. I would have shipped you off to some secluded location where no one would know to look for you." He produces a knife with a big ruby on its hilt from beneath his jacket. "I didn't want it to come to this, but you've left me no other choice."

I stare at him openmouthed. How can this be happening? I trusted him. My insides feel like they've been turned to gold. "You . . . you wouldn't," I stammer.

He glares at me. "At least you managed not to turn Captain Royce to gold, so I'll still have someone to pin your murder on."

I take jagged breaths as I stagger back around the table so we're on opposite sides. "Just let us go. You don't need us. You have the throne."

He shakes his head. "I have to explain the battle in the harbor somehow, and I won't spend my reign looking over my shoulder, waiting for you to return. I'm sorry, Kora, but this is how it has to end now." His jaw clenches as he tightens his grip on his knife. It's the same resolute look he always wears when his mind is made up.

I swallow and edge toward my father, my heartbeat thudding in my chest. I need to get him out of here—now—and for that, I still need a plan. I stall for time. "I'm surprised you're not like the rest of them," I say, "wanting to lock me away so I can turn anything you want to gold."

Pheus matches me step for step across the table.

My eyes dart to the balcony door. I hate that I'm leading him closer to my father, but I need to secure that gold. And as bulky as the chest is, it might act as a shield.

And if I can get to the balcony, someone might hear my cries for help.

My father mumbles and opens his eyes at my approach. A hazy fog clouds his eyes.

"Money makes men weak," Pheus says. "I'm not looking for unlimited wealth. I'll settle for the kingdom. I don't need gold that's destroyed everyone who's touched it, like that poor guard you condemned to die in the tower. He went crazy after what you did to him. You're a murderer, Kora, you're not any different than I am."

I shake my head. "No."

"That man drowned himself because of you."

It doesn't make any sense. I'd turned other people to gold and none of them had suffered such severe side effects. "You're lying."

"Am I? Or is that what you want to believe?" He takes several steps to keep in line with me.

"The gold doesn't do that to people. I know now what it can and can't do." It's not entirely true. But I know enough to know that turning him to gold for a few short seconds shouldn't have had that effect.

Pheus softly laughs. "Well, then you caught me. I killed him." He shrugs, like this admission carries no guilt, no remorse. "We would've lost the throne if he'd gone running around telling the world what kind of monster my niece was. I had to do it to protect us."

"You did it to protect yourself." I take a few more steps, keeping both him and the balcony door in sight. "There'll be no one protecting you when the kingdom learns what you've done." I'm nearing the end of the table. Then it's only a few feet of open space to the balcony door.

"That's why they're not going to find out."

The door to the room rattles. "Kora," a voice calls from the other side. "Kora, are you all right?" It's Royce.

I want to call out to him, but I make a better use of his distraction. I run to the balcony doors and throw them open, racing for the gold.

A strong wind tugs at me, promising to steal my pleas for help. Below, buildings and streets form a maze all the way to the ocean. It's dizzying. I focus on the chest, grabbing it quickly and hoisting it up. All my effort goes into keeping the chest aloft, especially when the cut on my arm starts to ache. I turn back toward the doorway, but Pheus is there, blocking my escape.

"You'll never be king," I spit. I'm trying to draw him out, get him away from my father for as long as possible.

His knife glints as he moves closer.

Knowing I can't hold the chest much longer or dodge his attacks under its weight, I hurl the chest at his head.

He ducks out of the way, and the chest sails through the doorway, smashing into a chair inside.

"You just threw away your only weapon," he says. "You never did have a head for strategy."

I charge at him. I try to wrestle the knife from him, but his other hand streaks out, grabbing my arm right where Captain Skulls sliced it.

I cry out. My knees buckle.

"One should always kneel before their king." He digs his fingers into the cut.

I try to get at least one of my legs around to kick him with, but he yanks down on my arm.

He points his knife between my collarbones. But before he can bury the blade in my throat, the pressure disappears from my arm as Pheus crashes to the ground at my feet. His knife goes sputtering across the balcony, and my first thought is that Royce has come to save me.

But it's not Royce towering over the figure of my uncle.

It's my father.

Somehow he's found the strength to stand. His hands are wrapped around the broken seat of a chair, and he pants with the effort it takes to remain upright. His hunched shoulders pull him closer to the ground, and I catch him in my arms as I stand. He's lost so much weight that he's not hard to hold.

He drops the splintered chair fragment. "Pheus told me you were dead," he says. He pulls me to his chest and wraps his arms around me as best he can. "I knew you weren't."

His scraggly beard scratches my forehead.

"I'm so sorry," he says. "All these years I thought I was doing you a favor by staying away where I couldn't hurt you anymore. This is all my fault." Tears splash down on my hair.

They're mirrored by my own tears. I swallow a lump in my throat. "Let's get you back inside where you can rest," I say. "There will be time for talking later." I prop my good arm under his shoulder as we move toward the door.

I hear something behind me. I turn just in time to see Pheus rise, blood running from the side of his face, as he picks up his knife.

"You never should've been king," he shouts, brandishing his weapon. "It always should have been me." He lumbers toward us.

I shove my father inside, and he lands on all fours inside the room. Then I duck as Pheus swipes his knife at me.

Wind whips at my dress as I stumble across the balcony for the chair fragment. I bring it up just in time to stop Pheus's dagger from digging into me. The metal rips through the wood, embedding itself.

Pheus fights to get his dagger free, but I keep my grip on the chair seat. Pheus uses that to his advantage and whips me around. We stumble toward the edge. He yanks back again, trying to free the knife, but it doesn't budge. Pheus switches tactics, using all his strength to drive the knife forward instead and sending me reeling backward to keep the blade from plunging farther through the wood and into my chest. The crumbling railing rears up. I cry out, but Pheus doesn't stop his mad drive. I barely register crashing into the low railing before his momentum carries us over in a cloud of broken stone. The world reels as we tumble over the ledge, and I lose my grip on the chair fragment.

I scramble for anything to hang on to. I catch one hand on the bottom of the remaining balcony railing and cry out as my arm jerks my body to a stop.

The wind takes Pheus's screams as he falls.

My arm burns, my fingers slip, and it takes every ounce of my willpower not to look down. I kick my legs against the slanted bottom of the balcony, feeling for some fragment to stabilize myself on. There's nothing. The wind readies itself to surge up and claim me too. It makes my legs sway like the headless bodies I'd seen on the Island of Lost Souls, and I struggle to keep my grip.

My fingers cramp up, and I realize the longer I hang here, the more strength I waste.

"Kora?" my father's voice filters out to me. "Where are you?"

His voice is the push I need.

I swing my other arm around and grab the balcony. I claw my way upward. Fire flashes through every inch of my arm, and all I can hear is the rushing of my blood as it courses through me.

Rough rock scrapes against my already scarred hands, and pebbles dig into my flesh. I get a hand wrapped around the top and cry out as I heave myself upward.

I crawl onto the balcony just as the door at the other end of the room splinters open and Royce bursts in. He rushes toward me, sweeping me into his arms. When he's set me firmly on the ground, I melt against him, letting his strength be enough for both of us.

Behind him, Rhat helps my father into a chair.

"Are you all right?" Royce asks. I can feel his heart pounding beneath his chest.

I nod, still shaking from the combination of hanging from the balcony and learning that my uncle has betrayed us all.

"I was so worried I'd lost you." Gently, he tilts my chin up. He leans forward, brushing his lips against mine. And unlike when I'd turned him to gold, he doesn't freeze at my touch. The way his lips press against me sends sparks flying around inside my body, almost as if I'd absorbed gold. Except this feels pure. This feels right.

All the coldness that the gold's brought to my life over the years has melted away, replaced by the heat left behind by being in Royce's arms.

Royce pulls away. His eyes open slowly. They find mine. He stares down at me and smiles.

"Well, that went better than last time," he says.

Despite everything that just happened, I smile back.

I spot the chest of gold sitting in a pile of broken wood, and behind it, the smashed door rests askew on its bottom hinge.

So many things have been broken. But now that I'm home, they can finally be repaired.

Behind Royce, Hettie enters the room. Her cheeks are flushed. She sheaths her sword and tries to tame the hairs that have fallen out of place during the scuffle in the hallway. The sword looks at home on her hip now, and I wonder if she'll ever take it off.

"Hettie . . ." I start to say.

"Don't." She holds up a hand. She blinks rapidly, fighting back tears. "I heard most of it, but I just had to know if . . ." Her voice cracks when she sees the empty balcony. She doesn't finish her sentence. Slowly, she backtracks through the room. She doesn't start running until she's out in the hallway.

Guilt flashes through me. I want to follow her, to comfort her, but I'm not sure she'll want to see me right now. I would've saved her father if I could have, and I know Hettie will recognize that. But I also know she'll need time to grieve, even for a father she claimed never loved her. So, although it tears me up inside not to go, I let Rhat be the one to rush after her. If there's anyone that can help her through this, it's him.

Sighing, I turn my attention back to my father.

Royce helps him over to me.

"Thank you," my father says to Royce. He gives me another long hug.

The three of us stand there looking out over the balcony. I squeeze Royce's hand and wrap my other arm around my father to help support him.

He's going to need all the support he can get in the coming months while he regains his strength. But I'll be there for him—and for Hettie. I'll be the princess I always should've been. United, we'll put the kingdom back together. We'll put our lives back together. We'll find a way to forget about the past.

And as the salty breeze drifts in, calling out to me, I know I'll answer that call—because as soon as things get back to normal, I'll set out to find a way to cleanse the cursed objects. I'll find a way to get rid of the power The Touch still has over me and my father once and for all.

ACKNOWLEDGMENTS

First and foremost, I have to thank and give all praise and glory to God, Jesus, the Blessed Virgin Mary, and the angels and Saints, without whom I wouldn't be here today.

Thank you to my amazing family—Dad (John), Mom (Meg), Katie, Patrick, Michael S., Danny, John, Maggie, Michael K., and Mittens—for always being there for me and making me who I am today. I love you all!

Special shout-out to my parents, who allowed me to dream and who have supported me through everything. To my dad for always supporting me and for inspiring me to travel the world, and to my mom for reading me so many fairy tales when I was a child. I wouldn't have the imagination I do without you. *SWAK*!

To my wonderful, loving, amazing sister, Katie, who gets her own separate paragraph for reading every single draft, for brainstorming with me, and for all those nights she stayed up super late to read. You're always my first reader, and I know I can always count on you to tell it like it is . . . and to find my silly mistakes.

Also, thanks to my extended family for your support! And to my niece and nephews for keeping me young. Your EE loves you!

Thank you to my agent extraordinaire, Christa Heschke. You took a chance on me, and I can't wait for our journey to continue together! I love your editorial eye and all you do to make my stories shine.

To my AMAZING editor, Jillian Manning. This book wouldn't be what it is without you. Your insights and ideas brought new life to it, and I'm so happy that I got to work with you.

To everyone at Blink—Hannah VanVels (thanks for your great and entertaining comments!), Jacque Alberta (what would I do without your eagle eyes???), Ron Huizinga, Marcus Drenth, Annette Bourland, and Sara Merritt. Your team made publishing my book such a seamless process.

To my amazing critique partner, Liz Osisek, who read countless drafts and other materials every hour of the day when I needed her to. I couldn't have done this without you and your insights. You dropped everything to help me, and I can't wait to do the same for you. I owe you more ice cream than you could ever eat.

Also, thank you to fellow writers and authors Jessica FairOwens and Triona Murphy for reading early drafts. You girls rock! Also to amazing fellow authors John Green, Dee Romito, Brenda Drake, Sarah Glenn Marsh, Emily R. King, Wendy Higgens, Ashley Poston, Elly Blake, Summer Heacock, Sarah Cannon, and Sarah Schmitt, who shared wisdom, advice, and friendship with me. Also to Jean Heck, Gavin Cahill, Gail Werner, Rebekah Snyder, Cathy Shouse, Whitney Eklof, Ashley Hearn, Bethany Robison, and Carla Luna Cullen for sharing their advice and friendship over the years.

To everyone (professors, faculty, and fellow students) at the Butler University MFA in Creative Writing program who helped me shape this novel into what it is today. I couldn't have done this without such a great program that encourages writers in every genre. Special shout-outs to my thesis advisors Michael Dahlie and Allison Lynn, who helped me see the potential in this novel early on. You both encouraged me, and I count myself lucky that you found your way to Butler.

To all those who prayed for me, especially my CRHP sisters, Father Jim, and Father Hunter!

To "the wind beneath my wings:" Ashley Zurcher, Laura Goldsberry, Jennifer Goldsmith, Clint Lahnen, and Tara Trubela. We make a great team! Also, please pay special attention to my use of the Oxford comma. Remember to use it wherever you go. Also to Paul Chen (@of_Mice_andChen), Eric Hurst, and Rachel Asuras. Thank you all for your help along the way!

To everyone at the Midwest Writers Workshop, but especially to Jama Bigger, for offering such an encouraging atmosphere to learn about writing and publishing. My book wouldn't be out in the world without your help! Thank you for all you do to help writers start and improve their careers.

To my friends who put up with me even when I was hermit while I revised the novel: Carolyn Johnson, Anna Vorsilak, Amy Dreischerf, Rose Jindal, Vinaya Bhatia, Brynn Hollingsworth, Emily Gorrell, Julia Stern and Nikki Mousdicas.

Un abrazo para mi familia en España—Sonia, Alfredo, Paula, y Carla.

To Brett Jonas, Julia Byers, and the rest of the #Ch1Con team for being awesome people and writers. Also, thanks for the great headshot, Julia.

To my teachers at St. Pius X, Brebeuf Jesuit Preparatory School, and Indiana University, but especially to Mrs. Taber, Mrs. Desautels, and Ms. Haffley, who made a difference in my life.

To everyone who liked my author page, shared my blog, or helped in some other way, you have no idea how much I appreciate it and how much you helped me achieve this dream.

And finally, to you, my dear readers—thank you! This book wouldn't exist without you, and I can't wait to share more of Kora's story with you. Always remember you're worth more than gold!

DISCUSSION
GUIDE FOR
A TOUCH OF GOLD

〉〉〉〉〉〉〉〉〉〉◉〈〈〈〈〈〈〈〈〈〈

1. What differences do you notice between the way the King Midas myth is presented in *A Touch of Gold* versus the older versions of the myth?

2. If you were given one wish like King Midas, what would you wish for? How do you think Dionysus might twist your words?

3. How does the author weave in other elements from Greek myths?

4. How does Kora's curse compare to that of her father?

5. If you had the power to turn things to gold, how would you use that power?

6. Which character did you most relate to? Why?

7. How has Kora's relationship with her father changed throughout the novel? How do you think it will continue to change?

8. Were there choices the characters made that you wouldn't have? Which ones?

9. Of all the characters who acted as antagonists, which one did you find the scariest? Why?

10. Which setting in the book would you most like to visit? Why?

11. Which scene or moment do you feel was the most pivotal for the plot? How would the book have differed without that scene?

12. What themes did you see play out while reading the book?

13. If you were Kora at the end of the novel, would you continue to outlaw gold in the palace and keep wearing gloves? If not, what would you do?

14. Which character changes the most throughout the course of the novel? Explain.

15. If you could ask the author one question, what would it be?

ABOUT THE AUTHOR

Annie Sullivan grew up in Indianapolis, Indiana. She received her master's degree in creative writing from Butler University. She loves fairy tales, everything Jane Austen, and traveling. Her wanderlust has taken her to every continent, where she's walked on the Great Wall of China, found four-leaf clovers in Ireland, waddled with penguins in Antarctica, and cage dived with great white sharks in South Africa.

You can follow her adventures on Twitter (@annsulliva) or on her blog: anniesullivanauthor.wordpress.com.